SON OF FRANCE

SON OF FRANCE

A CHRISTOPHER KRUSE NOVEL

TODD BABIAK

HARPERCOLLINS PUBLISHERS LTD

Published by HarperCollins Publishers Ltd

First edition

HarperCollins Publishers Ltd
2 Bloor Street East, 20th Floor
Toronto, Ontario, Canada
M4W 1A8

www.harpercollins.ca

Library and Archives Canada Cataloguing in Publication
information is available upon request.

ISBN 978-1-44344-382-1

Printed and bound in the U.S.A.
RRD 9 8 7 6 5 4 3 2 1

I guess it is strange to dedicate a novel like this to Gina and Avia and Esmé but I am doing it anyway.

ONE

Rue des Rosiers, Paris

THE WINTER AFTER HIS DAUGHTER DIED, CHRISTOPHER KRUSE SLEPT
poorly. He would awaken out of a dream at four in the morning, forget all but its mood, and jog through the park thinking of her. At this
time of day, only the most haunted were about the city. They walked
slowly, smoking cigarettes while he ran, but none of them were going
anywhere. He would do sit-ups and push-ups on the wet and cool
grass and shadowbox by the light of an old lantern near a monument
to the dead. No one watched him, or even noticed he was there. A mist
would rise up off the Seine or fall from the sky, and the phantom legs
of the tower would return him to the feeling of his forgotten dream. In
the fog, anything was possible. He spoke to his dead daughter. He
worried he was going crazy and then he stopped worrying.

There was enough time after his workout to shower and put on a
suit, to be the first customer at the bakery. He grew up with the church
and came to adore ritual if not faith. On his way from the apartment
on Avenue Bosquet to the bakery, through the dark of January and the

1

wind of February, the rains of March, through hot yeast and diesel exhaust, too much perfume, and the occasional flash of dog shit, he passed a travel agency. It was small and shabbily furnished. The woman at the desk in Voyages du Septième was always alone at this hour. She wore a crashing wave of teased-up white-blond hair and shoulder pads in her bright polyester dresses. In the absence of customers or even a book to read she stared out the window, her chin in her hand. Over time the woman began to recognize him, to seek him. It would not be French for her to smile or to wave, but now that spring had begun and there was enough light in the mornings, she would hold eye contact and exhale, faintly nod. They were together the loneliest people in Paris. All he had to do was open the heavy blue door, enter the fluorescent room decorated with tropical posters. Just buy a ticket, pack a bag, and *go home, you coward, where you belong.* There was nothing to pack but an urn, filled with his daughter's ashes, Lily's ashes, and seven suits. What remained of Evelyn was already in Toronto, buried in the Park Lawn Cemetery. He could follow her tomorrow. Today. This afternoon. Who needs the suits? There were plenty in the closet of the house on Foxbar Road. It would be dusty and quiet in there, quieter than quiet: no daughter, no wife, the hum of the refrigerator when he plugged it in and maybe, just maybe, the smell of them in the walls, on the beds and in the linens, in the cushions of the chesterfield where he had rocked his baby to sleep.

Kruse could not say this aloud to anyone but he stayed in France because Lily was here in the fog, around one of these corners, in one of these bakeries. She was older than when he had last seen her, on Halloween night, and her French was better. There would be no more mistakes. He would do everything correctly, with pure intentions. He would properly believe. He would bring her back to life.

If he walked into Voyages du Septième and bought a ticket from the lonely agent, if he carried the urn across the Atlantic, he would forfeit its magic. Lily would be gone forever.

While he did not need the money, Kruse worked: he protected the mayor and a few senators, potential leaders of potential parties, judges, executives, and four neglected Parisian wives on a sexual adventure in Antibes.

On the day it began again, the fourth of April, he had been thinking of the four neglected wives. He was on the metro, where it was important to have something to think about. They had flown down in a Learjet, drinking cocktails with vodka and shaved ginger and making suggestive comments he barely understood. The resort, a secret place, was on the water. All of the men were tall and young and tanned, free of scars, prostitutes with health benefits and five weeks' vacation. The women spent two nights in Antibes with these beautiful men and on the flight back to Paris they were quiet and miserable. It had not been what they had imagined. They were not better afterwards. Thinking of the women, he daydreamed his way past his metro stop and exited at the Chemin Vert station on the far side of Place des Vosges.

On his way to the restaurant he stopped in the plaza, lined with connected houses and arcades, a square of tan and peach gingerbread with morning smoke rising from the chimneys. Famous people had lived here, though he could not remember any of their names.

He walked along a thin, pleasant pedestrian street of boutiques, Rue des Francs-Bourgeois. Kruse decided to return with Anouk, to buy her a dress or a pair of shoes if her mother would allow it. The event was set to begin at eleven thirty and it was not yet ten. A few of the shopkeepers swept the sidewalk while others leaned on the doorways and smoked. The radio news, France Info, played through open windows above, along with the clank of cutlery on plates, laughter, an argument about funerals.

Baron Haussmann didn't get around to razing the medieval Jewish quarter, the Pletzl, in the nineteenth century, so the streets were narrow and lacking in epic vistas. In Paris this was where he felt the most magic, at dusk, when his eyes had not yet adjusted to the shift in light.

He could walk through any door, down any street, and find her waiting. "Papa," she would say, the little Frenchie. "I've been looking for you."

There were Stars of David on the baby blue awning above the restaurant on Rue des Rosiers. He checked the windows opposite Chez Sternbergh, the crossroads, the men's clothing store. He would not have chosen this restaurant, but no one had asked him.

In the late 1970s, his career moved from self-defence into the active defence of others. Most of these others were extraordinarily wealthy. His meetings with them were in luxury hotels, with harpsichord music playing at the right volume, or on the top floors of office towers in New York and Toronto. There was only one sort of camouflage in these places: he began wearing suits. Tzvi Meisels, his partner in Krav Maga, worked out an accounting solution so the company could purchase high-quality Italian wool suits for its principals; a man cannot fight in jeans. His wife, Evelyn, had not liked the men and women he protected. She had not liked his job. She had designed their unearned sabbatical in the South of France as a complete transformation. She had urged him to leave both fighting and his *fighting suits* in the walk-in closet of the house on Foxbar Road. Now, with his monthly stipend from the City of Paris and his freelance contracts, he had replenished his collection.

At the entrance a tiny woman in a mourning dress watched him. She wore a black wig and black stockings, and her eyebrows were painted on. From the briefing he knew this was Miriam Sternbergh. It was too cool to go without a jacket but she went without one, slightly hunched but also regal.

"Are you Monsieur Kruse?"

"I am."

The tiny woman stepped out onto the sidewalk, in a bulky set of high-heel shoes that echoed in the street. She shook his hand. "What dangers do you see?"

Security work was different in France because France was different. "They pay me to be paranoid, Madame Sternbergh."

"So . . ."

"I see dangers everywhere."

Madame Sternbergh took two steps back and leaned on the side of her restaurant. She pulled a package of cigarettes from a bulky pocket of her dress, fumbled one into her mouth. It felt wrong, as though she was a child with a toy handbag. In the briefing Kruse learned she had worn black her entire adult life. She had never married, though in the 1950s an affair with Jean-Paul Sartre had lent her a sheen of local fame. Her parents had opened the restaurant before the Second World War, and though she was just seventeen years old, she had taken over as proprietor afterwards. She was the only member of the Sternbergh family who had survived.

"My problem is I don't know what a danger looks like." Madame Sternbergh lit her cigarette with a match, and the scent filled their corner of Rue des Rosiers. "I can only tell you what it feels like. Feelings are my specialty. This has been my trouble, Monsieur Kruse, how I have become insufferable. Would you come in?"

"I shouldn't yet." The restaurant was on a corner and exposed on three sides, with plenty of windows.

"Monsieur Kruse, if someone wants to hurt us today he will hurt us. It has always been so."

This had been Evelyn's philosophy. "That doesn't leave me with many career prospects."

"Come talk to me. My leg hurts. I have to sit. Kruse—you're German?"

"Mennonite."

"Oh I like Mennonites. You don't hurt people."

"I'm a terrible Mennonite."

"If you will permit me, Monsieur Kruse, it is the contrary. By the look of your face you allow people to hurt you."

There were tulips on every table, which were covered in bright white cloths. He could smell cooking oil, roasted meat. From inside, the stencils on the windows made it difficult to see onto Rue des Rosiers or the cross street, Ferdinand Duval. Madame Sternbergh led him to the back of the restaurant, to the only table that was not set and decorated for the party. There was a simple soundboard on it. At the other end of the room, near the entrance, a podium and speakers. Kruse had fought against this placement, as it exposed the mayors to danger from behind, but the interests of the photographers and television cameras came before safety. These were vain and ambitious men, and elections were coming.

For a moment, somehow, the sun broke through and the sad restaurant turned jolly, the reds of the walls dancing with the tablecloths and tulips, the smoke. Madame Sternbergh clapped and sat up straight, but then the sun faded again to nothing. Now the restaurant seemed even darker. She put out her cigarette, sat back again, and sighed.

"You often work for the mayor?"

Kruse answered with a shrug.

A man in a tuxedo presented Kruse and Madame Sternbergh with two little coffees and a small plate of biscuits made with coconut.

"He's lived his entire life in Paris and this is his first time, his first time, in my family's restaurant." She pushed her lips out, emitted a gentle sound like *boeuf.* "Paris has rather a few restaurants, I understand. I understand. But you'd think, as a gesture."

"Does it please you to have him here?"

Madame Sternbergh flattened the creases in her wool dress. "Finally and enormously, yes. I am part of a committee, you see, trying to convince the mayor to apologize for the *rafle du Vel' d'Hiv.*"

Rafle he understood: roundup. The rest of the phrase was incomprehensible to him and, with an apology, he admitted it. This had not been in his briefing.

She picked up a biscuit, inspected it, and tossed it on the floor. Almost immediately, one of the waiters arrived with a broom. "This is what *infuriates* me. That a man like you does not know. That millions of you do not know. Thirteen thousand of us were arrested and held in the Vélodrome d'Hiver. I was just a girl. How can anyone not know?"

"When?"

"This was in 1942." She chose another cookie, smelled it, smiled in apology. "You know, before the war, I hated this food. I was a teenager. I didn't even care, frankly, if my blood was Jewish or Somali. I loved bacon. I was French, Monsieur."

Kruse was not French, not by blood. But he shared their shame, for sending their neighbours away, as his parents had taught him. Every one of us owns every atrocity. He could hardly look her in the eyes as she spoke. "Your family . . ."

"They had painted the glass roof of the velodrome blue, so the bombers wouldn't destroy the place. It was summer, and unbearably hot. There was no food, no toilets. All of us, we went from civilization into a hot bath of shit. Both my parents and my two brothers went to Auschwitz."

"The mayor had something to do with this?" It would not have surprised Kruse.

"He would have been a little boy in '42. But he does have the power to apologize for it, to tell the story to people like you, and he has not. You know what he says, our mayor? 'It wasn't us! Those weren't real Frenchmen who did that. The republic had dissolved. Those bad Vichy men . . .'"

"So you reopened the restaurant."

"When you have something to protect, Monsieur Kruse, you protect it."

"I'll speak to the mayor if I can."

"He is not only your employer? He is also your friend?"

"I would not say friend."

"People like him, I think, they do not have friends."

"Not the way you and I would define the word, Madame Sternbergh."

"And our guest of honour, do you know him?"

Pierre Cassin, the luncheon speaker, had been chosen to represent France in Brussels in some fashion. He was one of the politicians from across the country who had joined the mayor to build a new party, to save France from socialist ruin, restore it to glory. Kruse had worked many of their dinners and cocktail parties and tense conferences in miniature ballrooms. The conversations between the mayor and Monsieur Cassin were unofficial, too unofficial for the regular security machine. Kruse got the job not because the mayor trusted him, but because he and the mayor were bound to one another by ruinous secrets. The luncheon speaker, from what Kruse knew of him, was a much better man than the mayor. It would be his undoing. "I don't know him at all, Madame."

Again she shrugged, *boeuf.* Her small cup of coffee was empty but, for something to do, she lifted it to her mouth. Kruse was anxious to finish his work: identifying the weaknesses and finding ways to overcome them.

"Monsieur Kruse, I don't mean this as an insult, but you don't seem a bureaucrat."

"The bureaucrats are at another event today. He's a busy fellow, our mayor."

"Ah. So if this were football you would be *Ligue 2.*"

Kruse did not want to sound arrogant but he found the mayor's regular security team a collection of overconfident dullards. "Yes, Madame. I suppose."

"Do we still have spies and assassins? I was wondering this the other day, when they asked to book the restaurant." Madame Sternbergh snapped a biscuit in half and chewed it. "The wall has fallen. The Soviets are capitalists now."

"Perhaps Europeans felt similarly after the First World War."

"Touché. All right, Monsieur." She placed one of her hands on his for a moment. "Go do your job. I'll stop pestering you."

If he were honest, there was not much to do. He had already lost several arguments about how the luncheon was to proceed. With Tzvi he had invented a system of scenario testing, to think and act like Madame Sternbergh's spies and assassins, like terrorists, like the aggrieved maniac. Thinking like a maniac was, for him, the most rewarding. He did it on paper and he still had twenty minutes, so he browsed a children's shoe boutique down the street.

At eleven the men in suits and women in dresses began to arrive. Kruse inspected them, one by one, at a short distance. Most were in their fifties and sixties, calm and prosperous people without any hint of threat about them. This would not be a difficult assignment. Two thirty-something couples arrived together with small children. Madame Sternbergh knew them and said "*Coucou*" to the babies. The guest of honour showed up fifteen minutes early, unescorted. He was not a recognized star, so he was able to walk straight to the back of the restaurant and address himself to a bowl of cornichons. Even so, everyone turned to watch him. It was simply like that for some people.

Kruse introduced himself, congratulated the young man on his recent appointment. Cassin chewed a cornichon and stared at Kruse, amusement in his eyes. Pierre Cassin, mayor of Nancy and a newly appointed negotiator for the Maastricht Treaty in Brussels, carried no superficial glamour about him: no handlers, no portable phone. He was just under forty, with shiny Mediterranean skin and a full head of hair. For a politician he was short and slight, and his head appeared much too large for the rest of his body. Kruse had noticed this "lollipop effect" with Hollywood stars in his protection, and wondered if perhaps it was an evolutionary advantage, part of the chemistry that makes up charisma.

"An American security executive. If only this were to hit the papers. *More lousy foreigners taking jobs from Parisians.* A scandal for Monsieur le Maire."

"Canadian, actually."

"Our little cousins. That's okay, then. Where is His Highness?"

Kruse had been with these people long enough to know how they felt about the mayor of Paris. They were allies and enemies at once. Years of thwarted ambition were baked into every word Cassin said, and it would only get worse. The man had already lost some key battle;

the mayor of Paris would slowly ruin his fondest dreams and Cassin knew it and there was nothing he could do about it. Kruse carried no political hopes, but the mayor had similarly trapped him—had linked their futures. When the mayor succeeds, we all succeed. For a moment Kruse and Cassin spoke without speaking, the scent of sweet pickle in the air. "He's not far, Monsieur Cassin."

"No. No, he never is."

There was time to introduce Pierre Cassin to Madame Sternbergh, and they quietly chatted while Kruse returned to the door. Cassin eased in close as he spoke and made genuine eye contact. He asked questions. In half of the jobs Kruse had done for the mayor of Paris since December, the man himself had not shown up. There were always traffic problems. He was once out with an inner ear infection, and he missed the opening of a theatre because Muammar Gadhafi was in town and, at the last minute, the president requested his presence at a state dinner. These excuses were almost never genuine. The mayor had girlfriends, side projects, financial deals, off-the-books meetings.

Two of the mayor's assistants entered first and consulted with Kruse. The great man would introduce Cassin and leave immediately afterwards. A television crew was doing a story on top contenders for the next presidential election and they wanted an interview with him at the Grand Palais before his speech.

The mayor's car arrived, a black Renault. Kruse stepped out to meet it, opened the door for him, greeted him formally.

"Any media?" As he spoke to Kruse, the mayor scanned the little plaza. He smiled and waved to the locals.

"Not enough to justify the exposed position, Monsieur le Maire. It isn't too late to move the microphones to—"

"This is an in-and-out, it's nothing. I'd hoped for no reporters, to teach the *petit con* a lesson."

Kruse did take advantage of his special relationship to ask the sorts of questions no one else asked. "Then why are you doing it?"

The mayor's driver straightened his jacket for him, brushed his shoulders.

"His office insisted." The mayor watched a flash of dandruff fall to the cobblestones. "A magnificent entrance into the world of international diplomacy. Our little Cassin wants my job, you see. He wanted the announcement at the Grand Palais this afternoon. I think a Jewish restaurant is more his size."

"Your job? But he doesn't live here."

"Not my current job." The mayor stepped toward the open door. "My future job."

The mayor opened his arms to greet Madame Sternbergh with kisses as though they were the oldest and finest of friends. "One of my favourite spots in Paris," he told her, as three newspaper journalists made notes.

Kruse had expected her to take this with polite cynicism, but she turned pink before the mayor and stuttered that it was an honour and a thrill to have him. He shook every hand in the room and stepped up to the microphone. With a lovely blend of formality and informality, he welcomed his good friend Pierre Cassin to Paris, the historic Marais, and to the finest Jewish restaurant in the city.

"What we have before us, *mes chers compatriotes*, is the future of France. Her true soul. Pierre Cassin was born of a Muslim mother and a Jewish father. Yet he is one hundred per cent a Frenchman." The audience, many of them from the city's Jewish community, applauded.

Kruse understood the air of resignation about the guest of honour. This was not really a celebration of his achievement. It was the mayor's victory party. Cassin stood in the corner near the door to the kitchen. He waved them to their seats. "That's just who I *am*," he said, loud enough to be heard without a microphone. "Imagine what I'll *do*."

The mayor paused and looked away from Cassin, as though it were a moment of unspeakable vulgarity. Kruse thought for an instant he might roll his eyes. Then he spoke of Cassin's coming work on the

European Union, which would benefit France not only economically. It would also prevent what had happened in the 1930s and '40s on this continent, when good French families like the Sternberghs were destroyed by hate.

Madame Sternbergh yanked on Kruse's sleeve, to whisper in his ear. She was far enough away from the mayor that she was outside his spell. "Hear that? *Hate* destroyed my family. Not French policemen and their Nazi friends."

Kruse had no organized way to speak of the spirit world. But he would never forget the snap of panic that passed through him in the quiet before it happened. Madame Sternbergh's coffee-and-cigarettes breath hung in the air. She had more to say but he could not listen. There were footsteps outside the restaurant, in an irregular pace. He felt them before he heard them. At first he saw no one in the cluttered windows facing Rue des Rosiers. He would try to explain it to himself that night and in other miserable moments of darkness in Paris and he would fail. There was nothing yet to see or hear. Then he saw it—him. A man's head bobbed along the side of the restaurant, at a bizarre speed, not quite crooked but not straight either. He was in between walking and jogging. There was an instant, as he ran, that Kruse caught a look at more than the top of his head. Two of the windows broke, one after the other. And then two thumps, like dropped apples. He couldn't see where the apples had rolled but he shouted, "Get down and cover your ears!"

At the far end of the restaurant, Pierre Cassin dove.

The mayor's hands were up, to stop Kruse. "What are you doing?"

Kruse shoved the mayor out the open door of the restaurant, and he tripped and fell backwards onto the cobblestones. Inside, Cassin was too far away. Kruse couldn't see him. Madame Sternbergh was close so he tackled her into the near wall and she screamed and three flowerpots fell on top of them.

It began with a brief inhale, a contraction, as though the room were preparing to sneeze. The blast itself, two folded into one, was more powerful than he could have imagined. It was as though he had been kicked into the wall by the largest foot in the world, and when he removed his fingers from his ears there was blood on his hands and dirt from the flowerpots and Madame Sternbergh's face was a charred wreck. He tried to stand and he fell, dizzy from the blast. His head hurt and all he could hear was a high bee buzzing. He reached down to help Madame Sternbergh to her feet but she was unconscious.

A thick fog of hot ash filled the room. It felt like the hook of a coat hanger was stuck in his throat, and when he reached in to pull it out there was nothing. He threw up. Madame Sternbergh was not breathing. A woman stood directly in front of him, shouted in his face, but she was speaking underwater. *Cordite.* That was the word he was trying to remember. His left arm was wet with blood, and his hands. The fog began to settle. Kruse rubbed the ash from his eyes and, as he looked out at what the restaurant and its people had become, he reached for something to hold and tripped over a body and returned to the floor of Chez Sternbergh.

TWO

Rue du Champ de Mars

THE MAYOR'S SENIOR SECURITY MAN HAD POSTED HIMSELF OUTSIDE Chez Sternbergh. Instead of watching for threats he had sat in the car with the previous day's *Le Figaro*. He wept while the police questioned him. *Rien, Messieurs.* I saw nothing. My life is over. The paramedics inspected Kruse, wiped the blood and soot from his face and hair, none of it his, and poked him. Kruse had nothing helpful to tell the investigators. The man who threw the grenades was shorter than six feet and he had black hair, which narrowed their search to eight million men. He was young, or youngish. There was something about the way he had moved: crooked. How, he could not say. The man had straight posture but Kruse kept wanting to say *bossu*—hunchback. There had been five seconds. If he had followed the grenades instead of watching the top of the attacker's head he might have picked the bombs up and tossed them right back outside. The mayor was treated for a minor laceration, from his fall on the cobblestones. He stared at Kruse as the doctor worked on him, four stitches.

If Pierre Cassin had not jumped on the grenades it would have been much worse.

The survivors gathered to talk and to cry. An elderly woman with blood on the side of her face and in her hair said, to a man in a suit, wearing a knitted kippa, "It was a young Frenchman. A Frenchman in blue jeans and a light jacket."

A sooty man pointed his broken cigarette at her. "No, no, no, Madame. I saw an Arab running. It was an Arab in blue jeans."

Sirens, more sirens, overwhelmed the conversation. Madame Sternbergh had died of a cerebral hemorrhage, from the blast. One of the two babies had died and the other was on its way to the Hôtel-Dieu. When they were finished with him, Kruse refused a ride and walked north and west, up Rue Montmartre and along busy Boulevard Haussmann. It was pleasant to be among other people attending to their lives, sitting at cafés and reading newspapers, as his hearing returned to something like normal. An electric bird continued to coo in his ears, but not so insistently. He went farther north and west, away from his apartment.

Evelyn had commissioned a modern closet in the second-floor master bedroom of the house on Foxbar Road. When he opened the door the light turned on automatically, which never stopped feeling like sorcery. One of Evelyn's posters from her graduate school days hung at the end of the magic closet in a red IKEA frame: a reproduction of *Gare Saint-Lazare* by Claude Monet. Two locomotives rest under a triangular roof, with almost-people standing nearby and faintly, through the steam, a block of pretty apartments.

Hattemer, Anouk's school, was adjacent to Gare Saint-Lazare. The mayor of Paris had arranged it so Anouk could go for free, part of his payment to Annette and to Kruse. A train was starting toward Normandy when he arrived. The steam was gone, replaced by nuclear electricity, and Monet was dead and Evelyn was dead, but the almost-people and the buildings were here. He leaned over the wrought iron fence, near the end of Rue de Londres, and he watched the trains and then he watched the sidewalks and the windows. Hattemer was a private school, for the richest parents in Paris if not precisely for the children.

He was far enough away that they would not see him. The bell rang and Annette, who had been waiting in the lobby, emerged with Anouk. Three times in January he had picked her up, when Annette had still allowed it. The children were eerily quiet inside the school, even in the early grades. They would remain in their desks until Madame Fournier, the teacher, made eye contact with the chauffeurs in uniform and governesses in Dior, one by one.

Today was different. The parents had come. German town cars were parked up and down Rue de Londres. Mothers and fathers had emerged like prophets among the faithful. Word had already spread through Paris that a man had tossed grenades into a restaurant, that a baby had died.

Anouk had just turned five, two years older than Lily when she died. Five seemed impossibly old. She wore a big-girl backpack, simple pink canvas with no cartoon animals. Kruse could hear himself saying something bland to Evelyn, at Lily's fifth birthday party, about the astonishing speed of time. Anouk turned and said a formal goodbye to her teacher. The school vibrated with old values, methods, aesthetics, a sneer at the vulgarity of Mitterrand France. It wasn't a terribly relaxing place for a little girl. On the sidewalk Anouk exhaled as though she had been holding her breath all day.

Kruse followed Annette and Anouk down into Saint-Lazare station and watched them weave through the tiled columns of the rotunda. Even in the middle of the day the pillars carried the glow of soft lamps. They went through the turnstiles and he watched them until the last moment, the final flash of backpack pink. He stopped himself from running through and hugging them, kissing them, saying I love you without actually saying it. He returned to the street, feeling lonelier and more lost than before he had watched them. While he had trained himself to take a punch, the swing of a knife, a fall, even a bullet, Kruse had no idea how to survive a day like today. He walked south, conscious now that people stopped as he passed. They walked wide arcs around him, this man in a bloody, dusty blue suit. It was garbage. The paramedic had wiped a bit of brain from his shoulder.

On the Pont Alexandre III, just as he passed the gold winged statues, a police car pulled over. The two young flics appeared genuinely frightened. One was breathless, as though he had been sprinting, only he had just stepped out of the little white car. They insisted on driving him home because someone had called in to complain that a ghoul had just crossed the Champs-Élysées.

• • •

His wife would have been horrified to see him living in one of the great culinary cities of the world yet eating every day at the same little brasserie three blocks from his apartment, the same dinner: a salad with two modest rectangles of baked goat cheese. Café du Marché was a cramped, always-busy sort of place a Canadian has to learn to appreciate, as he was nearly always touching and smelling strangers, hearing them chew, sharing their secrets and their cigarette smoke. That night, the only free seat was at the bar. His neighbours wanted, even more than usual, to share a warm room with one another. It had been too late in the day for the explosion to make the afternoon papers but it was on every radio station and led the evening newscasts.

The story on France 2 began silently, with images from the explosion on Rue des Rosiers. Café du Marché was never quiet, but patrons shushed each other and the shushes spread through the main room and out to the covered terrace. Diners and drinkers stood and gathered to smoke and watch the television. Madeleine, the heavily tattooed rockabilly girl who spent all day every day behind the bar, turned the volume as high as it would go. More gathered at the entrance, under the awning.

Nine people were killed, twenty-two injured. The chief of police suggested another six Parisians were in precarious condition, which could affect the statistics. Shaky diners at Chez Sternbergh who had survived the attack were sure of what they had seen but no two of them could agree. A man or men had tossed the device into the restaurant, two of them or four of them, French or foreigner, as the mayor was introducing Pierre Cassin. No no, there were no men. It was hidden under a table all along. Someone shouted a prayer to Allah just before it blew up. No one had said a word. A man had laughed. A retired American intelligence agent in Paris tied the attack to the recent explosion in the parking garage of the World Trade Center in New York, which had killed six and injured over one thousand. If we are to understand why it is happening, he said, we need only remember the Munich Olympics. There is a diaspora of homeless and humiliated Palestinians out there and they have sons with money, foreign passports, and weapons.

One thing was certain: it would have been far worse if Pierre Cassin had not dived on top of the grenades.

The mayor of Paris appeared, surrounded by other survivors of the blast. It looked as though one of his handlers had mussed his hair, smeared a bit of ash on his forehead, tousled his suit and shirt so he would look battle-worn. The last Kruse saw him, behind the ambulance, the mayor had been much cleaner than this. His short speech, about how the people who did this have only made us stronger, was memorized from a script. "There is a murderer in Paris." The mayor looked around him, opened his arms. "But he is up against ten million of us, citizens of the most civilized city in the world. We will hunt him and we will find him."

Spontaneous applause erupted around him. It would play around the world, just as he had surely planned.

The segment ended with two short tributes, to Madame Sternbergh and to Cassin, who had a wife and two children, but when it was over the anchorman repeated two lines from the mayor's speech. He spoke of the hunt.

Madeleine turned off the television. Conversations in the room restarted low, in little more than whispers. The two men at the bar next to Kruse didn't speak at all, yet their silence was somehow louder than anything they might say. He hadn't noticed they were North African until now. No one said anything to them, not at first, but several people stared. They couldn't have ordered anything more French: a bottle of Sancerre and a plate of cured meats, nuts, and cheese. Madeleine slowly turned up the music, a violin concerto instead of her usual repertoire.

"I'm feeling sentimental." She winked at him, her regular.

The stares from behind were not driven by curiosity. Kruse could feel a sort of heat on his back and neck. Ten minutes after the news ended, the man next to Kruse, with a layer of sweat at his hairline, asked him if he would like to finish their bottle. They had decided to leave.

"Please don't." Madeleine put her hand on the bottle.

Kruse heard and felt the change behind him. A large man, red-faced with liquor, slid his chair away and stood up. Two others joined him. They murmured to each other and approached the bar.

"What do you say to that?" The bald man spoke to the backs of the North Africans. His forearms were thick and hairy and freckled.

Madeleine asked her clients to ignore the big man and his supporters. She tilted around and asked the soldier and his friends, with royal politesse, to sit down and enjoy their evening. A half-litre of whatever they were drinking would be on the house. The man next to Kruse was breathing quickly and shallowly. The other had closed his eyes.

"Look at me when I'm talking to you." The soldier waited. Neither of the men turned around. "We've been sitting here trying to figure you out. Why can't you debate, like the rest of us, instead of blowing up restaurants and office towers? You're cowards? Is that it?"

"Monsieur, I'm French." The one with the sweaty forehead turned slowly. "I was born here, in Paris. My parents were born in Paris. My father fought in the war. My first language is French and my second language is Italian."

"What about Arabic?"

"I'm proud to speak enough to make it through my prayers."

"And what do you pray for?" The soldier pointed to the television.

Madeleine cussed and looked around. Her fellow servers, two women and thin men with stylish haircuts, were no good to her at all. "I'm calling the police."

It was time for the soldiers to sit, but Kruse knew men like this. There was only one way.

"Get out." The soldier pointed to the door, at the street in the rain, as though the men were dogs who had soiled the floor.

"Let's go," said the sweaty man to his friend. "If Madame could package dinner for us."

Madeleine told the soldier and his compatriots to piss off, called them monsters, but they ignored her. She put a styrofoam package on the bar and the North African man who had not spoken to the soldier began filling it with the meat and pickles and dried figs and cheese. The leader folded his big arms. Kruse wiped his fingers and put his hand on the sweaty man's arm, asked him to stay.

"I don't want to stay. Not now."

Kruse slid off his stool and stood in front of the soldier, who was several inches taller and much thicker. But something in the soldier's eyes changed. Something always changed. Tzvi, his teacher, had taught him how to do this when he was not yet twenty, when his face was still free of scars, how to stand and how to stare. There was no anger in it, only the poise that comes with absolute confidence. Much of the bulk in the soldier's chest had migrated into his belly, as much as he tried to suck it in. Kruse took a step forward. "They're staying, Messieurs. I'm afraid you're not. Pay your bill and go."

"You're what? American? *Pay your bill and go*," said the soldier, mocking Kruse's accent. His friends laughed with him. "Sit down, Woody Allen."

Both of the men at the bar pleaded with Kruse to leave this alone. They were happy to leave. Madeleine was behind him, in the middle of phoning the police.

"What are you going to do, American? Fight three of us for your Arab boyfriends?"

"Yes, Monsieur. That is exactly what I'm going to do. Though I think we should do it in the rain, rather than break anything in here. We all like this place."

A few others stood up from their seats now, men and women, including a giant in a navy blue suit. The giant slipped past the soldiers and stood next to Kruse. All the soldiers could do now was find enough money in their pockets and, with some parting words about France becoming an Islamic republic, walk out into the rain.

There was a moment of relief, for those who had not wanted to see a fight. Madeleine vowed to report the men anyway, when the police arrived. The giant congratulated Kruse for doing what no one else would do, and returned to his seat. For two or three minutes the men remained at the bar with Kruse and then, without a word of deliberation with each other, they stood up. Kruse was careful not to make eye contact with them. He waited until they were on their way out before he said sorry.

The sweaty one who had spoken to the soldier, whose grandfather had fought in the war, shook his head. "Why are you apologizing, Monsieur?"

His French would never be subtle enough.

The men shook hands with Kruse, in the French fashion—limp, without ceremony—and opened their umbrellas at the door.

"I would have left too," said Madeleine.

Kruse nodded.

She pulled a couple of glasses down and poured a splash of the leftover Sancerre into each one. "Chin-chin," she said, and drank, and stared at him for a moment. "You weren't frightened?"

"You think I should have been?"

"He was as big as two of you and ugly and stupid as a turnip. He would have killed you. Plus, he had friends."

"Men like that don't actually fight."

The electric birdcall in his ears had mostly faded. One of the paramedics had told him it could take weeks, if not forever. The single sip of Sancerre had been enough, though he knew it would do him well to drink more, ease him into sleep. He did not want to leave but there was no reason to stay, apart from avoiding the silence of his apartment. He had furnished and decorated the second bedroom himself, with a small single bed and art Lily had loved: pictures of bugs, original sketches from *Alice in Wonderland* and *Winnie-the-Pooh*. All of the Astérix books were on the shelf, up to the point where René Goscinny died, and he had recently bought *Les Malheurs de Sophie*, a novel about a curious little girl who lives in a castle.

He stood up to leave, to say goodbye to Madeleine, but her eyes changed. She pointed behind him.

"My young friend. I just heard."

Only one man in Paris spoke to him in English. They met here, once a week, usually in a corner where no one would hear them. Kruse never understood why he had become a confessional for Joseph Mariani, who could hire as many real psychologists as he wanted, but he knew Joseph's heart: they were bound by what had happened to them in Aix-en-Provence, by blood.

Joseph joined him at the bar, switched to French for Madeleine's benefit. "You're abandoning a bottle of Sancerre?"

"I've tried to convince him to drink with me." She poured a glass for Joseph.

"He could use one."

"Why?"

"Surely you know our brave boy was in Chez Sternbergh today. He saved the life of our beloved mayor."

Madeleine looked at him.

"To you." Joseph touched the tip of Kruse's glass and drank.

"Nine people died. I made an error. If I'd focused on the grenades instead of the—"

"You saw him?"

"The top of his head."

Madeleine continued to stare at Kruse, even as one of the waiters waved for her attention. "What are you doing here, Christophe? Shouldn't you be . . . Where do you go when you've survived an explosion?"

"He comes with me. But first he takes a drink."

If he took a drink, a real drink, a red-cheeked racist from the military would swing and he would not see it. But this was not the genuine reason he avoided the Sancerre, which smelled faintly but deliciously of newly mowed grass.

"Where are we going?"

"You shall see."

Kruse pulled francs out of his wallet and Madeleine reached out, stopped him. "It's on me tonight."

"I don't deserve it."

She turned away from him, addressed the waiter. Kruse thanked her and she sighed, brushed him away as though he were a mosquito.

"Goat cheese salad and verbena tea. Jesus Christ, man." At the door, Joseph opened his umbrella and handed a second one to Kruse. It was an hour before sunset but it was dark. Rain roared on the cobblestones. Just beyond it, the sound of the pianist above the café who played with the window open: Brahms. He knew it was Brahms because his late wife, whom he had failed to protect, had taught him. He had learned to play it, though not nearly this well. The black Mercedes was parked illegally on Rue du Champ de Mars. Monsieur Claude, in his classic chauffeur's uniform, stood at attention.

If he had not dreaded the thought of being alone in the apartment, waiting for sleep to arrive, he would not have gone. The leather seats squeaked as he slid into place. It smelled of Joseph's cologne. "What's happening?"

Joseph pretended he had not heard the question.

THREE

Rue d'Andigné, Paris

KRUSE HAD NEVER BEEN INSIDE JOSEPH'S APARTMENT IN PARIS, BUT he had secretly followed him home so he would know where to find him. It was on the top floor of a stone building on Rue d'Andigné, in the sixteenth arrondissement. The street was lined with luxury sedans, German-made for one sort of Parisian and French-made for another. The apartment was a high-ceilinged four-thousand-square-foot art deco palace of dark wood and gold fixtures, pink highlights, curved ceilings, and streamlined appliances. The furniture was dark leather, as though it had come from a movie between the wars, and the massive chandelier hanging over the dining room table was the shape and colour of a honeycomb.

They weren't alone. A scent, a presence, made the tour difficult to follow: a list of designers, eras, famous guests who had been through. Joseph was leading him to something, to someone. A woman in soft-soled shoes and a black dress presented them with a tray of cheeses and a bottle of champagne, two full flutes.

"No, Madame, thank you."

"For Christ's sake, haven't you taken enough verbena tea for one night?" Joseph chose a glass. "This is Louis Roederer Cristal, the 1990."

"That means nothing to me."

"I could slap you."

"You could."

"Except I . . . couldn't."

Joseph adjusted his tie and continued. The bedrooms were named for famous Corsicans: Tino Rossi, Pasquale Paoli, Napoléon Bonaparte. The Mariani family was famous, but not for entertainment or statecraft. Joseph's father had worked in Bastia until the mid-1950s, when he moved the family business to Marseille: prostitution and protection, loan-sharking and illegal gambling, large-scale theft, and, eventually, the heroin trade. They invested the profits in legitimate ventures like real estate, restaurants, bars and nightclubs, tour companies, wineries, and luxury fashion. Now that Joseph's cruel father and sadistic brother were dead, he was selling off his family's traditional lines of business to focus on activities that would neither land him in jail for the rest of his life nor see him shot in the head and dumped in the Seine by rivals in the Brise de Mer gang. But Joseph Mariani had a few attachments to illegal activity he would never escape. At the end of the hall was a library and lounge. Joseph stopped him at the doorway.

"If this is . . . I'm sorry, Christopher."

"For what?"

"I didn't have a choice. They have me the way they have you."

"Who?"

Joseph led him into the room, and a stately woman stood up from a red-brown couch. Her eyes were small and fierce. In this light Kruse could only guess her age, somewhere between thirty and forty. She carried the severity and the confidence of a lawyer, but she did not wear a lawyer's clothes.

"I'm sorry it took so long to snatch him up, Madame Moquin. He wasn't at home. I had to do some detective work."

"It was as pleasant a wait as I could imagine." Madame Moquin wore a layered black dress with a hint of Gothic carnival about it. Her high boots and stockings completed the outfit: she was a raven. Her red hair had been clipped up extravagantly. She gestured toward her glass of champagne. "Thank you."

"Christophe Kruse, this is Zoé Moquin."

They shook hands and exchanged pleasantries. They sipped their drinks until the time was right for Joseph, as host, to explain why this raven of a woman was here, waiting. "She works with the Direction de la Protection et de la Sécurité de la Défense. *Le DPSD*, we call it. I think you have some experience with them."

Kruse had not only met men and women of the DPSD, one of France's clandestine agencies. He had escaped from them in a vat of wine. It was always his first thought when he smelled Beaujolais. "It's an honour to meet you, Madame Moquin."

"We have quite the file on you, Monsieur. As you can imagine."

Kruse could speak the language but he couldn't yet decipher the codes. He had no idea what he was supposed to be imagining. "Yes, Madame."

"Rather a large team is working on this, obviously. I should say teams."

"Working on what?"

The woman turned to Joseph and sipped. Then back to Kruse. "The attack on Chez Sternbergh. Joseph didn't tell you?"

"No."

"Our chief, the chief of the DPSD, furnished us all with a briefing one hour ago. While we have witnesses, none are terribly reliable."

"It was a young man with dark hair."

"I say this with the greatest affection, but every law enforcement agency in France will be falling over themselves and each other to solve this. And I fear, I know, Monsieur Kruse, from experience that . . ."

Zoé Moquin smiled weakly, turned to Joseph. "I wonder, Monsieur Mariani, if you might find us something to eat with our champagne."

There was a plate of cheese, crackers, tapenade, and grapes on the table. Joseph was careful not to look at it, to pretend it was not there. "The strawberries of Plougastel are in season, Madame. I believe we have a basket or two."

Once they could no longer hear Joseph's shoes on the wood, Zoé Moquin pulled a silver cigarette holder from her purse and offered him one. "Would you like to sit?"

"No, Madame."

"I've watched you, Monsieur Kruse. I've read everything."

He did not know how to respond to this so he didn't. "You work with the mayor?"

"Yes wouldn't be an entirely correct answer. Neither would no."

"If you work with Joseph you work with the mayor."

She looked away from him, at an oil painting of a long-ago street riot. "Maybe we should start over."

"If you can't tell me why I'm here, I'm not sure that would make a difference, Madame."

"The other security men come from another place. And I don't mean your Americanness sets you apart, necessarily."

"I'm not American."

"They're ignorant and empty. It's part of their training. I see you as different from them."

"Two of your colleagues, last fall—"

"I know. Your company in America. And yes, the ugly business some months ago. All you have lost. It's etched in your face." She ran a finger down her own cheek, the line of his longest scar. "What happened? Or is that a rude question?"

"Lots of things happened to my face."

"Let's leave it to my imagination, then." She smoked and sipped her champagne and watched him. "You and I have something in common,

Monsieur Kruse. Neither of us is obliged to work for financial reasons. We simply do, because it lends meaning to our lives. A sense of order, yes?"

The adrenaline of the day was suddenly draining from him, and the void was filling with annoyance. How did this woman know where his money came from? He was too tired for one of these conversations. "You've asked me to come here for a reason, Madame."

"These beasts killed a baby today. And for what? While we call in forensic experts from Lyon and London, and profilers from New York, and ask fat men behind computers to go through databases, the people who did this fly off to . . . wherever mass murderers go."

"What can I do?"

"You were there. You saw it and smelled it. You no doubt tasted it. Pierre Cassin was our friend. Madame Sternbergh and others from our Jewish community—have we not hurt them enough?"

"Madame Moquin, what do you want?"

She leaned forward over the heavy oak table and spoke slowly and quietly. "We want you to find out who did this."

"Why me?"

"Because you're nobody. You're not police or military. You work for the city, for the republic from time to time, but we don't know you. The press doesn't know you. You're a ghost."

"You think I can move faster than hundreds of investigators with credentials."

"We know you can. We want you to find them." Now she whispered: "And we want you to eliminate them."

Kruse waited a moment. "Madame, you've mistaken me for someone else. Our friend in common, Joseph Mariani, has access to—"

"He's not my friend, Monsieur Kruse."

"And I'm not in the elimination business."

She reached for his hand and took it in hers. Her skin was soft and cool and wet from the champagne flute. He could see down the front of her raven dress as she leaned forward, and she knew it. "I understand precisely who you are."

Perfume did not interest him, not normally. Walking through the scents in a department store gave him a faint headache. But the smell about her was different, like something he might encounter on a beach or in a forest that would inspire him to stop and try to remember. It was a thing he couldn't grasp. He liked having his hand in hers. "Thank you for this invitation, Madame. It was pleasant to meet you."

"Wait. Monsieur Kruse . . ."

He was already at the door and he kept walking.

Joseph was in the dining room alone, leaning on the back of a chair with his champagne flute at his mouth. "What do you think?"

"I think I'm not a murderer."

Joseph sighed, looked in the direction of the library. "What do you most love in the world?"

"My daughter. My wife."

"Of course. Nothing else?"

"You know what else, Joseph."

"Annette Laferrière and her daughter, Anouk, who live at number 5, Rue Valadon. And I am not the only one who knows. In my business, in Madame Moquin's business, with someone like you . . ."

"Someone like me?"

"A man who loves. It's all we—they—need to know. Why else have you stayed in Paris, my friend?"

Kruse walked to the door and did not respond or even slow his stride when Joseph called his name. When he reached the sidewalk and the rain he ignored Monsieur Claude's offer to drive him home and refused an umbrella.

• • •

It had snowed in Paris on Christmas Eve.

Annette invited Kruse to her apartment. He didn't know much about wine and food, compared with a genuine Frenchman, so he had asked his friends at Café du Marché to prepare something festive for him to take. With Anouk he decorated a little Christmas tree with homemade ornaments that would have seemed old-fashioned in Canada: popcorn, balls of coloured thread. Annette took pictures and drank good wine. After dinner he read to Anouk in English, *A Visit from St. Nicholas*. That morning he had found an eighty-year-old illustrated copy of the poem among the dust bunnies and cats at Shakespeare and Company. Then it was time to put Anouk to bed. He sang to her, one of the only songs he knew by heart, the inappropriate "Mammas Don't Let Your Babies Grow Up to Be Cowboys," and Annette had taken his hand in the almost-darkness. The wine in her breath was delicious to him, and the sound of Anouk's breathing, the warmth of her shoulder against his.

Anouk fell asleep and her mother leaned over to kiss him. There was no escaping it. Once they kissed it could not be undone. He wanted to kiss her, to stay in this apartment rather than return to the quiet of his own on Christmas Eve. But the elegance of Anouk's pink bedroom was manufactured, and not by them. The mayor owned this apartment—and he owned Kruse.

Annette Laferrière was a journalist when they met. She had wanted to write about his wife, Evelyn, who was at that time hiding somewhere in France. The police wanted to charge Evelyn for murdering her lover, and they weren't the only ones hunting her.

When he met Annette, Kruse was not sleeping, he was barely eating, trying to find and save his lost, unfaithful wife.

When it came time to publish the story—the truth about Evelyn May Kruse, her lover, and the people who had actually killed him—the mayor of Paris offered them a deal. Annette could remain quiet, give up journalism, and her daughter would go to the best school in the country. They would move from the worst apartment in Paris to one of the finest. Annette would have a rewarding career at the Carnavalet Museum, and a stipend from the city so she might live an altogether different life—the life of a rich woman. They would be safe from harm, forever.

The mayor of Paris guaranteed it. They would never ask for anything ugly or untoward from Kruse, from Annette, from Anouk.

He knew, back when they accepted the deal, that it was not possible. He knew as Annette leaned over to kiss him on Christmas Eve it was not possible. One of these days it would be more than a simple security job. If he had sipped a glass or two of wine at dinner, on the top floor of splendid number 5, Rue Valadon, Kruse would have pushed the calculation aside and he would have kissed her. He would have stayed the night.

How often he wished he had done it.

Instead Kruse put his hands on her shoulders, to stop her. He tried to whisper an explanation about how badly he wanted to kiss her. But Kruse knew they would come for him. He didn't want them to come for Annette and Anouk.

"You're too dangerous for me, are you? You've already brought psychopaths into our lives. How much worse can it be?"

"No. I just mean . . ."

"You don't have to explain, Christophe." Annette went on the balcony for a cigarette.

Kruse gave Anouk a kiss and he closed the door and he washed the dishes. He practised the words he would say. When Annette came back in Kruse said them. As he rolled up his sleeves to wash a casserole dish, Annette asked him to leave.

• • •

Kruse had followed her boyfriend home enough times, to and from work and from bars and brasseries and restaurants and lectures, to know plenty about him. Annette had introduced them at the produce market up Rue Cler. It was a village, this neighbourhood; they had met three or four times since then, greeted one another frostily as Anouk hugged Kruse and Annette crossed her arms. Étienne Bonnet was an editorial writer at *Le Figaro*, the oldest and most conservative national newspaper in France. He appeared on nightly current affairs programs, to argue with socialists, and he wore his influence and fame like a medal. Kruse had broken into Bonnet's white stone apartment twice, and had felt so miserable about it that he had not explored; the smell was enough. Bonnet was from such a steady line of wealth that money was charmingly irrelevant to him. His massive apartment was in an austere corner of the seventh arrondissement, though he would have referred to it by its more ancient, aristocratic name: le Faubourg. Étienne and Annette had met the second week of January at a conference on "smart cities" that both of them had deemed boring; the editorialist had found the story of their meeting so charming he had related it to Kruse twice.

On his walk home from Rue d'Andigné Kruse did it again. He broke into Étienne's apartment at the Place du Palais Bourbon and hated himself for it. Lights were out, but there was enough shine from the streets and from his small flashlight that Étienne's art collection, a blend of old and new, reminded him of what he had seen in the houses and penthouses of his clients in Toronto and New York: it was chosen by a professional, tasteful but impossible to love. The furniture was modern and the walls were white. Kruse startled himself when he walked into one of the bedrooms and shone a light on another man— himself. The walls were covered in mirrors, like a gym or a funhouse. The bed was round and in the middle of the room. He could see Annette in here, feeling . . . how would she feel?

Sick was how he felt, and blind and weak and limp and stupid. He didn't want to sit on or in anything, so he turned off his light and leaned against a wall in the semi-darkness.

Just after eleven the door opened and Étienne entered the apartment in mid-lecture. Kruse thought at first, with horror, that it was Annette. He prepared to leave by the nearest window. But it was another woman, someone new, and Étienne was preparing to give her the tour. First, the provenance of the place: René de Chambrun, the famous lawyer and businessman of the famille Pineton de Chambrun, had lived in these rooms. The young woman, who spoke in a small and awed voice, seemed to understand little of what Étienne said. Or no more than Kruse, anyway. The need to extract noble blood in a country that had given up on nobility was a quirk the editorialist shared with others Kruse had met since moving to France: two or three clients, some of the mayor's people. The man who had killed Lily, Jean-François de Musset, told similar stories after a bottle of wine. Everyone with ambition was secret royalty.

They moved from room to room, Étienne speaking with pretend humility about this *petit* piece or that *petit* discovery, vases and sculptures and paintings. They were nearing the room of mirrors when the woman asked if she might sneak into the bathroom for a moment. Kruse considered hiding, as Étienne Bonnet's hard leather shoes clopped toward the room, but decided against it. The light clicked on and Kruse wrapped his arm across Étienne's face, shushed his scream with his index finger in the mirror.

"Does Annette know?"

Étienne whispered too. "I am calling the police."

"Go ahead. Please."

The man breathed, considered. "What do you want?"

"If you're going to do this, break it off with Annette. She thinks—"

"We aren't married. She is free to do as she pleases, as I am." Released from his grip, Étienne stepped far from Kruse and looked at himself in the mirror. He was a tall and thin man who reminded Kruse of an adolescent bloodhound, with a face ready to sag into real dignity. "And you, lecturing me. A typical American, preaching ethics while invading a man's privacy. You're a criminal who has broken into my apartment, an ugly nobody without the courage to—"

"She has a daughter. She needs—"

The door opened down the hall.

"She needs *you*, Christophe? Then why has she chosen me?"

It was not a question he could answer.

Étienne fixed his tie. "You're pathetic."

Kruse slipped toward the doorway, to be sure the young woman would not see him. She walked in the wrong direction, in a small black dress. Blond and thin, short, with high heels. "Enjoy yourself, Étienne."

"Oh, I always do."

The editorialist waited until Kruse was nearly out the door before he called out. "Are you lost, sweet darling?"

FOUR

Avenue Bosquet, Paris

BY SIX IN THE MORNING, KRUSE HAD ALREADY JOGGED AROUND THE perimeter of Champ-de-Mars park. He had sprinted through the dewy grass. His sit-ups and push-ups were finished and because sunrise, that April morning, was an actual sunrise, he shadowboxed with a comically long adversary.

It was not really a job offer. Zoé Moquin could not un-say what she had said, and she had said too much. The Universal Declaration of Human Rights was signed across the river from his apartment. Instead of following the procedures and rituals of justice, the leading French security agency had sought the services of a mercenary. He could not un-know what he knew.

All he could do now was pack what he needed and fly to Toronto. It was a risk but he could not leave without a goodbye. He would wait on the sidewalk of Rue Valadon until they came down and he would pretend it was an accident and he would casually offer to walk Anouk to school.

He sweated in front of his own building on Avenue Bosquet, in his black hooded sweatshirt. There was a strong smell about the door. Kruse pulled the key out of the hole and stepped back. He crossed to the boulevard, then to the opposite boulevard, and looked up. It was still dark in the apartment, but in the sharp morning light, coming through the opposite windows, he saw a shadow move. The sweet smell remained in his nostrils, reminded him of something—someone. Men he knew in Paris who wore cologne did not wear this sort: the candy scent of a nightclub lineup, underneath the cigarette smoke. He thought about it for a moment and nearly smiled.

The smell was stronger in the stairwell, so strong that when he opened his apartment door he wondered if it would ever depart from his nostrils.

Tzvi Meisels stood in the kitchen, eating a croissant over a saucer. "This is not how I taught you to enter an apartment, Christopher. I was going to hide and jump out, like in the movies, test you. You would have failed. And then what?" Flakes of bread fell from his lips. "We would have to reconstruct our friendship."

"I smelled you from half a mile away, Tzvi."

"What do you mean?"

"Your cologne. When did you put it on?"

"After they phoned me. Before I left for the airport. It is a new scent. You think too robust?"

"I think too robust."

Though Tzvi had been his father since he was orphaned at seventeen, and though they had grappled and boxed and disarmed one another thousands of times, they had never actually hugged for the sake of hugging. It would have seemed bizarre to shake hands or to say "I'm so glad to see you," though Kruse was so glad to see him his eyes glistened with it.

"But it is favourable, you think? It smells favourably?"

"Welcome to Paris, Tzvi."

"You know this apartment is bugged. You know that, yes?"

Kruse did not know but he would not admit it now, out loud. It was as though he were carrying a piano up a long set of stairs and someone had finally offered to take it from him. He was comically tired. His legs were weak with the relief of seeing Tzvi. The front of his mentor's suit jacket and tie were sprinkled with the beige destruction of a croissant.

In an instant he thought over everything he had done and said in the apartment since December. Their company, MagaSecure, had bugged offices and a few houses for clients, so Kruse knew well enough where to look: behind and around paintings and mirrors, in light fixtures. It took him less than a minute to find a microphone on top of a nineteenth-century painting of a Provençal landscape: a hunter dressed in layers of brown, off-brown, and almost-yellow with his hound.

"I don't have visitors here. A few phone calls, but I've been careful."

"So they are serious, these Frenchies?"

Kruse shrugged.

"There is no reason to discuss here, is there? In your bugged penthouse?"

"No."

"It is a handsome home, I will admit." Since he had last seen him, Tzvi's accent sounded as though it had been dipped in glue. "You won the lottery?"

"Not exactly."

"You can tell me all about it on the way to my hotel."

"I'll shower and get dressed."

Tzvi walked across the kitchen and into the salon, stood next to him. He picked up a photograph of Lily and stared at it for some time. While he did, Kruse could not move. "Our beautiful girl." Tzvi took in a deep breath. "I have been worried about you, my boy."

If I leave, she dies.

"You are chasing phantoms in Paris, I think."

Instead of blubbering a response, Kruse lifted a finger—a moment, a moment—and walked to the shower. On his way he stopped in Anouk's bedroom, where she had never slept, which was really Lily's bedroom, and closed the door and breathed. Through Tzvi he understood that by any objective analysis he was half a step away from clinical insanity.

After the shower he dressed in his finest suit, a blue one, and stared at himself in the sweaty mirror. On the other side of the wall he could hear Tzvi rooting about in his drawers and closets, singing "Personal Jesus." Kruse couldn't remember the name of the band. One of those bands with men who wear eye makeup. It had been popular a few years earlier and Tzvi had come to love it, though he had the lyrics all wrong. "I am a believer," he sang. "You know I am at the gay bar."

Outside, the brief morning interlude of sunshine had transformed to light rain.

Kruse opened the bathroom door and, to interrupt and hopefully stop "Personal Jesus," shouted, "Where's your hotel?"

"The Morris."

"I've never heard of it. Where is it?"

"By the Louvre."

"You're staying at Le Meurice?"

"Well. Listen to you." Tzvi walked into the hallway, stood at the bathroom door, and mimed climbing an invisible wall. "*Le Meurice-uh.* Only the best of accommodations for me."

"Who's paying?"

Tzvi winked. "I am here for a bit of gentle tourism, my boy, that is all. I took the liberty of packing for you. All you need are toilet things."

"Toiletries."

"That."

"Where are we going, Tzvi?"

"Outside."

The wind had come up and tossed the soft rain into their faces. Kruse handed Tzvi the heavier umbrella. They walked east along Rue du Champ de Mars, past the aromatic cheese shop.

"Who called you here? The DPSD?"

"It is my profound love of architecture that called me here."

Kruse shook his head.

"You have not told me anything in a year. Not since you arrived in this bastard shithole of a country. Why should I tell *you* anything?"

They walked north toward the water, the Quai d'Orsay, where he hoped the new wind and the rain would overwhelm the tightness in his chest. The morning commute had not ended, so taxis were scarce. Tzvi vibrated with smugness. The city opened up at the river, past the roaring, honking madness at Les Invalides. The top third of the Eiffel Tower poked into a low cloud. In all their time together, Tzvi had avoided France. He would not forgive Parisians for betraying his uncle and sending him to Auschwitz, but when they arrived at the quay he whistled and slapped the concrete of the embankment and cussed and admitted defeat: he asked his protégé to hold his umbrella and took a photograph.

"What do you want to know?"

Tzvi looked at him the way he had always looked at him when he was slammed with *Canadian imprecision*. Then he looked up to the clouds. "How can I answer such a stupid question? I do not know what I want to know when I know nothing."

There was time, so Kruse told him everything. In Vaison-la-Romaine, their landlord had been a baker and local titan named Jean-François de Musset. He had planned to run for the National Front in the coming elections. Evelyn worked for Jean-François and for the party. She was also, Kruse learned in the press, sleeping with him. On Halloween night, Jean-François accidentally killed Lily with his car. He was drunk. More than drunk. And when that night Jean-François de Musset was murdered the police assumed it was Evelyn—his lover, roaring with revenge. Only it was not Evelyn.

"It was the gangsters."

"Yes."

"And the gangsters worked for the mayor of Paris."

"Yes."

Kruse hunted Evelyn, just as the police and the gangsters hunted her. And he failed to save her, just as he had failed to save Lily.

"None of it was supposed to happen." Kruse led him to the bridge. "They had drugged Jean-François, filled him with wine, hoping he would drive his Mercedes into a tree. This would end his political career. Only he didn't run into a tree. He ran into Lily."

"The mayor of Paris *ordered* this?"

"His chief of staff."

"And this was not a national scandal?"

"Only because the journalist who knew about it agreed not to write the story."

"At least de Musset is dead."

"It was not his fault."

"Only a Mennonite would defend his wife's lover and the murderer of his child. It's dangerous, the way you think."

"And I know the journalist."

He tumbled into embarrassment as he spoke of Anouk and Annette. It always pleased Tzvi to hear a confession. He folded his arm in with Kruse's and they shared one umbrella, walked like elderly lovers across the Pont de la Concorde, crammed with cars and tourist buses. They stopped for a moment to look down at the Seine. Tzvi asked for clarification: his apartment, Annette's apartment, their money, their deal, their "lifelong" protection deal from the City of Paris. All for holding on to their abominable secret. A *Bateau Mouche* hummed through the dark water.

"I am not a psychiatrist, Christopher, but you might have waited a few minutes before falling for another woman. A woman with a child, of all things. A dalliance I could see. Evelyn had betrayed you. You had ungentlemanly urges. But—"

"It wasn't intentional."

"What was not intentional?"

"Falling for her."

Tzvi lifted his nose, as though he had caught a whiff of the sewer. "Christopher?"

"Yes."

"You did not even dally with her, did you?"

His mentor and business partner did not carry the romance gene. Tzvi was bisexual and, in the twenty years Kruse had known him, had never extended a relationship beyond a week. To live as he had lived in Paris these past months, watching Annette from an irritating distance, waiting for—for what?—would be incomprehensible to Tzvi. On the bridge, presented with Tzvi's simple question, a question he would not answer, life since December was just as incomprehensible to Kruse.

"You wanted to keep them safe."

"Yes."

"So you reject them in some way, this little girl and her homely mother? To create a safe distance."

"She isn't homely." Kruse pulled Tzvi along, to cross the bridge. "But I knew they would come for me and I was right."

"You want to be the daddy."

"She's seeing another man."

"Of course. Of course she is. And I imagine he's dallying with her right now." Tzvi looked up at the clouds again, asked in Hebrew for God to send a lightning bolt of correcting wisdom down to his student. "My boy, if you had done the correct thing, if you had asked me for advice, this would not have happened. As you know and appreciate, smarter men than you, much smarter and much richer, pay me thousands of dollars for my counsel. For you it is always free. But no. You have to be Monsieur Lies and Secrets, Monsieur Heartbreak."

They passed the obelisk in Place de la Concorde and Tzvi tried to figure out where they must have put the guillotine for maximum theatrical impact.

To the right, at the fountain leading to the Tuileries and the Louvre, Kruse spotted a man in black walking into a grove of plane trees. He was the only one in the Tuileries without an umbrella, an amateur move, and he walked too quickly, on his tiptoes. He sneaked. Arm in arm again Kruse led Tzvi toward the fountain and positioned himself so he could watch the amateur spy and make it seem he was listening politely to the lecture about the importance of dallying-and-leaving and of listening to one's mentor. Men and women stared as they passed. It was against custom, this far from the Mediterranean, for men to be affectionate in public. Tzvi was not working, not seeking invisibility, so he smirked. He wore a brown suit, a blue tie, and gleaming shoes, all new since Kruse had left Toronto. His head was freshly shaved.

"Who are you watching?"

"No one."

"You can bullshit the Frenchies but you cannot bullshit me."

A waiter in a tuxedo leaned against the bar at one of the outdoor cafés, hugging a round tray. One silent couple sat under an umbrella with coffees, staring off in opposite directions. Kruse knew what Tzvi would say before he said it. They passed the fountain in silence, passed schoolchildren and busloads of seniors on their way to the Louvre.

"What kind of jackass builds a pyramid in the middle of all this?"

"The president of the republic."

"This is why I never trust a socialist."

"I like the pyramid."

"Yes and you should have dallied with this woman once, maybe twice, and you should have come back to me, for Christ's sake, because some of our clients—jackasses, yes, fools, the worst of them, the homosexuals and bored women—*request you*. It is so obvious, the truth of this: our Lily is gone. Gone, my darling Christopher. How did all of this machinery in your head go so wrong? And who are you looking for in the trees?"

"The people who phoned you."

"These ghosts you are hunting, perhaps we could talk about this. I know a psychologist in Brantford."

"Oh shut up, Tzvi."

They turned left and walked on the limestone gravel toward the terrace and the street, Rue de Rivoli. They jaywalked and Tzvi addressed the bellmen in front of Hôtel Le Meurice as though they were old friends: handshakes, instant jokes in English, winks, and pretend handgun shots.

They entered the hotel and Tzvi straightened his already stiff posture. He walked slowly, lordly, past tapestries and Renaissance paintings toward the dining room. It smelled of bacon, Tzvi's favourite, the angel and the devil married into slices of over-salted meat. Giant chandeliers hung over the white tablecloths and ornate tile floor. Outside, the cloud had thinned and the room glowed with golden light. They waited in silence for the maître d' to notice them and lead them to a table near the window overlooking the street and the trees. MagaSecure was a successful company but not this successful: in all of their travels together they had never stayed at a five-star hotel.

Kruse tried to keep the displeasure from his voice. "When did they phone you?"

"Define *they*. Define *phone*."

The waiter poured coffee in their cups and Kruse stared at Tzvi, a man who never smiled or laughed but whose eyes betrayed him.

"Yesterday. It was the middle of the afternoon. A client—you do remember those, I think?—had taken me for lunch at a sushi restaurant. I hate sushi, as you know, it is the food of the apocalypse, but what could I say? The green horseradish. If I could take that by itself, or with some brisket, then perhaps, perhaps. It was sometime after lunch when they called, as I was at the office being a bit sick. It was as though I could smell the dead fish of the Haifa port on a hot day, only it was inside me. What does Toronto have to do with Japanese fish? This is what I was thinking when they called."

"Was it a man or a woman?"

"A man. A friend of yours. He spoke with a British accent."

"Joseph."

"He did not identify himself. A businessman, certainly. But he did make an offer. I countered."

"Joseph works for the mayor of Paris."

"He is your colleague, then."

"His brother drugged the man who killed Lily. His brother killed Evelyn and he nearly killed me."

"And this Joseph is your friend?"

"He's the reason I'm still alive. His brother would have killed me. Joseph stopped it. He killed his own brother instead of me."

"And now you both work for the mayor."

Kruse leaned over the table and whispered, "I'm not a murderer."

"If you're working for the government, it isn't murder."

"What is it?"

"Justice."

"The man who phoned you, Joseph Mariani, is the head of a crime family."

"The question is, when someone offers you a million dollars, what is two million to them? Or ten? This is the morality of the story."

"The moral."

"Yes, yes."

"No."

The waiter returned to fill their cups with coffee and to take their orders. Kruse went for a French breakfast: bread, jam, a bit of cheese. Tzvi chose a variation on meat and eggs with menu language fancy enough to justify a three-hundred-franc price tag.

"My body thinks it is the middle of the night. But will that stop me from enjoying bacon? Negative."

Behind Tzvi there was a heavy red-and-yellow tapestry, and above that an oil painting that either celebrated or mocked the British royal

family as they prepared to ride out on horseback. Tzvi had a better view
of the room, which comforted Kruse almost as much as having the
view himself. His paranoia was, after all, a product of spending his life
with Tzvi. If they were to come, whoever *they* were, Kruse would pull
the tapestry down on them and open the window and go through the
Tuileries Garden and into the grey labyrinths of the city. Now that Tzvi
was here he was sure of it: they were watching, and if he refused this job
they would come. The life he had imagined in December, when he
allowed himself to do it, was as fanciful as the life Evelyn had imagined
for them in the South of France.

He would never live a life with Annette and Anouk in the seventh
arrondissement of Paris. No surgery would smooth his scars.

"My son."

"Yes." He realized Tzvi had been talking this whole time, about pork
and the one true religion in our hearts, and how taking the step of
eating pig while still loving God, the God of his own creation, made
him a human being. And this is what was wrong with his crazy long-
lost brothers of Arabia. They lacked the inner strength to say fuck it,
I'm my own man. God can either like it or he can shove it up his ass.
"Sorry, Tzvi. What?"

"Sure, it is completely halal to pick up a grenade and toss it into a
restaurant. God is a flexible and encouraging fellow when you want to
kill Jews. But bacon? No. No way. Not ever."

"I'm not doing it."

"*Someone* is going to do it. One of our competitors. And here is the
other trouble, which you have surely considered: *we know*. We cannot
know and not do it and go back to our lives."

"We protect people. We don't . . ." Kruse could not even say it out
loud. "We had a deal, when we started MagaSecure."

"No one ever asked us to hunt an anti-Semitic mass murderer."

"There is a reason for that. Why us, really, Tzvi?"

"You do not have to believe in evil, as an absolute. But there is no word in my vocabulary for what they did in that restaurant, if not *evil*. And you were in it."

"Revenge is—"

"It is not revenge, Christopher. It is justice. The simplest and most graceful justice. I'm not a young man anymore and there is something of my old work that I miss. We have protected some grotesque people. Why not un-protect some?"

"We don't know who did it."

"This is our job. Why us? No one is better suited."

Kruse did not want to talk about it and said so. An organ concerto played quietly in the background. Organ music reminded him unhappily of his parents, of how they had narrowed their short lives. If he regretted his choice in career, which had led him down every one of his dark alleys, the source of his regret was Allan and Nettie Kruse's religion. He did not know how, not precisely. If he had grown up regular, a regular boy with regular parents, he might have ended up an engineer.

"I had thirty minutes to pack. There was a chartered airplane waiting for me at Pearson, with a beautiful ageless server who spoke almost as many languages as me. My seat was a bed. She was not interested in joining me. At least that is what she said. We landed here and the Frogs picked me up at the airport. We negotiated *a bit*."

"If you want to call them Frogs please do it quietly."

"And they brought me here. A deluxe suite. I will show you after breakfast."

"You negotiated a bit. What does that mean, Tzvi?"

"They had negotiated with you. You had walked out. Somehow they knew I was empowered to negotiate on our behalf. They knew plenty about me."

"Joseph."

"And really. An Arab maniac blows up a bunch of Jews and my Christopher? This is difficult to refuse. Luckily, you had played your part."

"We don't know he was Arab. What was my part?"

"Hard to get. *La coquette.* I mean, they started with a million. I started with five."

"Oh God."

"We settled on three. You and I begin—"

"You. *You* begin." Kruse whispered, in Hebrew: "It is not in my heart to kill."

"My son. This century has brought us many things. Among them a truth I can relate with magnificent sincerity: it is in every heart."

It was raining heavily again. Tourists ran from the gardens to Rue de Rivoli, the canopies of Le Meurice. Mothers and fathers crossed the street with their children, carrying them, holding their hands. Kruse longed, as ever, to trade places with them. He would be a pear-shaped man in blue jeans and sneakers with a fanny pack and a striped windbreaker that says *POLO* in giant letters on the front, a little girl or a little boy to protect, a wife to surprise with flowers and trips, to hold hands with at the movies.

After the blast at Chez Sternbergh there had been bloody wanderers, confused in the smoke. An elderly man, charred and ashen, picked up body parts and dropped them into a filthy garbage bag until a woman in uniform stopped him. Another woman recited devotional poetry in the corner.

In every heart.

The deluxe suite on the sixth floor was decorated with old satiny opulence. It was vast and airy, ten times larger than most hotel rooms in the capital. Tall glass-plated doors opened over the gardens. Neither of them was interested in a drink from the mini-bar, and Kruse was reluctant to sit. He leaned against the rough wallpaper, in one of the only spots on the wall he could find without a painting. The room smelled of plummy cigar smoke, one of Tzvi's indulgences.

Neither of them removed their suit jackets. The way he was staring at him, with adoring menace, Kruse thought Tzvi might attack him for educational purposes.

"You heard about the World Trade Center?"

"Of course."

"These Arabs have figured it out—the new way to fight. With a few shekels and an endless supply of boys with below-average IQs, you can start and sustain a war. How do we patriots respond? War planes? An army? That costs billions. And it's exactly what the Arabs want."

"Again, we don't know it was Arabs."

"Persians maybe. Anyway, your Frenchies are smart. Goddamn brilliant to ask us. We find out who did this and we kill the lunatic in semi-gruesome fashion, snap some pics, and word gets around ever so gingerly among the intelligence organizations. Next thing you know, MagaSecure does two or three of these a year. We prevent mass murders. I do something truly meaningful with the back end of my life. You retire at fifty."

"I'm already retired."

"Tell me, Christopher, how you are retired. Your patron has given you an apartment and a monthly stipend. Yes?"

"Yes.

"Furnished. Their furniture?"

"Yes, Tzvi."

"Their furniture, their bugs. Maybe even video."

Kruse looked out the window, over the gardens. Rain fell and snapped on Rue de Rivoli. Two little sisters cried in it as their parents pulled them along toward shelter. He opened the window so he might hear them. Evelyn had hated the sound of a crying child, even the sound of Lily fighting against sleep. While it did not please Kruse, it did please him to ease her into stopping. The best: get her laughing while she is still in the middle of a cry.

"And the stipend. Allow me to conjecture. I set these deals up in Mossad. Perhaps they stole my model."

"Oh come on."

"They say it is for services rendered. It is your reward. Bon voyage! But then . . . oops, guess what, my foreign friend? We need you to do this little thing for us. If not, no more money and no more sexy apartment. And that family you care for, down the way, one worries about their safety."

"They haven't threatened me yet."

"What are you talking about? This woman—they will throw her out of her fancy new apartment and they will make sure she finds no suitable work. They will block all exits. They will invent crimes. I do not know how desperate they are but they could kidnap that little girl. She would be eating Nutella in a rented hotel room, watching *Bugs Lapin* with an agency goon. Close the window, please." Tzvi stared at him, his arms crossed over his chest. "You have a house in Toronto. What else do you have, apart from me? MagaSecure and me? You cannot love a woman who is with another man. And her daughter? The more you feel for her, as you know, the more you hurt her. This, my boy, *this job* is how you start over."

Tzvi had never said it, but when he spoke of his years as a government killer it was as though he were describing the best meals of his life. He was part of a group that had taken the name of the original Jewish assassins, the Sicarii, who tried to frighten the Romans out of Judea by slitting the throats of important men on the street and at parties.

But Tzvi had quit, fled, for reasons Kruse did not understand. When he discovered his teacher, in the little Krav Maga studio, Tzvi was not billing at three hundred dollars an hour. He had few students. He was a self-defence teacher with scant ambition and plenty of secret regrets, driving an eleven-year-old Volkswagen.

He said it so quietly he could not imagine his teacher would hear him. "We're just not—"

"I am." Tzvi moved across the room. He didn't attack. Instead he reached for Kruse's hand until he looked up and then he tenderly squeezed. "I always have been. And I trained you to be better than me."

"Trained, maybe. But—"

"It is in you. As deeply as it is in me, maybe more. Otherwise you would have stopped long ago."

Kruse wanted to argue but he did not know how. His parents had never believed him and neither had Evelyn. No matter what he said, they knew. And it frightened them. Why pretend with Tzvi?

"You can come in."

Kruse backed into the corner, prepared himself. "Who can come in?"

The door of the deluxe suite opened and two young men he did not recognize, in well-fitted suits, led Zoé Moquin into the room. Tzvi's French was imperfect but he understood everything and clients always understood him. His great talent, in other cultures, was a radical immersion into the manners of the place. For nearly two minutes he presented himself to Moquin and thanked her for the invitation and asked how she was faring this rainy morning. He complimented her on her red hair, pinned up again in a complex fashion, and her extraordinary dress. It was the colour of cream, the skirt shorter in the back than in the front, and open at the neck. It came with a wide and immaculate necklace.

Kruse tried so hard not to stare at Zoé that he knocked over an end table, interrupting the festival of politesse. "Why do you need us, Madame Moquin? Why not these perfectly capable men?"

Tzvi apologized for him and answered for her. "Because we are better. The best in the world. This is why they have hired us."

For the next half-hour Kruse listened to the briefing from a distance. Zoé Moquin looked up at him every few minutes. Her perfume battled with Tzvi's candy-factory cologne for supremacy in the room. When she suggested his apartment in the seventh would be the centre of operations, he said no. They would choose a hotel and submit the bill; it would do neither party any good to be listening in on each other. Kruse knew what Tzvi would say when they were alone and she was not listening: about her legs, her lips, the beauty mark under her left eye, the way she touched her neck when Kruse spoke to her. It was not complex, what she was asking of them. He had not closed the window all the way, and he listened to families on the sidewalk below calling out to one another. The fundamental anxiety in the marvellous lives of the British tourists, just now, was rainwater. Mothers and fathers were creatures of hope: soon it would stop and they would go back into the gardens, all the way to the Louvre. Rain doesn't last forever.

But it could last forever, said the children. It could.

FIVE

Rue Cujas

TZVI PROWLED THE LAMPLIT SALON OF THEIR SUITE LIKE A BOY WHO had just scored the winning goal. The childhood friend who had joined Mossad with him, and remained in Collections, was not being coy on the telephone.

"You must know this is a splendid gift you are giving me. It is a gift to me, and to you yourself, my friend, and to our great nation."

Instead of listening to Tzvi celebrate, Kruse inspected the art on the walls. Every painting was a portrait of a French industrialist in the 1920s. The captions were mini-biographies: each of these unsmiling men had become wealthy during and after the First World War, manufacturing and selling armaments, rebuilding in the north. Together the paintings were an alternative history of the city from the one Evelyn had taught him: Paris of the poor American artist. The men on one side of the room profited from collaboration in the Second World War. The other side chose not to collaborate and their assets were nationalized by Vichy.

Tzvi repeated one name over and over into the cordless receiver: *Khalil al-Faruqi*. Kruse made his way to the door jamb of his bedroom, his stomach tight with worry. It was supposed to take them weeks or months to find the man who had thrown the grenade. Even as they had gone over the plan in Le Meurice, he had hoped this day would never come. His bedroom was wallpapered in white with a pattern of blueprints for fifteenth-century war inventions: a cannon with three barrels, a giant crossbow, an armoured cart, a revolving bridge. Above his bed was a black chandelier like melting wax.

The call ended and Tzvi took his time walking across the carpets of the salon. He rubbed his hands for a while, feigned disinterest. "And how are you, *jeune homme*?"

"Tell me."

"You look a bit white. Have you contracted consumption in the last hour?"

"Tzvi."

"My boy, my wonderful boy, you will never guess what I have learned."

"You were right."

"Who might have guessed it? I was right! And it could not be more perfect. My oldest, filthiest bastard of an enemy, going back to Munich, did this to us. I cannot believe our luck—to earn three million dollars killing a man I have dreamed about killing since I was twenty. Christopher, sweetheart. When we find this *ben zona* I am going to cut a hole in him somewhere, maybe in his sternum, and fuck it."

"I won't allow that."

"Right in the sternum."

"You can't already be sure. You make one phone call and—"

"Mossad is the best in the world for a reason. They do not play by any sentimental rules. As for al-Faruqi, this is the work of his life. Some people build houses. Others work on computers. Maybe they are farmers, merchants, veterinarians, beekeepers. Khalil al-Faruqi kills Jews. We begin tomorrow."

"How would your contact know already that—"

"The French security apparatus, whatever it's called."

"Tzvi—in this, we are the French security apparatus. If someone in French intelligence has informed Mossad already, then how could they know what they know? And why wouldn't Madame Moquin pass it all to us?"

"You make me tired, Christopher. This is a Canadian disease you suffer from. It is like those happy maniacs who come by my house with their brochures and ask me to join their religion."

"The Mormons?"

"Not those happy maniacs."

"The Jehovahs?"

"Yes, those ones. The Witnesses of Jehovah. With photographs of lions and baboons and people of all different colours having a permanent cocktail hour together in paradise, only with no cocktails. There is no such place, no such world. Some people, my boy, are simply *bad people*."

"I think this is a dangerous line of reasoning, Tzvi."

He clapped his hands. "You make me tired. But not too tired to go out and celebrate. *On y va*."

"I have nothing to celebrate."

"The opportunity to eliminate a mass murderer and make three million dollars? You are a grump of astonishing passion."

"It's too fast."

"What's too fast?"

"They're paying us three million for nothing. If they know who did it . . ."

"No one knows. My old friend does not know. But he knows."

"How?"

"They listen in on *everything*, including this conversation you and I are having just presently. Hello, fat men with headphones and potato chips in Haifa! And whose Arabic is better? Your friends in French intelligence or my friends in Israeli intelligence?"

"It feels wrong."

"That feeling is fear. Come out with me. We shall dance it away."

Kruse shook his head and watched Tzvi walk down the narrow corridor in a dark suit, the walk of a man who has never been stopped. A splash of new cologne hung in the suite. Kruse stood in silence for a moment and then he called down for a bottle of red wine, whatever they recommended, and turned on the television. In the neighbourhood, Allan and Nettie Kruse were the only parents who didn't drink. There was a religious imperative, but neither of them were orthodox or even terribly rigid Mennonites. It was something else: fear of losing control.

He watched the news. In a town called Waco a religious group had done something to inspire a gigantic military siege. The woman who brought up the bottle, a Vacqueyras, spoke with a stutter. She had chosen it herself, she said, and stared at the scar on his cheek. The wine was a dehydrated plum. He turned off the television and sat in the couch and closed his eyes and remembered the man whose head had bobbed alongside Chez Sternbergh: his hair, his eyes, his nose, his ears.

For most of his life, he did not take a drink. It was not a fear of losing control that stopped him. He worried his senses would be dulled, that it would slow his feet and hands, make him a fool. But he was safe in the hotel, with nowhere to go. Nowhere to go until his third glass, just after midnight, when he decided to put his tie back on and go out.

The hotel was a converted thirteenth-century abbey with a clock tower on top. He walked backwards a few paces to watch it grow smaller in the pale evening spotlights. While he had no destination, there was nowhere else to go. He walked north and west through the tranquil old city, from the fifth to the seventh. It reminded him, after a certain hour, of a church: there were people on the streets but they spoke in careful murmurs, as though everything were a secret.

Rue Valadon was deserted. No people, no cars. He knew the code on the door by watching her, and though he didn't have the key he

didn't need one. In the foyer he took off his shoes. Piano played softly
toward the bedrooms. Annette had heard that falling asleep to classical
music taught children to concentrate in school or to be kinder to one
another, something. He stopped at her door and pushed it open wide
enough to see she was alone; Étienne was presumably out with one of
his other girlfriends.

Anouk's room smelled like her shampoo and conditioner, faintly of
apples. It had an en suite, and the humidity of a recent bath hung in
the air. Kruse sat against the wall, near her bed, and watched her in
what streetlight leaked in through the curtains. In December she had
been kidnapped. Anouk had watched a man without a nose strip her
mother naked and attach her arms to a hook on the ceiling. It was all
his doing and he knew, from daytime television talk shows, that episodes of fear and anxiety in childhood led to weakness and victimhood
later in life.

So in the dark, with the piano in the background, he whispered
strength to her.

By the time he heard the bare feet on the wood floor it was too late.
The only exits were windows: two in her bedroom and one in the
bathroom. Three glasses of wine had made it a philosophical option,
nothing more. What would it *mean* to sneak out a window?

Annette always slept in a long white T-shirt. She now had the money
to afford the finest lingerie in Paris, but instead she stayed with the
Johnny Hallyday shirt. To him, Johnny Hallyday represented French
extremes. They may have been more sophisticated than Canadians, but
when they were tasteless they were really tasteless.

She waved him out of the room and leaned against the wall in the
corridor, in between small works of what Étienne called *l'art-pompier*.
Her eyes were small in the light and he could tell she had just brushed
her hair.

"I could call the police."

"You could."

"This is an invasion. It is below you and an insult."

"I wanted to say goodbye."

She reached up for her black hair, pulled her fingers through her curls at the back. "What do you mean?"

"There's a job I have to do. And when I do it, I may not come back."

"Why not?"

"The apartment, what I have. They can take it away."

"Four months? Monsieur le Maire said we could have these forever."

"You can. I can't."

"I could still write the story, the truth about what the mayor's men did to you. To us."

"Monsieur le Maire has prepared himself, I'm sure."

Annette looked away, furrowed her brows as though she were working through a math problem. "You were chanting."

"Not chanting, not exactly."

"Another cowboy song?"

"No."

"Where are you going?"

"I don't know yet."

Annette's breathing sped up. When he fought, Kruse watched his opponents' chests. All but the best-trained fighters telegraphed with their breath. He knew when they were about to swing, and he always wanted to hit them before they hit him. Annette did not hit him. Her lips quivered and she reached up to block the view with her hand, as if there was something hideous in her teeth.

He knew someone like Zoé Moquin would arrive. Only it happened much sooner than he had imagined. But if he knew a Zoé Moquin would arrive, why didn't he just do what he had most wanted on Christmas Eve? If Kruse had lived here with them, whispering truths to Anouk in the night, whispering to Annette, everything would be the same. Tzvi would be out prowling. He would be thinking about a man named Khalil al-Faruqi. Everything would be the same but this: Annette standing before him with trembling lips, confused and hurt and perhaps worse.

Kruse had never kissed her but he had hoped to, someday. He had been a fool.

"I am sorry."

"For what?"

Kruse reached for her hand. Her skin was hot from sleep. Annette slept with her window opened, and did not smell of apples. She smelled of rain. For a few moments, magical moments, she allowed him to hold her hand. There was no way to say what he was thinking—*I will do anything to be sure you and this girl are safe*—without either sounding like an idiot or scaring her, so he said nothing.

Annette looked down at their hands, one in the other, and slowly pulled hers away. "It's very simple between men and women like you and me. You're either together or you're not. You can't be friends, not really. You're either in all the way, Christophe, or you're all the way out. It seems to me you're out."

"Maybe . . ."

"There are no maybes. And if you do this again I'll call the police."

It was not yet raining but soon it would. Thunder rumbled in the north. On the corner a new car gently rocked back and forth. Inside, two lovers moved on one another. Kruse arrived at the abbey just as the rain began to fall. The woman with the stutter, who had brought the Vacqueyras to the suite, asked how it was and offered him a towel for his hair. He said it was delicious and dangerous.

It took her a while to get it out but she said, "Like all the finest things."

• • •

The Salle Ovale of the National Library was as solemn as a cathedral. It smelled of dust and wood and of something that had been drenched long ago and might never dry. Natural light came in through the roof and a series of glass portholes to the sky. Yet like all of his favourite places in Paris the grand hall carried its beauty and grandeur with an unpretentious shrug. The scholars who showed up with him at ten in the morning to snatch their spots were hunched and unattractive. A few of them mumbled to themselves. These were Evelyn's, his wife's, people more than his, the doomed intellectuals, and as always he envied them for the simple ways they dove into complexity. He had queued with them in the courtyard, near the leaning statue of Jean-Paul Sartre, and when he had entered with them they rushed like roaches. The red-haired reference librarian with the freckles and the enormous wedding ring picked him out and pointed.

"One of these things is not like the other," she sang, in English, with an accent he would always find adorable.

"I forgot my plastic bag full of paper clips and discarded eyeglasses."

He and the librarian had never asked each other's names, but for months she had been helping him in the Salle Ovale. When Evelyn was on the run and he was trying to find her before the government and the Marianis, the librarian taught him the tricks of the place. Since then, preparing for client work, he came in once every couple of weeks. As long as they didn't know each other's names, her flirtation with him held its innocence.

"What is it today?"

Kruse did not have a regular spot. He was never here early enough to choose. The least attractive spaces were desks facing one another in the middle of the floor. He placed a pad of writing paper on the most attractive of the least attractive and pulled a piece from the top, wrote "Khalil al-Faruqi" on it.

For some time the librarian stared at the paper. She did not yet dye her hair, even though a two-centimetre-wide stripe of grey had appeared to the right of her forehead. If Kruse knew her well enough to say so he would tell her it was lovely. "I've just been reading about him."

"I wonder if I could look at that."

She winked at him and walked across the room. While he knew how to operate in a library, thanks to the academic he had married, the librarian had opened up new avenues. She had even taught him how to search on a computer. When she wasn't around, he was good. When she was around, Kruse found more than he ever needed.

The article was from *Le Monde Magazine*: a rundown of what had happened at the end of February in the basement of the World Trade Center. Two men drove a van filled with a six-hundred-kilogram bomb into the underground parking garage, lit a fuse, and ran. The men who did it had not acted alone. Someone had wired them money and advice; Khalil al-Faruqi was chief among the suspects.

"This is your man?"

"Yes."

One of her eyelids drooped just slightly lower than the other. The librarian wrote something in the small notebook she carried. "What would you like to know about him in particular?"

They split up the work of finding the books and magazines and newspapers that had not yet been transferred to microfiche. His table was soon stacked so high the librarian asked a porter to move him to a staff desk. This appeared to upset a few of her fellow librarians, who greeted him coolly. His option, in these moments, was to do what came naturally to him—apologize and thank them to the point of absurdity—or to do what a French person would do: pretend he didn't care.

Before she allowed him to sit, the librarian organized the material according to its comprehensiveness. On the top, a long profile about al-Faruqi in *The New Yorker*. The article came with a black-and-white photograph that at first appeared to be something else. Then he understood it: a pile of dead people, some in clothes and some not. It was artful and less gruesome than what he had seen in Chez Sternbergh, but once he realized what he was seeing it was similar enough that he could not breathe for a moment. He could taste the explosion in the back of his throat again. The caption described flatly that it was the result of a grenade attack on Israeli adolescents on a school exchange in Brussels: nine dead and seventy-four injured.

The librarian remained beside him. "Khalil al-Faruqi did that?"

"It seems so."

While they had never discussed his job in any precise way, the librarian knew he was not a journalist and not a bureaucrat. She called him a hunter. "I'd like to ask why you're interested in him. But I won't."

"Oh, it's just simple curiosity, Madame."

"That's what you always say." She looked at the awful photograph again. "In this case I do hope your curiosity, or someone's, leads to his capture."

Another woman, in a sweater with shoulder pads, arrived and whispered sternly to her. His librarian sighed, wished him luck, and followed her superior into the stacks.

The terrorist was born in Jaffa, probably in 1931. His father had been a doctor and had owned both an orange grove and a large share in a diamond business. Khalil al-Faruqi had several brothers and sisters, and his father had thirteen wives. He grew up in the ancient port city and, variously, in New York and Marseille and London. In 1948, with Palestine divided and Arab and Jewish militias fighting in the streets, blowing up cars and shops, the teenage son of wealth ended up in a refugee camp. His father was killed and the family ended up poor and miserable in Cairo. For several years he disappeared. Competing mythologies had al-Faruqi in jail in Saudi Arabia, working in Egypt, spying for the Ba'ath Party, launching an arms-smuggling enterprise. He helped plan the hostage-taking and massacre of Israeli athletes in Munich in 1972; Mossad would pursue him, unsuccessfully, for fifteen years.

In 1973, three weeks after the Yom Kippur War, al-Faruqi led a group called the New Arab Nation to hijack a Swissair flight between London and Geneva. Three Saudi Arabian government officials were killed, five Palestinian prisoners were released from Swiss prisons, and he got away with a "secret" payment of twelve million dollars from King Hussein of Jordan. In the next ten years he became the most feared Palestinian terrorist in the world, everywhere and nowhere at once, blowing people up in Europe and the Middle East. The peers of his youth softened into middle age, and al-Faruqi was ultimately rejected by movements easing toward political legitimacy: recognized parties, bank accounts, property.

The central question of the *New Yorker* article, from 1988, was whether or not al-Faruqi was still in business. It had always been his habit to claim an atrocity, to make a wily celebrity of himself. In recent years, unsolved attacks had led to al-Faruqi, yet he had remained silent and invisible. No one knew where he was, or even if he was still alive.

On his notepad, Kruse kept track of the number of people the Palestinian had admitted to murdering: it was over two hundred. It was not a successful expedition to the Salle Ovale; newspapers and magazines pegged al-Faruqi's location as somewhere on earth.

It was another rainy day, so far without rain. He used his umbrella as a cane and walked through the Tuileries. The tiny nightingales had arrived on their route from Nairobi to Oslo and serenaded him as he moved through the park. He chose Pont de la Concorde, not because it was the most beautiful but because of what he could see from it. A year in France had not made him immune to its beauty. Kruse had grown up in a house built after the Second World War among other houses built after the Second World War: boxy and efficient, with scant attention to beauty. For his parents, beauty was a cruel extravagance as long as children were going to bed hungry. He could never remember thinking, as a child: I live in an ugly place. If anything, he felt enveloped by warmth, if not beauty, and its pleasures were related. On Pont de la Concorde he did not feel warm. Every thought in his mind, when he reached the bridge, was of turmoil: bodies ripped apart by men who could, somehow, find a way to sleep at night. But from the bridge, with the Élysée Palace behind him and the Assemblée Nationale in front, the columns and statues and flecks of gold, beauty was a comfort. It was a government's trick, a religious feint. The citizens of Paris had been slaughtered many times. Heads had rolled into baskets. Babies had starved. But let us not forget the grand monuments of the republic.

Halfway across the bridge he saw her, standing next to a silver Audi with its four-way flashers blinking. The sedan was half on and half off the sidewalk. Zoé Moquin wore a bright yellow jacket over a blue dress with a swoop about the bottom, a hint of Spanish dancing about it. He could not imagine Zoé clapping her hands, stomping her heels, and spinning around a fire. The rain began to fall. Her driver, who walked crookedly and wore a hat that seemed too large for him, opened an umbrella and held it over her. His mouth was open and his breath seemed to be making a faint hum.

"Can we give you a lift?"

"I'm enjoying the walk, thank you, Madame Moquin. Another unforgettable dress. Bravo." Rain dripped from his nose.

She watched him and sighed. "You've had some early success with your research?"

"You know precisely what success we've had."

"He is a very bad man."

"How did you bug our room?"

"Room service. Your Tzvi must know."

"I have a theory, Madame Moquin."

"Would you like to share it?"

"We have had early success with our research because you gave it to us."

"I gave you money, not research."

The pedestrian and bicycle traffic on the bridge sped up around them as the rain fell harder. Her yellow jacket was immaculate. There was not even a speck on it. Zoé Moquin, he decided, did not have small children.

"You knew Tzvi would call his old colleagues in Mossad. You planted something."

"I wouldn't even know how to do that. You're paranoid, Monsieur Kruse."

It was strange to argue with a woman while a disabled man held an umbrella over her.

"You will pursue this bit of intelligence, I imagine. What will you need?"

"A car."

"Anything else?"

"Weapons. We'll contact you."

"You can't contact me, not about cars and weapons. There is a parking garage under the Louvre. I will leave an envelope at your suite, with the keys and instructions."

"If you know who did this, Madame Moquin, why have you hired us at all?"

"First of all, I know nothing. We're bound by certain laws and conventions, as you know. Whereas you and Monsieur Meisels . . ." She looked to her right, toward Notre-Dame. Its towers were hidden by the cloud that had dropped on the city.

"We'll look into it."

"And then . . ."

"Your instructions to us were quite clear, Madame. You were watching me at the library?"

"Not me. But yes."

"Can you stop that, please?" Kruse walked past her, toward the grey Assemblée Nationale. The heavy rain bounced on its stone steps.

"Let us drive you." Her voice sounded different when she raised it: "You may not like me but that's no reason to soak yourself."

Kruse soaked himself.

SIX

Allée Pierre et Marie Curie, Clichy-sous-Bois

ZOÉ MOQUIN HAD LEFT THE CAR IN A TIDY UNDERGROUND PARKING
lot east of the Louvre. It was one twenty in the morning yet ballet-
class piano played from hidden speakers. Kruse had a thin line of
sweat along his hairline, remnants of his warm-up in the flat. It had
been his tradition in Toronto, before they went out to a job: shadowbox the anxiety away. The car was supposed to be forgettable, a plain
brown Renault with a dent in the driver's door. But Moquin or her
staff had tucked it in a crowd of immaculate black and silver German
sedans. To park here for a day, between the palace and Les Halles, was
over one thousand francs. It was not the natural habitat for a plain
brown Renault.

Kruse slid their bags into the trunk next to a brown suitcase. There
were two semi-automatic pistols inside the suitcase, two assault rifles,
and two enormous knives.

"Jesus Christ." Tzvi carried it into the passenger seat with him, tossed
it in the back. "Who are these people?"

It felt natural to ease off into the darkness with Tzvi, the way another man might feel about going for a beer with a college pal. They had created nine strategies, based on what they might find in Clichy-sous-Bois. It was a lovely name for a suburb, but they expected everything but beauty. Tzvi, the navigator, whistled and opened the map. Kruse had studied the route and he knew the city well enough—if not *les banlieues*.

MagaSecure did dangerous work and he had the scars to prove it, but they had never before set forth on a job knowing that if they were successful someone would be dead before morning. It was a grotesque word: *assassin*. He could feel the blood pumping through his fragile stomach, but it nearly always felt this way on the night of a job—no matter what they were about to do. Kruse would not admit it aloud but Tzvi was right; he was surprised at his own confidence. He was a man of violence, no matter how much poetry he had read to please Evelyn.

The only other cars at this hour, on the north bank of the inky Seine, were taxis. The road was named after Georges Pompidou, whom Tzvi had met at a summit of European leaders in Israel after the Six Day War.

"He was prime minister at the time, the quietest. The least likely of them all, I thought, to be assassinated. He smoked a lot of cigarettes and wore too much cologne, like an awkward teenager."

"I know someone like that."

"Tiny mistress, minuscule, an elf princess."

Lights twinkled off the water. Drunks and lovers walked along the quay. This is what Kruse had imagined, when he and Evelyn had planned a year in France to change their lives: quiet walks along the water, holding hands, kissing where it seemed right, returning to their apartment to dismiss the babysitter and peek on sleeping Lily.

At the walls of Bercy Park, another concrete city emerged. The splendour and peculiarity of Paris turned banal and modern and efficient, an everywhere and nowhere city, a place for cars. Paris became Canada, an almost-America, and it comforted him. He expected to see a Home Depot and a Wal-Mart. He turned onto the Périphérique and weaved between two all-night transport trucks. Tzvi did what he always did on his way to a job: he spoke his way through their progress, eventuality by eventuality. He did it with his eyes closed and moved his hands, acted it out, climbed the stairs they would climb, kicked in the door. They drove north and then northeast, on the autoroute that would take them all the way to Brussels or, if they liked, to London. The national highway was quieter than the Périphérique and the quay, with rectangular box buildings and more miserable trees, uglier signs for less-appetizing food and wares, nowhere to walk. Tzvi confirmed the last few turns and they entered a neighbourhood of long nine- and ten-storey apartment complexes, random piles of garbage, burned-out cars. On the ground floor, gathered around steps, young men and women stood drinking and smoking in the darkness. American hip hop played from a ghetto blaster. They turned to meet the headlights and their eyes shone.

Tzvi had spent another hour and a half on the phone with his contact in Mossad, going through the research the agency had collected on al-Faruqi and his French network, where he might be today. While he did, Kruse had stood on the balcony of the old abbey and looked out on the street: businesspeople with cellular phones, men and women with shopping bags, the white-haired Parisians out for a stroll, the after-school children in blazers and shirts and shorts. He envied every businessman with a briefcase, every man picking up a baguette and a basket of strawberries on his way home, every exhausted father on the cobblestones.

Their destination was down an alley and through a crumbling lot named after Marie and Pierre Curie. Someone had planted aspen trees unevenly along the fence. A narrow river of discarded water bottles, magazines, and beer cans had collected between them. For night jobs, Kruse and Tzvi wore dark grey and brown, the invisibility cloaks of vagrants, instead of black. They never wanted to be mistaken for police or commandos. To take the shine off his head, Tzvi had bought a knitted skullcap from an Arab merchant near Les Halles. It gave him the air of a devotee. The entrance was not marked with an address but it matched the description. Glass had long departed from the windows on the main floor, replaced by wood and cardboard and tape. No one loved the building enough, or hated it enough, to tag it with graffiti.

They put on their night goggles and armed themselves with the sharp, heavy, discreet knives Tzvi had brought from home. Unless there was a need for snipers, Tzvi's philosophy was that a trained fighter always brings a knife to a gunfight. And not the Rambo bear-skinner with a compass that Zoé Moquin had included in their care package. If you have a gun or a machete, either you'll use it or someone will use it on you. In their work, they were always outnumbered; the fewer guns in a theatre the better.

Kruse climbed the communications tower and disabled telephone service while Tzvi kept watch. They entered the building as they entered every building: silently, calmly, with authority, like telephone repair-men. The door did not have a lock and the elevator was out of order. Someone had abandoned a broken television set inside. Kruse found the electrical room at the back and popped off the breakers. Tzvi scanned the floor with his penlight to be sure there were no abandoned needles. Bits of thin glass from fluorescent tubes lay on the stairs. It smelled of fresh urine. In an alcove on the second floor a man wrapped in blankets rocked and murmured to himself.

They had expected a guard somewhere. The Mossad agent had said it was no longer a place to live so much as a gathering place for violent young men pretending to be refugees as they planned their next assault. The hallway was empty but for a cat and its shirtless owner passed out near an open door.

"Well, I am only a pretend scholar but that seems terribly un-Islamic," said Tzvi.

Kruse dragged the man into the apartment and tried to close the door. It was broken, half off its hinges. The cat followed him inside and then back into the hall, meowed at him, rubbed against his legs as he walked. Kruse picked up the cat, loved it into a purr, and returned it to the apartment, told it to stay. He listened at each door, for French and for Arabic. Halfway down the corridor, they had heard nothing but the snores of the shirtless man.

If they were successful, if by some miracle Khalil al-Faruqi was here, their job was to "eliminate" him and take a photograph of his dead body. On every job there was a potential that someone would be killed. This is what Tzvi had told him, when he was fifteen, and what they told every student and every client: treat every fight like a fight to the death. While there was nothing his Mennonite parents could support about what he had chosen to become, Kruse tried to honour them in tonight's true mission. If they can walk in and walk out with the information they came for and without killing any violent young men pretending to be refugees, they succeed. They remain good.

If Tzvi knew how he felt, he would try to forbid it. The spice of what they intended to do, here and elsewhere, hung heavily in the hall. They weren't rescuing anyone or protecting anyone or preventing an attack, no matter what he tried to tell himself. Kruse stopped to breathe a moment. Tzvi pulled out the photographs one last time to shine his light on them, to stamp the images in their eyes. He kissed Kruse on the cheek. "Welcome back, my son. And to your future."

The door of apartment 322 was, like the others, hollow. Tzvi pressed his ear to it and tried the handle. There was no point picking the lock of a door like this, so he stepped aside and counted down from five, in Hebrew. It was, as ever, Kruse's job to kick it in. At *achat* he kicked and the door swung open and Tzvi whispered "My son" again and they sprinted into the apartment, into position. The main room was empty and so was the kitchen. Kruse set up. Streetlights flooded the room in flat yellow. A woman shouted in the darkness of the bedroom and a man mumbled.

Then a baby began to cry.

Tzvi cussed and ran into the bedroom. The woman screamed again but Tzvi shushed her, in Arabic. The baby cried louder. Kruse shone his light into the bedroom and opened the curtains. Tzvi was in position on the bed, behind the man. The woman—in a long white night-gown—cowered in the corner with the crying baby in her arms.

"He made a call. Fucking cell phones."

"Should we take him out of here? Into the hall? Into the car?"

"Too late." Tzvi addressed the man, bearded and handsome, with a Roman haircut. "We are looking for your boss, Mr. Khalil. Nothing sinister. He is an old friend from the country club."

"Go ahead and kill me."

Kruse sighed.

"I hate it when people say that." Tzvi slammed his hand into the man's ear. "Where are they coming from? This building or elsewhere?"

The man started to pray. Tzvi gave him five seconds to shut up and the man prayed all the way through. The woman joined him, rock-ing with her baby. Tzvi gave the man one last warning and knocked him out. The woman screamed, called them ugly devils. Kruse gently guided her by the arm out of the bedroom, and she shouted in his ear in Arabic. He was a motherless dog, an unbeliever, a murderer. She spit in his face and he calmed himself, fought his instincts. He low-ered her to the couch with her baby, whispering.

It was a modest but clean apartment, a place of dignity, and when she stopped screaming Tzvi complimented her.

"You saw what just happened to your husband."

She did not respond. The baby had stopped crying.

Tzvi pulled out his knife. "This is what I do for a living. I am paid to do it, by people who will ensure I never go to prison no matter what I do. Do you understand, Madame?"

"My baby."

"Do you understand?"

Her voice shook. "Yes."

"We are not here to hurt you. We love babies. We are mad for babies. We want your baby to be the president of the republic. We are only here for information. We want to leave you and your baby to get back to sleep. Your husband will wake up eventually, with a mild headache, but he will be fine too. Okay?"

"Yes."

Kruse went into the kitchen and drew a glass of water for her, wiped the warm spittle from his face. He checked his watch. Speaking calmly had worked. The baby had fallen asleep in her arms. A girl, if the pink blankets meant anything. Kruse watched from afar. He did not want to crowd the woman.

"Now, the men your husband called." Tzvi sat next to her. "When will they arrive?"

"They are a few kilometres away."

"How many will come?"

"Ten, perhaps."

"Now this is very important. Khalil al-Faruqi—where is he?"

"Monsieur, no one tells me things like this. He's not here. Not in Paris. He is far from Paris."

"But you have met him?"

"I have had that honour."

"Does he travel with many men?"

"He is very wealthy. There are men and women, children."

"Thank you. Thank you, Madame. The men who are coming, will they know where to find him?"

She looked up and prayed.

Kruse returned to the main room. "It's a girl?"

"A girl."

"Madame, Khalil al-Faruqi is not a real Muslim. He is an infidel himself, worse than us. He pretends. In reality, he is only a businessman." Kruse handed her the glass of water. The baby had long eyelashes and, in the streetlight glow, a pink nose. Kruse nearly said aloud that he was always astonished by the perfection of a baby's skin. "Think of your baby. Al-Faruqi is not mad for babies, like us. He kills them. That is his business."

"All of you kill babies."

Tzvi hid the woman in the closet, with her child. She insisted on covering her head, with men on the way. Tzvi tied up the groggy husband and slid a heavy bureau in front of the closet door while Kruse prepared his trap in the hall. He returned to the room and looked out the window while Tzvi stretched.

"They are coming to kill us, Christopher."

"I know."

"They will torture us, if they can."

"I know."

"They are little sadists. Ninety per cent chance they will fuck you in the ass with an inanimate object. No lube. Do you want that?"

"Tzvi."

"You cannot be thoughtful about this."

"No."

"I outlaw it. No thoughtfulness."

"All right."

"I spent a good part of my life, some of my finest years, training you to—"

"Yes yes yes." The windows were open in the apartment. A wind had come up and it twinkled through the leaves of the parking lot aspens. The night air entered the room and cooled his neck.

"Listen to me. You know damn well why I am saying this. This is not like anything we have done before. To stop these men, you have to stop them."

"I'll stop them."

"So they do not have another chance. No revenge. Not later tonight, not tomorrow, not ever."

A white van arrived and skidded to a stop in front of the building. Seven armed men jumped out. Tzvi asked for details on the weapons and Kruse reported semi-automatic handguns, no automatic rifles, no flashlights. Tzvi kissed him on the mouth.

"Christopher, my boy, my son."

"Yes, Tzvi. Yes."

Tzvi slapped him. "Do not fuck around."

Through the closet door he could hear the woman praying. He envied her. He could feel Tzvi watching him as he left the room. In the corridor he tested his trap again and crouched into position. He looked back toward the doorway at Tzvi, who winked and put his night goggles back on.

Kruse heard the clumsy, tentative footsteps on the stairs. His hands were cold, as always before a fight, and his face was hot. He willed his heart to slow. If he were to die, he was pleased he had visited Anouk one last time. He had held Annette's hand for a moment, in her apartment. It was something.

The men were at the top of the stairwell now, quietly arguing with one another in the dark about who might go first, a communal beast of anxiety. Arabic was the fourth language Tzvi had forced him to learn, in his teens and early twenties, and it was by far the hardest to trick his mouth into speaking. But it was his favourite. One of the young men opened the door and squinted in the darkness, his chest heaving. He sprinted immediately down the hall, toward apartment 322 and Tzvi. There were no windows, so apart from some streetlight seeping under the doors it was altogether dark. The man didn't make it. Blindly he ran straight into the taut metal cord Kruse had stretched across the hall, at neck height, and the back of his head hit the concrete floor with a hollow *thock* Kruse had heard too many times. The young man twitched once and lay still. Kruse gently moved him to one side of the hall.

The men whisper-shouted into each other's faces, spun like little boys at the lake mustering the courage to jump into the cold water. They called out for him. Ahmed! Ahmed! One punched another in the shoulder and ordered him to go. This one ran too, though he was still conscious when he hit the floor. He called out for help before Kruse could silence him. What Tzvi wanted him to do now was to finish each of them. The idea was nauseating. More shouting and calling out from the end of the hall. Ahmed! Naseer?

It took two years, when he was a teenager, to teach calm to his body. Before a fight or during a fight, when a larger man was mauling him, when every fibre in his brain was given to panic, he learned to breathe himself into stillness. Somehow the process had a smell, of the bamboo mat in the entrance of the Krav Maga studio off St. Clair Avenue in Toronto. It was nearly always wet, from melting snow in the winter and rain in the other three seasons, and fragrant. The third most courageous of the young men jogged into the rope and stumbled, hooted and swung at imaginary foes. Kruse took him down and covered him with a blood choke. The man hummed and squirmed and scratched at Kruse, tried to bite him until he went limp.

That left four, the four most frightened, to argue and call out for their fallen friends. One of them stepped forward and aimed into the darkness and shot three times. One of the bullets was so close Kruse could feel it pass.

"Who is it?" The shortest and stockiest of them had a deep voice. He switched from Arabic to simple French. "Who are you? What do you want?"

Kruse would not reveal his location or his accent. As quietly as he could manage, he disarmed and stacked the three fallen men against the wall to leave the corridor open. He crouched down again, the night vision goggles heavy on his face. The one who had spoken fell to his knees and crawled, feeling around as he made progress down the hall. Every five or six seconds, in a rhythm, he called back to his partners, "All is clear, all is clear."

They would need someone to interrogate, so Kruse waited to see if this one would make it past him and his comrades. It was a wide hallway. The young man paused for a moment as he passed, but just for a moment. His fallen friends were breathing but the others at the back of the hall were questioning him incessantly. "What do you see, Walid? Who is there?"

Walid crawled through the corridor and touched nothing but the thin, filthy carpet underneath him, calling back, simply, "All is clear," until it wasn't.

At the end of the hall, Tzvi pounced on him and dragged him into the apartment.

It sounded like a gulp and a thump, and the other three shouted for him, for Walid, whose voice had been a comfort. The tallest pounded at the dead light switch and asked God to intervene. The other two did not bother to shut him up. They would not come, so Kruse sneaked toward them. No one spoke, not in words, but there was a muffled roar from the other end of the hall. Walid! The tall one took three bold steps and two timid ones. He took his gun back from his comrade and lifted it. There were tears in his eyes. With his free hand he reached out and swept invisible things aside. He was far enough from the others, so Kruse disarmed him, broke his arm, and knocked him out with hardly a whisper. His head hit the floor with another awful sound, which was enough for the remaining two. They were poorly trained, adolescents in a haunted house, feeling around for the stairwell door. The first man opened it. Kruse intercepted the second and he shrieked in fear. There was a pop and he stiffened and went limp in Kruse's hands. In his panic the man had shot himself in the neck. Kruse wanted to undo it somehow, to start over. No, let's try this again. But the man was dead. Kruse whispered a quick, barely conscious plea and dropped him and ran down the stairs, where he found the last of them on the first-floor landing, feeling around for the handrail.

He took the gun away from the last man and informed him, in Arabic, they were going back up the stairs together.

"I speak French, asshole," the man said as he climbed. "Who are you?"

"A friend of Khalil al-Faruqi."

"A friend? Have you killed my—"

"Please believe me. I really don't want to hurt you."

"You're not al-Faruqi's friend."

"Do you want to tell me where he is? I have a few questions to ask him. Then you'll be my friend."

The young man laughed. "I don't want to die."

"You won't die. I promise."

At the top of the stairs Kruse led him toward the suite at the end of the hall. He stopped to remove the trap. There was a shout and several shots from behind them. Kruse's cheek burned and he spun around, knocked the gun out of the tall man's hands and kicked him in the face. The one he had been escorting lay in the hall, two holes in his back and one in the back of his head.

He had promised.

Just outside apartment 322, dragging the unconscious tall one, Kruse realized the blood dripping from his face was his own. One of the bullets had grazed his cheek.

Tzvi shone a flashlight on him. "What the hell?"

"This one shot me."

"How? When?"

"A moment ago."

"How did he see you?"

"He shot blindly. Killed his friend."

"I peeked out just a minute ago and this son of a bitch was on the floor. How could he have shot you?"

"He came to."

"*Came to* from what? From death? The others out there, might they also come to? And what was he doing with a gun?"

Kruse showed Tzvi his collection of automatic handguns, tucked into the waist of his pants. "I have them all now."

Walid was tied to a chair in the middle of the apartment, lolling and drooling. The tall one lay face-first on the floor, the end of the Persian carpet folded up in his hair. Tzvi turned him over.

"Press a wet towel to your disgusting face. We will have to stitch you."

"Did you learn anything?"

"I learned that my beloved protégé lacks courage. Courage and intelligence."

Kruse pointed at Walid, who looked as though he had fallen asleep in the chair.

"This is not how I raised you."

"Enough."

"None of those men in the hall should be alive."

"Tzvi—"

"None! You are lucky the idiot did not kill you first and then walk in here and kill me. A man pulls a gun on you, you dispatch him. Quietly, carefully, coolly. It is legal, in fact! How do we walk past them now?"

"Quietly, carefully, coolly. What about the interrogation?"

"Al-Faruqi is on the continent somewhere, in France or Spain or Portugal. Maybe Italy. Super-helpful conversation." Tzvi kicked the chair over. Walid hit the floor, head-first, and shouted that he would violate their mothers sexually. "Our pal here speaks Persian better than Arabic. He's Iranian, it turns out. You know where he was last March? Buenos Aires. Do you know what he did? He convinced one of his lunatic pals to blow himself up at the Israeli embassy. He bragged about it! He called me a dirty Jew, right to my face. An absolute charmer, this one."

"Walid."

"What?"

"That's his name, Walid."

"Why do you know his name?"

"His friends were calling out to him."

"My son, my dear son: his friends, all of them armed with handguns, drove across town to kill you. Why were they *calling out* in your vicinity? Now we have to walk through the hall, on our way out of here, and I don't know how many of them are awake or asleep, dead or alive. Who has a gun?"

"No one."

"Who will slit my wrist as I walk past?"

"Tzvi—"

"Ten minutes ago we discussed this."

Kruse walked across the room and stood over Walid. The wound on his face throbbed as he bent over the young man.

"Walid, my friend."

"Fuck you."

"I can cut you out of here. I can let you stretch, drink a glass of water."

He revived somewhat, wriggled against the ropes. "Yes. Yes. Let me go. I won't hurt you."

"No, no, you won't hurt me, Walid."

"But I can't tell you anything. I don't know!"

"I know your name and I know where to find you."

"Liar." A moment later, he squinted. "How do you know that?"

"Your friends in the hall, they decided to help me. And for my part, I don't care if I leave you dead or alive. You did something terrible in Buenos Aires. My partner wants to make you suffer, then die."

"He's a Jew."

"Oh just kill him," said Tzvi. "Or I will."

"Where is al-Faruqi?"

"Fuck you."

Tzvi took out his knife and leaned over Walid. He prepared to dig into the young man's right eye. Walid screamed and Kruse pretended to hold back Tzvi.

"Wait," said Walid. "Wait wait."

"I can't hold him back much longer."

Tzvi grunted, insulted the size of Walid's penis in Persian, reached around Kruse and dug his fingers into the man's face.

"He's in Spain!"

"Where?"

"Castilla-La Mancha."

Kruse sat up and Tzvi backed away. Castilla-La Mancha was a region, not a province or a town or a city. "Where in Castilla-La Mancha?"

"We're not to know."

"Who does know?"

"No one."

Tzvi booted him in the side of the head.

"I forget the name of it. I forget!"

"The name of what, Walid?"

"There's a bunch of them at an old farm or an old village. I was only there once."

"It's in Castilla-La Mancha?"

"Yes. Now let me go."

Tzvi rummaged about for a map.

"Oh just kill me."

"Don't worry, Walid. They'll never know you told me." Kruse lay next to him. He whispered. "No one will tell them. I promise."

Walid began to cry.

SEVEN

Paseo de la Alameda, Sigüenza

THE SIGNS IN CATALAN FADED AND DISAPPEARED. THEN CAME THE black bulls of Aragon. Kruse stopped the rented Jeep at a highway restaurant near Zaragoza and Tzvi woke up, refreshed from his nap and famished. They had both worked in Spain, and Tzvi openly complained, in the restaurant, that in recent years the enterprising Iberians had discovered a new strategy to keep the Jews away: menus.

"Ham with ham on the side with a delicate slice of ham on top, starting with a ham salad and concluding with a delightful slice of ham over melon and a steaming hot cup of ham."

There was a forest fire in the hills; the cloudless blue sky glowed red beneath the smoke. Castilla-La Mancha was the arid world of the *Don Quixote* novel that had been on Evelyn's list of books for him to read. Kruse had tried, but the story was sad in a way he did not like. Tzvi was asleep again; in a car, on the highway, he was like a baby.

It made no sense, living here. This province was central yet remote, with land too dry for decent farming and few rivers. Villages and towns were far apart. Yet it made wonderful sense, living here, if you didn't want to be found. Just beyond the smoke of the fires, Kruse turned off the main highway and detoured north along a white-bleached secondary road. More hills, bald but for a few dark bushes, and the Jeep descended into a valley and a small city with a massive but plain medieval castle on the hill.

The outskirts of Sigüenza were dominated by warehouses and men at work in shirts that were once white. When they reached the medieval quarter Kruse pulled over in front of the right sort of hotel, El Doncel. Inside the dark lobby, set before a dark restaurant, he paid for two rooms.

The woman at the desk, in a red blazer that matched her lipstick and fingernails almost too perfectly, tilted her head at him. "Where are you from, Señor, originally? Your accent?"

Ethnicity, he had learned, was a European obsession. "What's your guess?"

"Not American. Americans can't speak other languages."

"I don't know if that's true, Señora."

"You're trying so hard, enunciating so carefully. My first guess was Swiss German but you're dressed like, I don't know, a Belgian?" She squinted at the left side of his face, the new stitches from the gunshot, his scars. "Danish. You're Danish."

He wrote their made-up surnames, Olsen and Blum, on the registration card. "Does that help?"

"No, not French. Unless . . ."

Tzvi walked into the lobby. He winked at the woman behind the counter and slapped Kruse on the shoulder. "Where the hell are we?"

The clerk pointed. "Americans!"

They ate in the plaza, the only patrons, as bats flickered in the yellow-lit emptiness. Two adolescent boys, not yet old enough to care about appearances, leaned against the restaurant windows in football outfits and watched them, listened to them speak English. Tzvi chose the egg dish again, this one mixed with black pudding and peanuts and dried tomatoes. Kruse opened the map of the province of Guadalajara, where Walid had identified the compound, and that was the end of jokes about food.

Just before dawn, they drove through a protected park and, off-road, to the peak of a hill with the ruins of a Moorish tower. There was no movement about the houses and outbuildings below the tower. It was the best time of day to scout a place: in the light, before anyone was awake.

In his notebook Kruse sketched the buildings, set around a deserted chapel: three stone houses, freshly painted white and orange, with terracotta shingles and flowerpots in the courtyard. A modern yet more decrepit warehouse was on the edge of the grounds. They were delighted to find no dogs. Kruse had better eyes, so he kept watch with a rifle while Tzvi crept to the warehouse and toured the estate. Inside the warehouse, in a tidy corner, there was a long table and a chair with a computer and a printer, a fax machine. He tested doors, climbed ladders, and peeked into the windows of the hacienda.

A few automatic weapons were propped up against the wall. Tzvi spotted three women but no children, though he could not be certain. Two of the women looked young, late teens or early twenties.

"Did you see him?"

"Two of the girls were in bed with him, the bastard. There were two jugs, not bottles, of wine on the floor. A marijuana pipe on the bedside table. I might have walked into the room and smothered him with a pillow."

They drove back into Sigüenza and completed the plan of al-Faruqi's compound. It was a sleepy day, warm and cloudy. They visited the cathedral and the castle, spoke in near whispers, outlined their strategy. The El Doncel restaurant was mostly deserted, as the tourist season had not yet begun and, as the hotel manager had confirmed with a hint of anguish in her voice, Sigüenza was a detour for *Don Quixote* enthusiasts and few others. Baroque music played quietly. They sat by the window as the sun set over the tidy little city. Tzvi had grown tired of complaining and mocking the ham in every dish, and decided to order the house specialty no matter what was in it. Across the street, on the corner, black-haired lovers ducked into a doorway and kissed. In their walk through Sigüenza they had discovered that the calm and wise page of Queen Isabella, Martín Vázquez de Arce, had been killed in Grenada. With the rest of the Spanish army, he had been trying to wipe out the Moors. In the Gothic cathedral there was a statue of Vázquez de Arce, El Doncel, the Queen's page, reading a book.

Kruse had waited for the correct moment. "If anything happens to me tomorrow—"

"A lot is going to happen. You're going to wipe out some terrorists, bring great glory to MagaSecure and to the civilized world."

"We're on a mission to—"

"If you're killing a killer, it's not murder."

"Oh no?"

"It's an act of grace."

"You say that like you actually mean it." Kruse could not summon an appetite. The house specialty, a wine-drenched stew of meat and vege-tables, looked and tasted and smelled like resignation. He stirred it, moved chunks of potato and turnip. "When that boy shot himself in front of me—"

"Everyone has to sleep at night."

What Kruse could not explain to Tzvi is that he felt, felt or imag-ined, Lily watching him. She watched him from somewhere. And what could she see but a thug, splattered with another man's blood? "A thug's act of grace."

"What?"

"Nothing."

"You know, in India, for hundreds of years, one of the finest things a low-born man could be was a thug. It was a calling. You had to train with a guru and if you were good enough and your heart was true enough, you would be accepted into the tribe."

"And the point of this tribe?" Having spent a good part of his adult life with a PhD in philosophy who was not remotely proud of her husband's profession, Kruse knew the answer to this question. It paid for her Gucci shoes.

"To eliminate the enemies of civilization so the children can sleep unharassed in their cozy beds tonight."

"Very poetic. And entirely untrue."

"I am comfortable with *thug* if it means stopping men like Khalil al-Faruqi." Tzvi swirled his glass of wine unnecessarily, sighed. "Now, my tender savage, you were saying. If anything happens to you?"

"I want you to have the house in Toronto." Kruse slid a letter he had prepared, as a will, along with his bank account information. "Please take care of Annette and Anouk in Paris."

"Take care of them? I can't take care of me."

"Pretend they're clients. The fee is my house."

Tzvi looked at the letter for a moment, folded it, and put it in his inside pocket. "No one can hurt us. We can even sleep a few hours. Dream ourselves into it, like always."

"I've never done this."

"In December you walked into an apartment full of professionals to do what? Oh yes, to kill a nose-less psychopath."

"I walked into that apartment to rescue a woman and her daughter. And I didn't kill the psychopath."

"You just gave him permanent brain damage."

"His own brother killed him, Tzvi."

"Unharassed in their cozy beds tonight."

• • •

Kruse could not sleep after two in the morning, when the first crack of thunder woke him into worry. He shadowboxed to an all-night political talk show on the radio and nearly fainted with hunger. If there was a heaven, a committee of judgment, he was not afraid of God. He was afraid of what his daughter would feel and what his Mennonite parents would say, watching him prepare to murder a man for money. Allan and Nettie would petition the Lord for a well-timed bolt of lightning, a heart attack, to prevent it. This was essential to their calculation: murder is evil, but if God chooses to kill a man it is a divine welcome.

The air was still but charged at four thirty, when they stepped out of the lobby of El Doncel into the darkness and quiet of Sigüenza. Not a drop of rain had fallen, but the smell of wet dust was in the air. Tzvi closed his eyes, whispered to himself like an Orthodox student. They passed through the park without seeing another vehicle. The rain began to fall, first in sprinkles and then in a torrent, as they neared the Moorish hill.

Already the soil had gone muddy. The Jeep slithered up to their parking spot on the distant side of the tower. He closed his eyes, breathed.

"Christopher. You are prepared?"

"Probably not."

Tzvi rubbed his hands together. "You want me to tell you why I quit?"

"One never quits Mossad."

Tzvi made quotation marks with his fingers. "Quit Mossad."

Kruse turned off the Jeep and its wipers.

"An Israeli diplomat, a trade representative for agriculture, was in the embassy in London in 1972. He opened a letter. This was a bomb. His name was Shachori. He had known my father. Black September claimed it, and we tortured an asshole in Damascus until he ratted out the killer. I mean, the actual man who manufactured and sent the thing, the scientist. He lived in Cairo. We did our research, like this, we watched the place. Who goes in and who goes out. In the middle of the night we broke into the apartment like a couple of squirrels. There was no one else in the suite, we were sure of it. Until there was."

"Who?"

"A boy. Eleven years old. He walked down the hall in his underwear. Nothing in our research suggested he would be in the apartment. But he was."

"And?"

"The kid was tall. He did not look like a kid, not in the light we had." Tzvi paused for a long time, so long that Kruse thought this was perhaps the end of the story. Then he took a deep breath and touched the digital clock on the truck radio. "I killed him. I killed him, and his father walked out of his bedroom, naked. It was a hot night. He knew we would come, the father. He did not beg for his life or try to fight us or escape. There were no declarations, no prayers. It no longer mattered that we were in his home. He bent over his son and rubbed his hair and wept so quietly, with—I do not know what to call it—terrible nobility."

"What did you do?"

"I waited until he looked up at me and I told him who I was and I shot him in the forehead."

Kruse watched him.

"So what, Christopher, can you do with that?"

It was not a question to answer but Kruse didn't move for a few minutes as they watched the compound below, in the rain. When he was ready, Tzvi said so. There was nothing more to discuss about their plan, about what they would do first, then second, so they put on their grey rain jackets and gathered their weapons. They wished each other good luck and opened the doors and stepped into the mud. It was a blessing: the rain and the low cloud extended the night and drowned the noise of their footsteps. They entered the courtyard, freshly painted and decorated with spring flowers. There was a well in the middle of it, not a fountain, which seemed just then the difference between a French and a Spanish village: water is not worth celebrating if you cannot find any. No one stood guard, not in the rain and not in any of the windows. Tzvi crept around the well, and Kruse, who had been thinking it all morning, put his hand on his master's wet shoulder and whispered, "This is wrong."

Tzvi wiped the rain from his face. "Of course it is. And it is right too, Christopher."

"We can go back."

"We cannot go back. If it helps, for it does help me, think of all the people—*children*—he murdered. Or do not think of it as revenge at all. It is simply what we do. We are mountain vipers. In the village is our breakfast. We feel nothing. We kill and we go."

Kruse stood in the rain.

"This is what I trained you to do." If any of the men or women woke up and walked to the window they would be caught, but Tzvi waited at the well and held his eyes on Kruse's until he nodded. "Yes?"

There was no way to answer.

"It will be over quickly. You can weep in the car."

Tzvi ran over the wet stones to the open door of the stable, attached to the complex of two-storey houses. They removed their noisy rain jackets and their boots. It smelled of shit in the stable but there was only a cat and her kittens, curled up in the corner. The chickens slept elsewhere.

The first building, connected to the stable, was the kitchen. It was still a mess from the night before, or perhaps the night before that. Dirty dishes were stacked on both sides of the sink, and food that belonged in the refrigerator, yogurt and meat, sat open and stinking on the counter. Cockroaches moved over the dishes. Kruse walked past and a hidden world of fruit flies flew up in a cloud. Four men were sleeping in the living room, two on old chesterfields and two on slabs of foam. The wooden floor was cracked and dry and needed a sweep. There was a cache of six firearms—two rifles and four handguns—against the wall. None of the men was over twenty-five. They were pimply fraternity boys sleeping off last night's kegger, dreaming of little victories. The room itself seemed to sleep. It smelled of last night's wine, of cigarettes and marijuana and underarms, and it helped him hate them. This was an anteroom of hell. Tzvi crept to them and Kruse followed. They went back to the stable and buried the guns in a pile of hay, frightening two of the bony kittens, who stood up and stretched and went back to sleep. The next door led to a bedroom, not Khalil al-Faruqi's but that of another man of his generation, perhaps sixty, sleeping with a very young woman with bleached blond hair. He snored unevenly, each inhalation a surprise.

At the other end of the bedroom, lousy with wine jugs and clothes and a pizza box, Tzvi reached the next door and pulled it open. The door creaked and a woman opened her eyes. Kruse put his finger to his lips and for an instant it seemed she would accept it, remain quiet and go back to sleep. She closed her eyes and opened them again, and this time she believed.

It was too dark in the room to make out much of what she saw, but she saw enough and turned to the man sleeping next to her. He wore a grey beard. The thick black hair, from the photographs of his youth, had disappeared from the top of his head. He snored noisily. Kruse had imagined a larger and more powerful man, muscles and battle scars. In the photographs he wore the fatigues of a revolutionary, like Fidel Castro, but he had the presence—even sleeping—of a flabby politician.

Before she could speak, Kruse put his hand over her mouth and dragged her off the bed. She only struggled for a moment. Tzvi opened the French doors and Kruse carried her out onto the balcony. She was naked and slight, just over five feet tall. Her skin felt and smelled warm with sleep. Tzvi closed the doors behind them. In the rain and the wind he could immediately feel her turning cold. In Spanish he called himself a soldier. He explained what they had come to do: to take away this man, a mass murderer. Her choice was simple: she could remain quiet out here or she could go to prison.

Kruse went back inside, yanked a blanket from the bed, and threw it out to the woman—the girl—on the balcony. Tzvi had pulled a little knife from the holster on his ankle. "I will wake him up first. He has to see my face."

"Just do it."

"Close the door."

Kruse reached for the handle and saw movement in the adjacent room. The woman with the dyed blond hair reached for something beside the bed and lay back again, pretended to be asleep. He sprinted for her but not quickly enough and she sat up with a handgun. There was a yellow bruise under her left eye.

"Give it to me, Señora," he whispered in Spanish. "No one will hurt you again."

The woman glanced down at the man in bed, still snoring, and said, "Señorita."

Kruse tiptoed around the bed, kept his distance. The woman was older than the other two but not by much. Perhaps she was twenty. She slipped out of bed, in panties and socks, and kept the gun on him. "What are you doing here?"

"We came for Khalil."

"Americans?"

"Yes."

"You will pay me how much to stay quiet?"

He was at the opposite door now. On the other side of the woman Tzvi crept into the room. His eyes were wide and hungry, as they always were before a fight. When it happened, it happened quickly: the wet girl walked into the room without any hesitation, her own eyes hungry, and startled Tzvi. He turned and hit her with the blunt end of the knife and she fell. The blond woman pulled the trigger before Kruse could hop out of the way completely and his left shoulder burned as he hit the floor. By the time he was back on his feet the fat man, al-Faruqi's sweaty contemporary, held his own gun. Tzvi's hands were up.

Before the thud came from behind, his shoulders tingled with it, with his error. He should have hopped on the blond woman in her bed. He should have thrown the other one over the balcony and onto the cobblestones. He should have slit al-Faruqi's throat himself. They would have been halfway back to Sigüenza by now. They would have been halfway up the mountain with their meal.

• • •

Kruse emerged from a concussion the same way every time. It felt to him like hours had passed when it might only have been a minute or two. He woke out of a dream of the puppet theatre, Guignol and his friends mocking the kings and aristocrats, Lily laughing, Anouk.

His wrists were tied securely behind him to a straight-backed wooden chair. There were ropes around his ankles but they weren't secured to anything. He could stand if he had to stand.

Kruse was in the corner of the living room where the men had been sleeping. One of them, with a wispy moustache and zigzags shaved in the side of his head, wore a dirty red T-shirt that said *Fly Emirates*. He stood smoking a cigarette. There was something in his free hand. "Good morning, American," he said, in heavily accented English.

Pavarotti was singing "Nessun Dorma" in the kitchen. The opera itself, *Turandot*, didn't make sense to him as a story but he could listen to "Nessun Dorma" all day. In this version, the chorus was sung by women— not just covered by violins. The aria rose to its marvellous conclusion and Kruse closed his eyes again, sleep on just the other side. Guignol and his little stick, whacking the fat king and flirting with the queen. Unlike Tzvi, who had always spoken of an epic battle, Kruse had always hoped to die anticlimactically, old and broken, in the palliative care unit of a Toronto hospital. Lily would have flown in from Paris or London or New York or Amsterdam to be with him. Evelyn would have brought his slippers from home. Somehow they would still be in love. She would read those poems he had always pretended to understand, Auden or someone, by a soft lamp. Maybe "Nessun Dorma" would be playing.

On the other side of his guard, in the distant bedroom, the muffled shrieks in Arabic: "You have one minute to think!"

The gauze had cleared from his view of the room. His head thumped. He could see now what the young man held: Lily's little turtle, her *doudou*. Kruse carried it everywhere. It had become a part of him.

"Give the turtle to me."

"Where did you Jews hide our guns?" The young man reached back and stuffed the *doudou* in his pocket. Then he opened a leather holster on his belt and pulled out a knife. It had an olive-wood handle, like the ones he had seen at the market in Vaison-la-Romaine. The young man stepped forward and leaned over Kruse, the cigarette in his mouth. With one hand he squeezed Kruse's chin, digging deeply with his fingers. "Where?"

He placed the knife against Kruse's cheek, at the bone. He pressed into the flesh, into the stitches from the bullet, and exhaled with a squeak of ecstasy. The blood dripped down the blade and onto his hand. A hot worm of it slid down Kruse's face and neck and chest.

"Can I have a cigarette?" Kruse tried not to flinch, and to speak calmly. "Before you cut me again?"

The question seemed to stump the young man. He looked around but there was no one to ask.

"Smoking helps me remember where I hid things."

The young man put the knife on the windowsill and reached again into his back pocket. For an instant Kruse thought he was going to pull out the *doudou* and hurt it in some way. In the distant bedroom, Tzvi shouted in Arabic cuss words and howled in pain and laughed—something like a laugh. Kruse closed his eyes, breathed himself out of panic. He wanted to call out to Tzvi, tell him he loved him, tell him God loved him, because he knew Tzvi's secret. Secretly, Tzvi believed. It was like a sputtering engine, Tzvi's moans in the distant room.

"What are they doing to him?"

"Cutting him up. And when they are done, they will cut you up. Then they will find your family and cut them up—everyone you love.

This is what Ustaaz does to his enemies. If you hurt him he hurts you ten times."

The young man pulled out a soft pack of cigarettes and a silver Zippo lighter. He put a smoke into Kruse's mouth and flicked at the flint. The moment it was lit, Kruse thrust himself back in the chair and kicked up with all the force he could gather. His feet planted solidly in the young man's groin and he squeaked and fell, dropped the cigarette and lighter. Kruse shoved himself forward and tumbled onto his side, slithered back until he could reach the lighter. The young man rolled in pain, then onto his hands and knees. He vomited and rolled onto his opposite side, told Kruse he was going to cut his fucking eyes out.

Kruse flicked the lighter on and held it as close to the rope as he could manage. The smell of his skin burning behind his back was stronger than the smell of the rope on fire but he could not stop. The young man was on his hands and knees again, spitting and mumbling. It was not a thick rope. It came free just when he thought he couldn't take the flame another instant. He waited a moment, for the young man to retch again, and he reached quickly forward to burn the rope at his ankles.

"Wait." The young man pointed at him, tried to stand. He spoke softly and eyed the door, worried perhaps that someone might come in and catch him in his shame. "Wait wait wait a minute."

Kruse was up on his feet before his guard could manage it, and took two steps before he kicked him in the head. The young man didn't move. Kruse rolled him over and pulled the *doudou* out of his pocket, kissed it, told it things, and put it in his jacket where it belonged. The young man had disarmed Kruse. His knives were on the coffee table, lined up like materials confiscated from a crime scene.

There was no more shouting in the distant bedroom but a man was speaking, softly and declaratively. "This is how it's going to be, my friend."

The door was half open. The room was crowded with the men who had been sleeping. Kruse could not see Tzvi. He could not see the blond woman. Khalil al-Faruqi wore a white robe, from a Ritz-Carlton, and matching white slippers. He pulled at his beard, as though he were trying to summon a bit of evidence. He held a tiny espresso cup between two fingers, as daintily as a prince. Kruse scanned the room for weapons.

From where he stood he could not see Tzvi but when he moved a few steps closer he could hear him breathing hoarsely.

"Give me a name or we move on to the next arm, my friend."

His head crunched with each beat of his heart. Behind al-Faruqi and his men: the balcony where he had taken al-Faruqi's escort. Kruse crept back and, when he was far enough away, he ran through the living room and the kitchen. "Nessun Dorma" was finished. Pavarotti was on to that one from *Tosca*. He was halfway through the kitchen when he realized there were two men at a small table, eating eggs. The first to stand was a bit of a muscle man. He swung with everything he had and Kruse dodged it, pulled him off balance and stomped his knee from the side. Before the man could scream Kruse put his knee into his jaw. The second one was up and jabbed at Kruse with a knife. With his own knife Kruse simply sliced at the inside of the man's wrist three times, up-down-up, and blood sprayed. The man backed away and ran for a tea towel, praying. Kruse knocked him out with the handle of his knife.

The balcony was just low enough to reach with a hop. Kruse pulled himself up and onto it as smoothly as he could manage and peeked into the room.

Tzvi stood in front of the opposite wall, his right arm tied to the bedpost. They had stripped him naked. There was something wrong with his left arm, hidden. It took time to understand Tzvi's left arm was half gone. Pieces of it lay in a wretched pile of blood and flesh. From what remained of his arm, a fast drip. Tzvi stared at al-Faruqi with something like defiance. But Kruse could see what was behind it. Tzvi knew it was over. He was going to die.

The trick was to slow himself, to think. He breathed in the rain, scanned the room, made his plans. The blond woman was weeping. She held a massive set of bolt cutters.

"Cut again."

"No!" The woman cried. The floor was uneven and the blood ran like twenty fingers. She stepped away so it would not touch her bare feet.

One of the younger men gripped the stub that remained of Tzvi's arm and the woman lifted the bolt cutters.

"Unless you want to tell me who sent you, my old friend. There isn't much left of this arm. We'll switch to the other one after this? Then we'll go for your little zayin. One little chop. *Chip chop*." Khalil al-Faruqi looked around. "Yes?"

The men around him were not as keen as he was.

Only one of them had a gun: the man in his sixties who had been sleeping with the blonde. He held it on Tzvi.

The French doors were open slightly. Kruse entered, the sound camouflaged by the rain, and the only one who saw him, at first, was Tzvi. His eyes changed.

This was precisely what Allan and Nettie Kruse had spoken of, night after night, after he had begun his training. To fight back is weakness. It is the road to damnation. The only honour is in leaving the weapon on the table and closing your eyes and praying when the murderers come for you. You ask the Lord to forgive them. Then you. It is the finest achievement of the human heart, to die with the dignity that comes with saying no. I will die in pain, in flames, rather than hurt another.

At the bamboo-scented Krav Maga studio where he grew up there was a practice wall for small but heavy knives like the one he held, forged without handles. He had thrown knives the way other teenagers skateboarded. Kruse moved behind one of the young men and threw his knife. It hit the old man with the gun in the side of the neck just as he turned and pulled the trigger. The young man, Kruse's shield, fell before him. Kruse drew his second knife, the one he cut with, and he cut them as they came. Al-Faruqi tried to run and Kruse tripped him. The two younger women ran out of the room, over al-Faruqi, as Kruse finished the other men. One of them had trained. He cut Kruse in the chest and in his roaring confidence he said something vile about fucking him. Kruse cut his throat. They were finished, all but al-Faruqi, and the blond woman was on her knees holding the bolt cutters like a teddy bear and apologizing to the bloody floor.

Tzvi spoke like a drunk man. "I can wait."

Kruse put the guns on the balcony, in the rain, and ordered the blond woman to untie Tzvi, to find clean towels and ice, and when she hesitated he wanted to kick her into the wall but instead he embraced her for a moment and she shivered in his arms and she said, "I want my mom. Will you take me to her?"

"Whatever you like." He spoke sweetly into her ear. "But first the towels, the ice."

In the living room, Khalil al-Faruqi stood at the window with the olive-handled knife the young man had used to cut Kruse's face. "Stay back."

Kruse did not stay back.

"I have money." He held the knife up, close to his body. He understood how to fight better than his guards, even if he had not done it in decades. "I have proof."

"Proof of what?"

"You will see. The most glorious proof. We can work together."

"Where were you on April fourth?"

"Almost seven million pesetas. Some American money. How about that? Just let me go and it's all yours."

"April fourth."

"Here! I'm always here, Mossad. You saw the girls. They can't get enough of me. I'm an old man with wine and girls, favoured by God.

Why would I go anywhere?" Khalil al-Faruqi dropped the knife and lowered himself to his knees and took off the robe so he was as naked as Tzvi. The blond woman passed behind him, with the ice and towels. The two younger women watched from the kitchen doorway. The only guns on that side of the hacienda were buried in the hay, but he wanted to be sure.

"Come in here, where I can see you."

At first they didn't move, or respond. Kruse had a vivid imagination but he knew there was no way to conjure what these men had done to them. Together they huddled in the corner, where he pointed.

Al-Faruqi ignored the women as they padded across the filthy room in bare feet.

"Everything I have done—it has been in a state of war. In war everything is permissible, Mossad. You know that. Who knows better than Israelis?"

"I'm Canadian."

"Bullshit."

"We're here for the restaurant."

"What restaurant?"

"You know what restaurant. In Paris. Rue des Rosiers. Chez Sternbergh."

Al-Faruqi sighed. "I have ordered many things. I have . . . killed men, of course, in war."

"And women. And children. Babies."

"In war! In war! Someone blows up my children and I blow up their children. But I did not order any operation in Paris, not for years. It was not me. I swear it, Mossad, I didn't blow up any Jew restaurant. And if you kill me here, naked, like a thief, a dog, *like a fucking bitch*, you are killing an innocent man."

He looked up at Kruse, wiping the tears from his eyes. There were no scars on Khalil al-Faruqi, not on his face or on his arms or on his chest. He was clean and rich, and he would live a long life with teenage girls and good food, jugs of wine and pipes of dope. For a time he lowered his head and his body quivered and Kruse thought he was crying. Then al-Faruqi looked up and laughed.

• • •

His grandfather, Heinrich Kruse, had arrived in Canada as a Krause. He was the son of a grain farmer and that is what he did in Canada, first in a Mennonite community in southern Manitoba. It was not a story anyone told in full, but Heinrich became involved with a married woman and was either banished or fled to Ontario, where he dropped a vowel from his name and went back to work. One afternoon at harvest season, on his forty acres, the swather picked up a tree branch. It was large enough to stop the blades. Heinrich climbed down off the old swather and reached in to dislodge the branch. The machine lurched forward and one of the rusted blades bit deeply into his arm.

At this time he was not yet married. It was only a bit of luck that he was discovered at all, by a neighbour who had come to borrow—of all things—a Bible. The gentleman was hosting a prayer session that evening and he wanted a few on hand, as inevitably one of the attendees would forget. The neighbour untangled Heinrich from the blades and carried him to his car and drove him to the Stratford General Hospital.

On the way to Guadalajara, Kruse formulated the story he would tell and practised it on the blond woman who lay shivering under a blanket in the back. The two black-haired women had fled south in a Toyota truck. It was different for her. She had been forced to cut a man's arm off, in three pieces. Her name was Bianca.

Tzvi lay in the reclined front seat of the dirty Jeep, the stub of his arm wrapped and sitting in a bowl of ice. He mumbled a story about the day his parents had taken him to swim in the Sea of Galilee and a little boy drowned. They were about the same age. Ever since that day he knew God was either cruel or an imagined thing, like Mickey Mouse, and that none of us was special and one day he would die in some banal, absurd manner. Some stringy-haired woman would cut his limbs off in a farmhouse in dusty ham-laden Spain and he would bleed to death in a Jeep. "But, my friend, *but* when the bitch—sorry, Bianca, I cannot forgive you—was cutting me and I thought I would die I could feel him out in the rain. He was on the margins of my senses. Can I say that? He was out there, knocking gentle at my door, waiting for me to let him in. Christopher?"

"Yes, Tzvi?"

"What do you think of that?"

"Bianca was cutting off your arm at the time."

"Prevarication. You are afraid of the great truths. I was like that once. I was like that two hours ago. I think I can still eat bacon. It felt to me like he—*He*—was agnostic about that."

Bianca had told him to go to Guadalajara instead of Sigüenza. It was not much farther and the hospital was finer. On the way, Kruse saw a few grain farms. It was plausible. He noted landmarks and learned the word in Spanish for swather by describing it to her: *hileradora*.

The concussion and blood loss, the lack of food in his belly, the panic, Tzvi's talk of God and bacon, the men he had killed, whatever it was, threw a wave of dizziness at him. On the outskirts of the town of Valdenoches he pulled over and threw up. Then he opened his window and the faster he drove the better he felt. It was still morning, some-how. His chest and arm had finally stopped bleeding and all he needed on his face was a few more stitches. Tzvi was in and out of conscious-ness now that Guadalajara was visible in the distance. He told Kruse he was his father and that he loved him. Tzvi coughed and grasped at something. The bowl of ice tumbled on the floor. Kruse reached over and took his master's free hand in his and kissed it and sang "Mammas Don't Let Your Babies Grow Up to Be Cowboys." He remembered the first part of "You Are My Sunshine" so he sang it three times. He sang as loud as he could sing, to keep Tzvi awake.

"You are crazy people," said Bianca.

His parents encountered Tzvi only once, in his second year of train-ing. A blizzard and a transit strike had arrived on the same night. Kruse had walked across the city to arrive at the studio with mild frostbite on his left cheek, the one with the open stitches, and for three hours Tzvi taught him to break arms. It was dark when they were finished. Eventually it would be part of his training, learning to drive, but for now he was too young. Tzvi had just bought a used four-wheel-drive Land Cruiser, dark sky-blue, Israel blue, and as he drove across Toronto he quizzed him, in Russian, on what they had been discussing in the strategic portion of their time together: how to sneak into a well-guarded foreign palace. When they arrived at their little house on the east side, Allan Kruse ran out to fetch his son. He had been waiting at the window, watching what he could watch for in the blizzard.

His father, who would be dead in less than two years, and this man who would become his father, did not speak. Allan did not thank Tzvi for driving him home. Kruse was still a teenager but he understood how his choices had hurt and had shamed his parents, who did not have many rules other than *help ever, hurt never*, which was not an official Mennonite axiom or a line from the Bible but words on a post-card the missionaries of an Indian guru had left in their mailbox. From his Land Cruiser, in the blizzard, Tzvi did not ingratiate himself or even say hello to Allan. They were, Kruse understood, competitors. He opened the door of the Land Cruiser while his father stood in a cheap grey sweater on the sidewalk and his mother wrapped a shawl around herself on the front steps. Tzvi reached over the gearbox and took his hand for a moment and squeezed in the cold, squeezed like this.

The university hospital was on the east side of Guadalajara. He stopped fully at every intersection, drove the speed limit into the hos-pital complex, hemmed in by stained concrete and fir trees. Kruse parked in the employees' area, as close to the emergency room as he could manage, and released Tzvi's hand. A garbage truck designed for needles backed up the hill. A woman pushed an elderly man past him, in a wheelchair.

He took off his bloody shirt and put on a clean one. Bianca watched him in the rear-view mirror.

"Do you want to go inside?"

"I'm not hurt, Señor."

Bianca had cried, shivered, and talked to herself for at least half of the drive from the bloody hacienda to the hospital. "It might help to talk to someone."

"Talk about what? I don't want to be arrested with you lunatics."

"You're right. That's not a terrific idea."

She opened the back door and held up the two stacks of bills he had given her—two hundred thousand pesetas. "I want more."

The wet one, the one Tzvi had hit, knew where al-Faruqi had hidden the money. The peseta was a weak currency—seven million was less than seventy thousand American—but two hundred thousand would give each of the women a start.

Kruse ran to the front door of the hospital, where two wheelchairs sat abandoned. He pushed one back to the Jeep and gently lowered Tzvi into it.

"I could have killed you, Señor. The gun was on the floor, just sitting there."

There were two backpacks full of money in the back of the Jeep, and a black leather briefcase. "If you speak of us, to anyone, I'll come for you."

"I've already forgotten."

He pulled another five stacks of pesetas out of the backpack and she stuffed them into her pockets. She jogged across the parking lot toward a chain-link fence. Bianca had told them everything she knew: Khalil al-Faruqi had spoken on satellite and cellular phones, a lot. Arabic and English, mostly. And it was true: on April 4 he had been at home in Spain, stoned or drunk or both, watching some awful American movie dubbed into a language she did not speak.

Khalil al-Faruqi had kept a file. *The proof*, he had called it. When they were leaving, Kruse stuffed the proof into the briefcase.

Inside the emergency room he prepared to stutter his way through a shaky, emotional explanation of what had happened. He shook up his Spanish, weakened it. His friend's arm had been caught in the damned *hileradora*. They rushed Tzvi down the hall.

Passports, yes, of course. Medical insurance? They had rushed here! Who thinks of insurance when a man's arm has been cut off by the blades of a tractor? He had cash. Yes, he had cut his own face extracting his friend from the blades. No, no he was fine. Well, he could use a bottle of peroxide and some cotton balls, maybe some stitches.

In the washroom Kruse took off his shirt. The gunshot wound on his shoulder was a mess. His chest was not so bad and his face was still his face.

An intern stitched him up. She said she didn't believe the story about the swather blades. It took three hours for the news to arrive: his friend would have months of therapy ahead of him but he would survive. Tzvi was sedated. If Kruse wanted to go, spend the night in Guadalajara and come back the next morning, he could visit his friend. They regretted to inform him that if his friend was not insured, the procedures and his stay in the hospital would cost approximately two and a half million pesetas.

The outer circle of Guadalajara was 1960s precast concrete apartment complexes, bland row houses, parking lots, gas stations, cheap hotels, and unwelcome restaurants. At the train station he rented a locker and stuffed *the proof* inside.

It had arrived only a month earlier.

Back in Sigüenza Kruse had known there wasn't much time for Tzvi. He held the terrorist to the floor and locked his arm at the elbow. The women stood next to them in the corner. He could smell their perfume. One looked away, out the window, and mumbled to herself. The other watched. Hungrily, he might say. When the man did not answer quickly enough, Kruse turned his arm to the point of snapping the tendons. The woman who watched clapped her hands softly. "Do it, Señor."

Khalil al-Faruqi laughed and cussed. Why did it matter who had given him the money? "Just take it, Mossad."

"I'll ruin your right arm first." Kruse turned it. "And then—"

He screamed. "It was your people—the CIA, you asshole. Mossad doesn't speak to the CIA? You *can't* break my arm. You *can't* kill me. We're allies." Spittle leapt onto his beard. "These kids who blew up the parking garage in the towers, in New York—these aren't my people. You think I'm a man of God? I'm like you. Ask these women what I did to them last night."

The woman who looked out the window covered her ears.

"Mossad, who told you it was me who attacked your restaurant?" Khalil al-Faruqi tried to look up, to meet Kruse's eyes.

Before he had a chance to reflect on Mossad, on French clandestine services, Kruse thought of one man: somehow, impossibly, Monsieur le Maire.

"This man who told you—think of him."

It was quiet in the house but for Tzvi drowsily telling Bianca how to bandage the stub of his arm.

"I kept all the paperwork. When they were last here, I had my men take the papers from them. I know things about you, about what your government is doing."

"My government?"

"Señor." The woman who watched stepped forward, touched Kruse's shoulder. "He made a request. Ask us what he did to us last night."

In a monotone she described how he had routinely violated them, two sisters it turned out, from Valladolid. When she was finished she said what he had done to them the night before was not unique. All they hoped, night after night, was that he would be too drunk or too stoned.

"Why didn't you leave?"

"He said he would have us killed. His boys with the guns. First they would fuck us with their guns and then they would kill us. Then our brother and our parents. What he says, Señor, about being innocent? He is not innocent."

"I didn't blow up any Jew restaurant. And these girls . . . it was sex talk."

"It was not sex talk."

Kruse had learned all he was going to learn from Khalil al-Faruqi. In the adjacent room there was a thump.

"Señor!" the blond woman called out. "Your friend fainted!"

The camera was in his vest. He carried four knives. Kruse released the killer's arm and stood up off him and pulled out his favourite knife. It was quiet for an instant. The dark-haired woman, the one who had been watching, had gone into the kitchen. Kruse suppressed an urge to pray, to make a ritual of this.

Al-Faruqi scrambled to his skinny knees, naked and hairy, put his hands together. "I will do anything, say anything. Whatever they're paying you I can find so much more."

Kruse heard the woman walk back into the room behind him. He turned, prepared to protect himself from her, but she walked past him and with a scream thrust a kitchen knife into Khalil al-Faruqi's right eye. The man fell on his back, his hands on his face, and she leapt on him and thrust it into his stomach nine times. They were both naked and covered in blood. She rolled off him and stood up and he reached and gurgled. She dropped the knife and turned to her sister and said, "I'll need a shower. Then we can go."

Kruse shot him with one of the guns from the balcony, to finish it, and took the photographs. The bloody sister cleared her throat. "What he said about the Americans was true. They came. He was helping them."

"With what?"

"The men who set the bomb in the tower in New York. Señor Khalil knows who did it and how to find them. They wanted to work out something else with him, for money. It was going to make him very rich. It is all locked in a cabinet in the computer room."

Kruse carried Tzvi out to the Jeep. The woman followed him.

"And I know where he hid the key."

In the medieval centre of Guadalajara Kruse parked and found a copy shop. It was a modest place, designed for small entrepreneurs, students. There were no surveillance cameras inside or outside. He had taken twelve instant photographs of Khalil al-Faruqi on the floor of the hacienda salon. Three of them, taken together, were definitive. He blew them up and faxed them to the number Zoé Moquin had provided, without a covering letter.

He paid his bill and he was about to leave when the clerk called out to him. A fax had come in, a rare occurrence, and it was in French. Perhaps it was for him?

It was written in cursive, on an otherwise blank sheet.

Revenez immédiatement. Come back immediately.

• • •

Santillana del Mar is a town built with old yellow stones on the North Atlantic coast of Spain. In 1879, in a cave not far from the town, a little girl discovered red paintings by paleolithic people. Between the cave and the town there is a five-star private convalescent home called Hospital Altamira. Kruse had followed the ambulance in the Jeep, a little longer than four hours. He could practically hear Tzvi cussing in Hebrew every time they hit a bump. It was not so terrible. What remained of his arm was in traction and he was attached to draining tubes; the nurse was not being miserly with painkillers.

According to their passports they were Swiss Germans, the only sort of German Tzvi could allow himself to impersonate. His convalescent name was Hans Miller.

The room was vast and overlooked cliffs, grand rocks, the ocean. Kruse left him with a stack of pesetas but the bill was prepaid for three weeks. Tzvi insisted on kissing him before he left.

Kruse had already said he was sorry, hundreds of times. He knew how to disarm a woman with a gun just as he knew how to run across the street when he suspected a white Mercedes might slam into his daughter. But some miserable corner of his brain, some defect in his heart, inspired him to hesitate, and here they were. The window overlooking the sea was nearly the whole of the wall. The buttery tile was so clean the light shone off it, and soft techno music played through invisible speakers. Tzvi's room smelled of eucalyptus. When he had arrived, a little card announced the thread count of his sheets and contained a small biography of this month's guest chef—a Michelin-starred woman from Lyon. At five o'clock, if it all agreed with Señor Miller's pharmaceutical cocktail, a porter would arrive with a glass of champagne.

"My life is over," he whispered.

This had been a common theme: a one-armed man could no longer earn a living as a protector of the innocent.

But little of what they did amounted to actual protection, and few of their clients were innocent. They were planners, strategy guys. The rest was usually theatre. "Stop saying that, Tzvi."

"In the ambulance, do you know what I thought about? What devilled me for five hours?"

"Tzvi, stop."

"Hans. I am Hans from fucking Zürich."

"Sorry. Hans from Zürich. Stop speaking nonsense, Hans."

"I hope you are sorry."

"Hans, every cell in my body is sorry."

"I will never make love again, unless I pay for it. That. That is what I thought about. I think you know me. You know Hans. I am not given to wallowing."

"But the morphine."

"This is not the morphine. I am not wallowing. It is a fact. And even if I discover some ugly creature who wants, actually *wants* to make love to me, to gimpy old Hans, how ever will I do it? How do I balance myself on the bed, if I want to do it conventionally on some moonlit night?"

Kruse did not want to say anything false. He had his own obsessions to contend with, on his drive north from Guadalajara.

"Are you thinking *prosthetics*? If you are, you are poorer at thinking than ever I imagined."

"I was thinking Zoé Moquin will give us a lot of money. You don't have to worry about work for some time, if ever. And love, if I am honest, Hans, has never been among your top considerations."

"So the morphine is having an effect." He looked out the big window. The sun was a couple of hours from setting and the light was dully spectacular on the water. "I will use some of those pesetas, if I can. Perhaps a nurse will let me experiment."

"Perhaps, Hans. Perhaps."

Again they embraced, all this hugging after years of no hugging at all, and Kruse vowed he would be back soon. On his way out, he spoke with the hospital director about Hans. If any of the nurses or orderlies or doctors or physiotherapists or janitors or . . . accountants, *anyone* discovers herself, or himself, being propositioned by Hans they should not feel harassed. Not ideally. The morphine was having a curious effect on him.

The director stared at him a moment, put a hand on his arm. "I understand."

On his way down to the Jeep, Kruse was certain he had made an error. It was an "I understand" filled with the sort of nuance he could not decipher in Spanish. He worried that by the time he was out of the parking lot someone would have quietly offered Hans a blowjob.

It was a six-hour drive to Barcelona, to drop off the bloody Jeep and rent a room in an airport hotel. He thought of Anouk and he thought of Annette, how he had now and forever exempted himself from their lives. There would be a smell about him, assassin smell, and all good and pure people would know it. He returned to the moment he climbed

onto the balcony of the hacienda: the blond woman, Bianca with the
bolt cutters, and gore dripping from where Tzvi's elbow ought to have
been. If he had hopped back down, abandoned his mentor to death
instead of walking in and slaughtering the masochists, would he feel
better? Would he have held on to something? It grew dark and the
routes were tricky in the mountains. Goats and cows were on the highway. The little war was over and there would be no more. In war we do
not want to kill but we must, to protect our dear ones. He turned up
the radio.

EIGHT

Place du Colonel Fabien, Paris

ZOÉ MOQUIN SAT ALONG THE WALL OF THE EMPTY CAFÉ, BATHED IN grey light. It had rained constantly since Kruse's return to Paris but just now the skies were not as dark. The clouds would soon break to allow the drowned tulips a moment to breathe. Back home they had clients in government and politics—in Toronto and Ottawa and in Washington—but none of them had ever looked like Zoé. Kruse did not know if he could make any generalizations about her: while she did not carry herself like a fashion model, she dressed like she was on a runway, with bulbs flashing about her. Her dresses were a combination of elegance and imagination he lacked the words to describe. This one: blue and soft and shimmering, with a matching hat. When he was close enough he could see the little dots on the fabric were not dots at all: they were moths, with visible legs and antennae. Insects. The blue of the dress matched the blue of her eyes. Weeks later he would congratulate himself when he remembered his thought, in this tired café of the tenth arrondissement: *Surely you can't buy a dress like that in a store.*

She did not stand to greet him when he arrived and she did not smile. In front of her, an empty espresso cup and half a glass of sparkling water. There was no music in the café, so he could hear the little echo of fizz inside the Badoit bottle. So far they had communicated only by fax: the photographs, the commandment to come back, a question, an answer.

By the time he had reached his hotel room in Barcelona it was midnight and he was exhausted. He turned on CNN International. A story on the five men arrested for the World Trade Center bombing led into news of the mysterious death of Khalil al-Faruqi, a terrorist best known for hijackings and explosions and assassinations in the 1970s and '80s. He had been linked to the Black September attacks at the Munich Olympics and the murder of an Israeli diplomat in Britain. One of his photos, doctored to avoid the grotesque, was included in the item. There were unconfirmed reports and rumours that the French government was planning a press conference to declare al-Faruqi the mastermind of the Chez Sternbergh bombing.

A woman with a British accent, a specialist in Middle Eastern affairs, declared al-Faruqi was murdered by either clandestine service operatives or, perhaps more likely, another terrorist group. The Americans could have done it, the Israelis, even the French if they were committed. Or perhaps, if he had executed the attack in Paris, al-Faruqi had done it without permission from the reigning extremists in the Middle East. "The idea that these people are united is nonsense. You can't find two of them who agree, which is probably a blessing for the West. Al-Faruqi was not a well-loved man."

The segment ended with the presenter delivering some dopey aphorisms about living and dying by the sword, and a photomontage of al-Faruqi dressed like Fidel Castro, like John Travolta in *Saturday Night Fever*, with a small boy on his knee, and, finally, like a drunken gangster of the movies with a pot-belly.

Zoé Moquin's posture was as perfect as her lipstick. "Tell me how it happened."

It was something he wanted to cut out of himself. But he was honest enough. They might have been in and out like samurai in slippers. Instead it was chaos, with shrieks and with blood spraying against walls, new horrors to join with old ones that gathered in his mind before sleep.

It did not matter to her, what they had done to Tzvi. She had waved him past it. "Tell me how he died."

"He begged."

"You see, these men are so tough when they are doing the killing."

"He claimed he was innocent. He said he knew nothing of the explosion on Rue des Rosiers."

"Really?"

"I would say I believed him."

"A professional liar is bound to be good, Monsieur Kruse. And even if he were telling the truth, this was no innocent man."

"The DPSD is going to send assassins to find all the men you've judged?"

"You saw what he was doing with your friend, with the bolt cutters? That was a specialty of his." Her cheeks went red as she spoke. She slid her knuckles along the zinc tabletop. "It was of no strategic consequence. He would do these things, and videotape them, simply to show the Muslim Brotherhood—his clients—he was serious, cruel, that he lacked compassion. It was business. Like a job interview."

Apart from the Badoit bottle, the only noise in the café now was the dying rain, diesel engines on the roundabout of the plaza.

"*But what if he didn't do it?*"

"Didn't do what, Monsieur Kruse?"

"Chez Sternbergh."

Zoé took a deep breath, righted her already stiff posture. The colour in her cheeks had faded to a soft pink. "There will be a press conference. We will neither confirm nor deny. But we will strongly hint."

"But what if he didn't do it?"

She investigated the fingernails of her left hand. "What if, indeed? What are you asking, Monsieur Kruse? You want me to pay you and then hire you to go after someone else? This is your operation. Is it complete or is it incomplete?"

"I'm doing this for one reason."

"Not three million reasons?"

"Annette and Anouk."

"Yes. They are in your file. What about them?"

"I want a guarantee."

"What sort of guarantee? I don't understand."

"You said they were in danger if I didn't . . . take the job."

"I didn't say that. Monsieur Kruse, I work for the Republic of France. I would never, never threaten the lives of innocent citizens. As what? Leverage? The money was my leverage."

The waiter arrived with another little coffee and bottle of Badoit.

Zoé Moquin sighed. "It pleases me that the prostitute attacked him."

"Why?"

"That it was a woman, that is all. Thank you for allowing that to happen."

"One thing he did say, Madame Moquin, and the women confirmed it. The CIA had paid him for information about the World Trade Center bombing. They had plans to do other work together. He had what he called *proof*. I don't know if—"

"Give it to me."

"I don't have it."

"Where was he keeping this proof?"

"Somewhere on the compound."

"We'll take care of it." She dabbed her face with the white serviette and stood up.

"Madame. Do you have other suspects?"

"Do we have other suspects? Again, this was your operation. It sounds to me like you have other suspects. Are you finished? If you are finished

I will pay you and you will not hear from me again. It sounds to me like you aren't finished." She stepped away from the table. "Let me know, Monsieur Kruse." Without saying goodbye she walked out of the café, her new heels clacking on the old wooden floor.

Kruse drank his little coffee. When he stood up to leave he was no longer alone. Joseph stood in the doorway, in another of his crisp navy suits.

"Good morning, my friend. It's such a lovely coincidence to find you here, at one of my favourite cafés. And congratulations. I knew they were right to contact us. It was smooth, I imagine?"

"You saw the news."

"Did Madame Moquin pay you?"

"Not yet."

"Well, that's not so smooth. Not so smooth at all. And that face! More damned scars."

Kruse was so exhausted he nearly laughed.

"I have an idea." Joseph snapped his fingers. "How about Monsieur Claude and I drive you home?

Outside, Joseph opened his umbrella and held it over both of them. He led Kruse across the street, past a couple of plane trees and a bus stop. There was a patch of grass and some shrubbery, then a bit of public art he could not fathom. On the other side of it, a rather bland modern building made of glass.

"You know this place, Christopher?"

"No."

"It was a big deal when they first constructed it. Even in Marseille, where I was living at the time, it was in the news. The architect was a foreigner, a sympathizer to the cause. This, my friend, is the headquarters of the Communist Party of France."

The word *communist*, to a Canadian, was an altogether different word than it would be to a Frenchman. Communists were movie monsters. Kruse remembered thinking, as a boy in bed, that every airplane passing overhead was a missile launched from the Soviets to destroy Toronto. He would die in the night, vaporized without a chance to say goodbye to his parents. In the end he did miss the chance to say good-bye to Allan and Nettie Kruse, but not because of Leonid Brezhnev.

Although the president was still a socialist, these were not jolly times for the left wing in France. In the legislative elections, at the end of March, the Parti Socialiste had collapsed and voters had not chosen the communists as an alternative. The Soviet Union, which had once seemed a rival society, had fallen apart. The headquarters of the Communist Party was a capital of gloom.

"Shortly after you left, I received an anonymous call. Now, who calls me anonymously? Who knows my phone number? I can't say. It was a woman, and her number was untraceable."

"The call was about Khalil al-Faruqi?"

"That's it, Christopher—it wasn't. The call was about one of these men." Joseph pointed at the Communist Party headquarters. "He's rather a loud figure, in the news quite often. A communist who is some-times a socialist. Loud! Whenever you have a debate show, in the eve-nings, about unions and abortions and military spending, there he is."

Kruse could not remember his name but he could see him: a pudgy, red-faced, extraordinarily articulate man who leaned over tables and pointed as he spoke. In America he would not have been a politician at all. He would have been a talk show host.

Before Joseph was through his first name, Kruse was with him. They finished it together: "Réné Chatel."

"What about Réné Chatel?"

Joseph put his hand gently on Kruse's back and they walked up the smooth concrete walk, past the blobs and sticks of white art in front of the building. They were not alone. Even in the rain, giddy American tourists took pictures. *Just think of it, Helen: real life, actual commu-nists.* A large poster of Georges Marchais, leader of the party, remained in one of the central windows. In the poster his finger was up in the air, as though he was just about to deliver a devastating rebuttal.

"That's it, old man. I don't know. This woman said she knew it concerned me. How? I can't say. She spoke with an accent. A breathy German, maybe, like in the movies. She said she had evidence Réné Chatel had something to do with the Chez Sternbergh attack."

"Why?"

"Why did she phone me? I don't know. A vendetta against him? Guilt?"

"No, I mean why would someone like Réné Chatel want to blow up a restaurant?"

"Our dear mayor, as you know, is doing extraordinarily well. If the right can get it together, Christopher, these people—the socialists, the communists—may be finished. And I don't mean an election cycle. I mean a generation."

Our dear mayor. "Can we get a meeting with him?"

"Him?"

"Monsieur le Maire."

"Why?"

"How about this for *why*? My oldest friend was nearly killed, and so was I. A lot of others, none of them terribly good people, I'll admit, are dead. Why? The mayor and his friends in the DPSD set it up. Set me up. Why, if they weren't sure al-Faruqi did it?"

"Let's forget about the mayor. He's the innocent party in this."

Kruse nearly laughed, to think of the mayor as an innocent party in anything. A man and a woman walked toward them on the sidewalk in thin matching raincoats. They spoke English. Kruse and Joseph stood on the fringe of the sidewalk while they passed. "A man like Chatel, a famous man, decides to risk his life and his legacy by blowing up a restaurant? It doesn't make sense."

Joseph shrugged. "My mother is rather a devoted Catholic. Not a lick of it is rational, if you sit down and go through it with pen and paper. But my dear mother isn't alone. There's another billion of them.

Religion, politics, the stock market—it's all hocus pocus, more or less. Add some crazy into the mix."

His right side was getting quite wet, as Joseph talked with his hands and the umbrella did not remain in place. Monsieur Claude pulled up in the Mercedes, got out, and opened the door for them.

Kruse was sure Réné Chatel had not done it himself. Why would a politician and tier-three media star hire someone to toss a couple of grenades into a restaurant? Communists in France weren't typically racist. The legislative elections were finished. The mayor of Nancy had been popular and their patron was certainly powerful, but both men were instantly replaceable. To think eliminating one or both of them would harm or cripple Gaullism or even French conservatism seemed absurd.

Monsieur Claude pulled up in front of the apartment on Avenue Bosquet. Kruse thanked him for going out of his way, and Monsieur Claude stated it was, as ever, an honour to have him in the car.

"My friend." Joseph squeezed his forearm. "It's a time to celebrate."

Kruse had nothing to celebrate: Tzvi was in pain on the Atlantic coast of Spain and every time he tried to sleep he was haunted by the faces of the young men he had killed in the hacienda. "One thing, Joseph."

"Yes, my friend?"

"I asked Zoé about Annette and Anouk. As you know, I didn't do this for the money."

"Of course not."

"I'm a murderer. Tzvi lost his arm. So I wanted to know, is it *over*? Are they safe now?"

"And what did she say?"

"I expect you know what she said."

Joseph leaned back in the seat of the Mercedes. "She hires assassins but she wouldn't *think* of threatening a woman and her daughter. Is that it?"

"That's it."

"Well, maybe you are finished. Maybe you aren't. But I'd get that part straight with them."

"But they never said it. That's what I realized."

"Said what?"

"That Annette and Anouk were in danger if I didn't take the job. It was you, Joseph. You said it."

Joseph prepared to answer and then turned away, as though his response were interrupted by something more important.

"Who am I working for? This woman? The mayor? You? Someone else?"

Joseph looked up at the rear-view mirror and Monsieur Claude understood it was time to exit the car. He walked around to open the door.

Kruse went into the bakery, his bakery, which smelled almost like home, and bought a baguette. It was the middle of the afternoon. The woman in Voyages du Septième was staring out the window. Soon he would have business for her.

NINE
Rue du Louvre, Paris

ONE OF MAGASECURE'S NEW YORK CLIENTS WAS A SEVENTY-YEAR-
old architect whose life had transformed, overnight, when she designed
a glass office tower in London. Her instant fame was not of the envi-
able sort. Londoners despised the tower so much she received forty
imaginative death threats the week after it opened. She was so nervous
all she could do in the fall of 1988 was walk around New York with
Kruse, arm in arm, teaching him about architecture. Thanks to her,
Kruse knew the offices of *Le Figaro*, in a prosperous quarter of the city
north and east of the Palais-Royal, were art deco.

Number 37, Rue du Louvre was thin, the colour of vanilla pudding,
with scooters and motorcycles parked on either side. Kruse waited in
the lobby for the editorialist to come down. Étienne Bonnet was ten
minutes late. Most people in France were late, though of course they
would say ten minutes late counted as early. If you threw a dinner party
and wanted people to come at an appointed hour you would add
"English Time" to your invitation.

A tiny elevator opened eighteen minutes after English Time and Étienne greeted Kruse with a broad smile, called him *jeune homme* as though they had gone to college together. The editorialist was not alone. Men and women in dark business suits and dresses were watching. He briefly introduced his American friend Christophe Kruse and explained that the group with him had just met with the editorial board of *Le Figaro*: they were newly elected members of an exciting political party called the Union for French Democracy.

"Congratulations." Kruse softly shook their hands. He was learning the French grip: gentle, with all the masculine competitiveness buried in other gestures. "But I'm actually Canadian."

"With that accent?" said a beautiful woman whose eyes had been stretched into severity by plastic surgery.

"Some of us in Canada grow up speaking English."

On their way out, the politicians enlightened one another with anecdotes about the difference between *North* America and *America*. Étienne led Kruse through a door and up a set of marble stairs. Now that they were alone, they stopped acting.

"Fifteen minutes. That's all, Christophe. I have a deadline."

"It's all I need."

"And a social tip. You're the only one in Europe who cares about the distinction between America and Canada. Just let it go."

"Thank you, Étienne."

"Did you shave with a machete?"

Even on stairs, Étienne carried himself as though photographers were chronicling his adventures. His movements were majestic and unnecessary. He opened doors with a flourish, lifted his chin.

The library was on the third floor of the old building, lit by a chandelier. Table lamps warmed the newsroom. The desks, the floor, and the shelves were a marriage of dark wood and gold. A man in an unfashionably tight-fitting suit slumped at a workstation with a computer, a microfiche reader, and a pile of foreign newspapers. The air about him smelled of corned beef.

Étienne invited Kruse to sit by the window. "I assume this is about Annette."

"Actually—"

"It's been difficult to concentrate, I admit. I have been imagining, all morning, that you've finally schemed up a satisfying way to blackmail me. Let me tell you this, before you begin. You can tell her anything you like about me. It won't matter. And here's why, my naive American friend—"

"It's about Réné Chatel."

At first it seemed Étienne did not hear. Then as his mind processed what Kruse had said, his face mirrored doubt, confusion, revelation, skepticism, confusion again.

"I *would* like to hear how Annette and Anouk are doing, of course."

Étienne spoke in a quiet monotone. "They're fine, I think. Nothing to report. How do you . . . Christophe—what exactly do you do?"

"I'm in the security business."

"This is what I thought. So why would you be interested in Réné Chatel? You do mean Chatel the communist."

"Yes."

"What, is he a *client*?" Étienne said *client* the way a Canadian would say *communist*. He did not have to work. His parents did not have to work. His grandfather had made enough money for several generations to coast on interest, as long as they had been somewhat careful about investments. He did work, in a job that paid much more in prestige and influence than in salary. It was almost honourable.

Kruse did not like to speak to Étienne any more than he liked to break into his apartment. But he didn't know many people in Paris outside his government clients, Joseph, and the people who sold him bread and coffee and salad. He had little choice.

"I'm doing work for another client and Monsieur Chatel has come up."

"As what?"

"Someone to investigate. I want to know more about him, that's all.

At the library, when I searched him, *Le Figaro* came up many times. I saw that you had written rather a bit about Monsieur Chatel."

"He's a maniac."

Kruse looked down at his notepad. This was certainly information, though not useful enough to write down. "You've known him a long time."

"We went to school together. Our parents knew each other."

"He grew up wealthy?"

"Like most devoted communists, yes, he grew up in a wealthy family. Then his father was taken in a Ponzi scheme based in London. We were in high school together when it all fell apart. They lost everything and more."

"A good high school?"

He smiled. "Lycée Janson de Sailly."

"The best."

"I would say so."

"This must have been humiliating for the Chatels."

"The family moved to Nantes. None of us heard from Réné until he showed up in the National Assembly—a communist! The first communist *jansonien*, I would think. And his undignified television interviews. He was always a clown but today I wonder if perhaps he has suffered a mental crisis." Étienne paused long enough to blink a couple of times. "What is the nature of your investigation?"

"Do you think Monsieur Chatel could be dangerous?"

"To French politics? No. What did the communists get in the legislative elections? They're as relevant as the Berlin Wall. Even *they* aren't crazy enough to make Réné leader. Besides, he lost his seat."

"I don't mean dangerous economic policies."

"What do you mean?"

"Could he hurt someone?"

Étienne took in a long breath and exhaled thoughtfully, one of his tics. It was designed, Kruse thought, to hold his attention. "I remember saying to my editor-in-chief, after Réné and I had last spoken, I wouldn't be surprised to see him in our pages very soon, and not for his political observations." Étienne spoke without any of the irony or grandeur he tended to carry with him. "The fall of the Soviet Union has been hard on him, I would say. And we're already dealing with a fragile mind. So yes. I would even say I predicted it."

"When did you last speak?"

"Two months ago, perhaps—just before the election. He wanted to have lunch. I don't know why. He knows *Le Figaro* would never, in one hundred million years, publish a positive editorial about the Parti Communiste."

"Was he worried he'd lose his seat?"

"He was resigned to it. Of course, there was a right-wing conspiracy against him. This is what he wanted me to write about, a systematic effort by the Office of the Mayor and by the Gaullists to destroy him."

"Just him?"

"The party in general. But of course, he sees himself as the party. *L'état, c'est lui.*"

"He mentioned the mayor. Anyone else in particular?"

"The mayor wants to create a coalition of centrist and centre-right political parties, as I'm sure you know as a devoted reader of *Le Figaro*. But that isn't enough, according to Réné. The mayor will not be satisfied until he and his people destroy the Left forever."

"Would you say he was obsessed with the mayor?"

"I would say that."

"And at the end of this meeting you worried about him."

"For his sanity, yes."

Kruse sat back in his chair, looked down over the quiet street below. Two adolescent girls in school uniforms walked arm in arm. One of them carried a leash and a small dog pranced ahead. He could not stop playing his game: one of the girls, the one with the dog, was Lily. She had done so well in school that he had rewarded her with what she had wanted for years: a Yorkshire terrier.

"Can I help you in some way, Christophe?"

"You can help me find him."

"This is not . . . you've not been hired to harm Réné?"

"No."

"If there's a story here, you have to tell me first. If he's done something. Yes?"

"There's no story."

Étienne stood up and walked past the researcher, who sighed loudly. On his way back Étienne whispered something to the man, which seemed to placate him. "We're hiring interns from the provinces now, to 'broaden our voice.' This one's from a ridiculous little town in Franche-Comté. It used to be enough that we ate their cheese. Now we have to endure their inbred sons and daughters."

As ever with Étienne, Kruse reached a point where all he wanted to do was throw him out the nearest window. The editorialist slid a business card across the table. It was Réné Chatel's National Assembly card with a phone number, written in ink, across the top.

"You didn't get it from me. I wouldn't call him a source, but I don't want word getting around that I can't be trusted."

"Oh I'm sure most people know that."

Étienne extended his hand for a shake. "Would you like another social tip?"

"Let me guess. Stop breaking into your house."

They were still shaking hands. Étienne pulled his away and wiped it on his pants. "You lost her. I won. Look at yourself, Christophe. It isn't just your latest wound. When did you last sleep? Perhaps you could stand in the sun from time to time, or smile, or simply work to make someone in your presence feel good."

If Kruse wanted to confide in Étienne he might say he was quite certain he had seen ghosts of the men he had killed in Spain walking across the floor of his bedroom last night. They did not speak. The dead men were confused, searching for something they had lost. Kruse was a man in his thirties hiding under his covers.

• • •

His first thought, when he saw the man in the atrium of *Le Figaro*, was that he was homeless. The receptionist was simply being kind, allowing him a respite from the rain. But it was not raining. The homeless man, in a wrinkled grey suit and what appeared to be a bunch of garbage bags stitched into an overcoat, stood up and waved.

"Mr. Kruse, hello. I was hoping to introduce myself." The man spoke English with an American accent: Georgia, Alabama, Mississippi. "Raymond Peach."

"Hello, Mr. Peach."

It was a different sort of handshake: unnecessarily strong, a return to the New World.

"How do you know my name?"

"You're investigating folks. I'm investigating you. It's a simple thing, really. And I figured, just now, instead of following you around and sniffing where you piss, maybe I'll just come clean and introduce myself. I'm an employee of an organization called the Central Intelligence Agency."

"I believe I've heard of it."

"Have you? Well." Peach had a wild mess of grey-blond hair, whorled in a nest on the otherwise bald top of his head. "For the last couple of years I've been here in the hexagon, like you I think, Mr. Kruse, learn-ing how to be French. My counterparts, the DGSE, gave me a little office to call my own. You familiar with them?"

"Direction générale de la . . ."

"Very good. All these goddamn French acronyms. De la sécurité extérieure. They've got me on Boulevard Mortier. There's a lot of streets in Paris, and this one ain't nowhere pretty. Way out by the ring road. I don't understand what makes it a boulevard. Anyway, shit."

Kruse had dealt with the CIA in New York, in Washington, once in New Orleans. If MagaSecure work ever crossed into their territory, they would show up and ask them out for cocktails in a hotel bar and threaten them with hearty smiles on their faces. Tzvi, who had worked for so long in Mossad and knew the tricks, generally did all of the talking. All of the insulting. Agent Peach was a couple of inches taller than Kruse, and portly. He had the air of a slow-moving man who was briefly quick; in high school, perhaps, when he had played offensive tackle. One thing he had learned from Tzvi was to not initiate conversation.

Raymond Peach smiled a dimple into his cheek. "Can I take you for a drink?"

"I'm not much of a drinker, Agent Peach."

"Yes, I know that about you. But you're willing to break that rule from time to time, aren't you? Come on, just a quick one."

People in France didn't do this: pressure each other to go for a drink. *Non* was no. And the agent was only pretending. Kruse had the choice, he could say no, but Agent Peach would make things difficult for him. He and Tzvi had never turned them down, but they had tried to learn more, in each of the meetings, than the CIA learned from them.

"There's a nice little brasserie at the end of the street." Peach led him out the door. "The barmaid dresses like an actual barmaid. One of those poofy white shirts unbuttoned a bit low, and a short black dress. It'll be a scream."

The brasserie was a point on a busy intersection. All the way, jaywalking when they could, Peach talked about Canada. He had a sister in Edmonton who worked as an engineer—a lady engineer!—and absolutely loved hockey. "A girl from Mississippi who talks only of hockey. The Oilers lose and she's goddamn distraught. Whoever could have figured that? But she couldn't get away from home fast enough. It was tough, growing up the way we did, in that time. So many changes! I'm all for change now. This is my sixth foreign posting. But when you're eleven and you see and feel and hear, right in front of you and in all the newspapers, that everything your parents taught you was wrong, or at least half wrong, boy, Mr. Kruse, it does something to you."

Agent Peach lacked the reserve of other CIA agents he had known. But Kruse had never met with the CIA after killing people. Maybe this was a technique, what they do before they arrest you.

"Change doesn't know it's being cruel, does it? You lost a daughter. You lost a daughter and a wife, am I right, Mr. Kruse?"

"Yes."

Peach opened the door of the brasserie. It was busy and smoky inside, in the middle of the morning. The bar chairs were taken by retired men drinking petit blanc. Only the rich could retire this young in Canada. Kruse nearly said so, to test the mood, as it was surely just as true in Mississippi. Peach had been right about the bartender. She dressed in what seemed to be historical clothes. Perhaps it was a theme bar. Would they arrest him in a theme bar? They sat at a booth against the cool window.

"You must be wondering, why me?"

Kruse shrugged.

"We got a bit of a file on you and on your man Tzvi Meisels. A bit of a file! It's our job to have files, of course. But your move to France. It didn't make a lot of sense to me, going through the information. What were you planning to do here?"

"Bake bread. Make wine. Sell cheese."

"Seriously?"

"My wife wanted me to change my life. Get out of security."

"That's Evelyn."

"Yes."

"Now: what happened to your beloved wife, Mr. Kruse?"

Kruse didn't answer.

"I'm sorry to have brought it up. I just wanted to see what you'd say." Agent Peach pretended one hand was a notebook, the other a pen. "*Subject is uncommunicative.* Is it too early, do you think, for a pastis?" The way he said the word, it nearly rhymed with *fastest*.

The waiter arrived with a tray. He wore a regular cheap tuxedo. It was not a theme bar. Peach ordered a Ricard and Kruse asked for a sparkling mineral water.

"And your daughter. Jesus. I know you wanted to change your life, but this can't be what you were thinking."

Kruse looked at his watch. It was a quarter to eleven. He was eager to phone Réné Chatel.

Peach looked at him looking at his watch and smiled some more. "This is fun, speaking English, hey?"

"Get to it, Agent Peach."

"What were you doing in Sigüenza last week? What business did you have with Khalil al-motherfucking-Faruqi?"

"I've never heard of him."

For perhaps two minutes, as long as it took for the waiter to arrive with a pastis and a Perrier, Peach stared at Kruse. He wasn't smiling anymore. This was the face he had worn on the offensive line. The waiter seemed to enjoy the tension. He took his time leaving the two drinks. He lingered to wipe the table.

Peach poured the pastis and water, stirred them with ice. "I know you know us. We've had run-ins. Maybe you're thinking, oh, this is just like all the other times. My boy Tzvi and I are a faint nuisance to another low-level CIA man. Well, Mr. Kruse, I've come to tell you this morning that you're wrong about that. I'm not that man. And Khalil al-Faruqi was not yours to kill. He was a key witness in maybe the most important investigation in the last ten years."

"I don't know who or what you're talking about."

"Yeah. Yeah, I'm flying to Santander tomorrow. I'm going to rent a car and drive to . . ." Peach pulled a pair of reading glasses out of the inside pocket of his garbage bag coat. "Santillana del Mar. When I get there, I'm going to park my rental and ask to see my chum in room 219, and then you know what I'm going to do?"

"No."

"I'm going to sexually assault your one-armed business partner."

"That's against the law, Agent Peach. You should reconsider."

"If that doesn't satisfy me, and I fear it won't, I'll ask a few of my friends in the DGSE, the ones like me with inadequate grooming habits, and they'll hold you down in that fancy apartment of yours and I'll sexually assault you too. Again and again. Until you tell me who hired you to assassinate Khalil al-Faruqi. There were some documents at the compound, documents that weren't yours to take, property of the Central Intelligence Agency."

"I am astounded, Agent Peach. Confused and astounded by this conversation."

"And I am a man of liberal understanding. I don't need to know anything more than I need to know. You give me a name, and that paperwork, and *whoosh*. *Whoosh*, Chris. Can I call you Chris?"

"No."

"*Whoosh*. I disappear back into the alleys of Paris."

"I've never heard of . . . what's the name you're saying? The man who was assassinated? I'm afraid my Arabic is as inadequate as your grooming habits, Agent Peach."

"You're a liar. Even about *that* you're a liar. How do you sleep at night, lying like you do? Betraying America like you do?"

Kruse stood up and placed a fifty-franc note on the table. "I don't sleep, Agent Peach. Nothing you say can make it worse, I'm afraid."

"I'm coming for you." Peach repeated his threat in French and the men at the bar laughed at him.

• • •

Two men and a woman painted the puppet theatre in Luxembourg Gardens. They wore white coveralls, splattered with abstract art, and matching conductor's hats. On a small folding card table, a beat-up silver ghetto blaster played a song so American it conjured four-by-four trucks and light beer: "Achy Breaky Heart." Before he arrived in France he would have assumed violently tasteless things—this sort of music, graffiti, television commercials for grotesquely large portions of french fries and soda, city men in cowboy boots—were particular to his part of the world, his people. Kruse passed to the other side of the theatre to flee the music and to note the performance times. One day Annette would call, stranded. She and Étienne would be on their way to one of his properties in Provence or the Dordogne and she would have no choice but to ask: could he take Anouk for a couple of days?

It was late afternoon and, for the first time in many days, warm. The sun shone over the gardens; the high wail of a thousand shrieking children rose up with the smell of flowers and popcorn. There was a lineup for the pony rides, and in the pool all the little sailboats tipped and zipped in the light wind. Men and women sat alone in the green chairs that dotted the manicured forest, reading and listening to Walkman stereos and doing crossword puzzles or nothing at all.

His plan was simple: before he called Zoé Moquin to declare himself finished, he would meet with Réné Chatel. He did not like to be manipulated, even if Khalil al-Faruqi was a mass murderer. If the communist had done it he would collect the money and fly back to Toronto with Tzvi. From Pearson airport he would phone the police first. Then he would give Joseph a courtesy call. It would be his turn to throw a grenade.

Réné Chatel had agreed to meet him at the statue of Margaret of Anjou. It was both public and private at once, as the crowds did not venture to this otherwise featureless corner of the park. He had run past the statue hundreds of times, during his morning exercises, but he had never really looked at it: a boy hugging his mother's waist as she both comforts him and extends a hand in a spirit of defence. *Come near him and I will destroy you.*

"A Frenchwoman, obviously."

The man who spoke had seemed, a moment earlier, to be walking past and reading a copy of *Le Monde* at the same time. Now he looked up at the statue, just behind Kruse.

"She was married to Henry the Fifth. The mad king, they say. But it's not quite correct to call him a madman, because he was sweetly insane, a man of compassion. But Margaret was strong where he was weak. She ruled, not him. And do you know why the boy is included in the statue?"

"I know nothing, Monsieur. Monsieur Chatel?"

"She worried about Richard, one of your Shakespeare Richards, becoming too powerful—*even king*—while her husband was in the midst of one of his episodes. Worry became war—the Wars of the Roses. Of course, in her efforts to protect her son, prepare the way for him, she killed him. He died in battle, you see, among many thousands of others. And in the end, her efforts allowed her enemies—the Yorkists—to take over the British monarchy."

"All of it was to protect a little boy?"

"There are worse reasons to start wars." The man, who wore a moustache and a cravat with his beige suit, shrugged. "It is a theory. Obviously, the sculptor believed in it, its emotional power. And would we not, all of us parents, do the same?"

"You have children, Monsieur Chatel?"

"Two sons, both of them in *collège* now. And you, Monsieur Gibenus?"

It took Kruse a moment, to adjust to the name he had used on the phone: Mathieu Gibenus. "No."

Réné Chatel was a short man in the middle of middle age, with carefully manicured hair and hands. He was not at all what Kruse had been expecting. A communist who remained a communist after the great failure of communism wore, in his mind, layers of dusty grey canvas. He dressed like Agent Peach. But Réné Chatel's linen suit appeared new, and tailored. All he needed was a cane.

"You said you have information for me, Monsieur Gibenus."

"I wanted to ask you about the mayor."

The man lifted his shoulders, stiffened. His breathing changed and so did his eyes. "What about the mayor? Why should I be considered

an interview subject for a man I do not know? First, if you're a journalist, where is your notepad?"

"I use a recorder."

"Is it recording?" He looked around. "You do *not* have permission to
record this conversation. I have already informed my lawyer that you
had asked to meet me. A dossier: there is a dossier, Monsieur. Anglo-
Saxons are not the only ones on this planet who can be litigious. If you
publish anything I have said up to now, let me just say . . ."

For the next several minutes, Réné Chatel followed many tangents.
The press was keen to destroy him because the mayor of Paris, who has
a personal vendetta against him, owns the press. Or his friends do.
They own everything. Free will is an illusion in a city where the mayor
sees everything, controls everything. He could not and would not say
anything specifically about Freemasons but to assume they did not play
a role in this was dangerously naive. Réné Chatel was not afraid because
he was a walking symbol: for freedom, of course, and for the dignity of
the worker. His lawyer was considering lawsuits against the Office of
the Mayor of Paris and against the republic, as it was not at all clear
that he had actually lost his seat in the National Assembly. Why should
he simply assume that because the government says it is so that it is so?
The government does not represent the will of the people. It represents
only capital.

After some time, his monologue ended. Kruse had stopped paying
careful attention when Chatel veered deeper into Freemasonry and
touched on how Monsieur's government, the American government,
had faked the moon landing *just because it could*. And if they can do
that, they can do anything. Kruse had waited for a pause, to ask about
some of the other statues of French queens, to calm the politician, but
there were no pauses.

From time to time, men and women with money hired MagaSecure to
act as therapists more than protectors. They would arrive to complete an
analysis and it would be clear the clients were not under any threat, apart

from whatever had gone wrong with the subtle machinery in their brains. Tzvi had set up a protocol in this situation: the money comes up front. If there is enough money, they listen. They listen for as long as the client needs to speak. But it drew the energy out of Kruse like an invisible syringe. He preferred a three-hour fistfight to three hours of paranoia.

When he couldn't stand another moment of Réné Chatel, Kruse put up his hands. "Monsieur Chatel. I'm sorry."

It worked. The communist stopped speaking for a moment. "For what?"

"For wasting your time."

"But you . . . What is your article about? The party? Me?"

"It's about the explosion at Chez Sternbergh, Monsieur Chatel."

Réné Chatel took two careful steps back into the trees. Without looking away from Kruse he reached into an inside pocket. "It's you."

"What?"

"You. An American. The letter said you would come." The communist did not pull a letter from his jacket. It was a knife with a homemade sheath on its blade, made with newspaper and clear tape. He pulled the newspaper free and tossed it on the crushed gravel. "The letter said I would have no choice."

"Monsieur Chatel—"

"Kill or be killed." He held the knife in his right hand and his yellow and black polka-dot pocket square in his left, which he used to dab his forehead. *"But if you do wrong, be afraid, for he does not bear the sword in vain. For he is the servant of God, an avenger who carries out God's wrath on the wrongdoer."*

"Your letter was incorrect, Monsieur. I don't know what you're talking about. Please believe me: I am only here to speak with you."

"It said you would have a warrior's face." Chatel stepped forward. "That you do."

While this was not a popular place to gather, the statues of the queens were the way into the park for some people. Others simply walked the

path. By the time Chatel had begun quoting from scripture, two people stood and watched. Now there were five. Someone ran on the
gravel. Kruse did not turn away, in case the awkward man lunged.
"Please, Monsieur. Think of your sons."

"I am thinking of them. I shall see them again."

Kruse now believed Chatel was capable of anything, but this was not
the bobbing head of the man who threw the grenades into Chez
Sternbergh. "Do you know who blew up the restaurant?"

"You see. You see, it's proof." He spoke to the growing crowd around
him. "This was foretold."

"Monsieur Chatel, this letter . . . who wrote it?"

"Everything that has been foretold in the letter is coming true,"
Chatel called out to the audience. "He will slaughter me in front of you
all, like an ox!"

Kruse, whose hands had been out the whole time and who backed up
as Chatel stepped forward, did not have to defend himself. Men and
women called out to the communist to drop the knife. Then there were
shouts and a break in the crowd and two policemen, in their tilted hats,
arrived to stand on either side of Kruse. They were not gentle with
Chatel. One and then the other ordered him to drop his knife.

"You're not real. You're with him. Someone call the real police!"

Then they shouted over each other, the police and Chatel. He
ordered them to leave. The audience could save his life, save all their
lives, save France by calling *real police*. Kruse stepped back and into the
crowd, walked backwards until it happened: Réné Chatel shouted a
curse and lunged at a policeman. The policeman leapt back into the
crowd and stumbled. The other drew his gun. "Put down the knife!
Now!" He screamed at the crowd on the other side of Chatel to dis-
perse and they did.

The policeman who had fallen stood up again and Chatel took a step
toward him with the knife. Those who had not yet run away ran away.

"Put down the knife!"

Chatel reached for the policeman who had fallen, not with the knife but with his handkerchief, and said something Kruse did not hear. And the other man shot him. People screamed. Kruse did not run, not at first.

Dust had collected on the shoes he had just shined. Dust, somehow, in this damp place. A brief gust of wind moved through the trees and white petals drifted past and it smelled of flowers. No one was following him. From time to time, when he worried for children or when he longed to share a surprise, a joke, a moment of beauty, Lily and Anouk would fuse into one girl. He would close his eyes and return to the backyard of his house on Foxbar Road, with his daughter among the magnolia blossoms, and she would become Anouk in the puppet theatre of Luxembourg Gardens on his knee so she might see over the head of the woman in front of them.

Still, no one was following him.

Even in the sunshine the soft lamps in the windows of the Luxembourg Palace were on, and men and women in suits and dresses—senators—walked back and forth with glasses of wine. Kruse walked toward the palace, into the soft wind. No one was following him. He thought about knocking on the door, asking to address the Senate with humble truths about the republic. The police had not followed him. No one he recognized from the mayor's office or the DPSD was in the park. No one watched him. Kruse turned left. Among the elm trees, men in blue overalls with yellow stripes wiped the seats of the green chairs, moved them into strategic positions on the white gravel like artisans of leisure. He walked north out of the park. At Place Saint-Sulpice there were trailers and white tents for a film shoot. He joined the crowd. Two actors he did not recognize stood at the Fountain of the Four Bishops. A woman shouted "Action!" and they began speaking. They looked awkward together but they were supposed to be lovers. No one walked or drove past, looking for him.

On Rue Bonaparte the boutiques were for millionaires. He would soon be one of them. In the movies, people always accepted bags and briefcases full of money. But what did they actually do with it all? Could he pay his French credit card with a stack of American bills?

He ended up near the river. The financial solution would involve Switzerland. He could forget about Réné Chatel, forget about Agent Peach, gather up Tzvi and fly back to Canada—first class. No, business class. People in Canada didn't allow themselves to say "first class" because it was unfair to the second and third class. In Canada it was easy. He did what a Canadian would do. On Rue du Bac he walked into a quiet brasserie with a red door and ordered a beer. There was a gold-ringed mirror across from him. He needed to sleep. His warrior's face, the sound of the gunshot echoing in his ears, inspired him to cross his arms and put his face on them and cry in public.

* * *

At just after ten in the morning a tall woman walked out of the apartment on Rue d'Andigné. Her cocktail dress was black and sparkling. It would have been magical in the soft light of the evening, in front of the opera house. But it was a bright morning, the second in a row, and the sun was high enough that she had to raise a hand. Her high heels echoed through the street. She nearly jogged. Though Kruse had been in the country only for a year, he could already see the beautiful woman was no more French than he was. The driver, Monsieur Claude, folded his *Figaro* and rushed around to open the back door of the Mercedes. Like the other imported cars on the block it was freshly washed despite the April rain. The woman's blond hair was long and straight, gently dishevelled. She put on a pair of large sunglasses.

Monsieur Claude remained at the door. Two minutes later, Joseph walked out in a grey suit, and the valiant sound of his leather soles also filled the corridor. That was how a Frenchman walked: quickly and confidently, looking everywhere and at everyone with studied indifference. Monsieur Claude dished him a quick thumbs-up, the most casual gesture he had seen between them.

"And how are you this fine sunny morning, Monsieur Claude?"

"Very well, Monsieur Mariani, thank you."

Kruse sneaked between the cars and entered the Mercedes from the opposite side, ordered the woman to move to the middle just as Joseph sat down.

"My partner in the doing of good deeds. This is a delicious surprise."

Monsieur Claude bent down on the sidewalk beside Joseph, the door open. His job was to prevent this sort of thing from happening, with the others on protection detail. But he had been lazy this morning and flashes of panic and failure and resignation passed over his face. Without looking back, Joseph reached up and touched Monsieur Claude's chest. "*Ça va, mon ami. Ça va.*"

Kruse introduced himself to the woman, who looked straight ahead as though none of this were happening. She did not take his hand.

"She doesn't speak French. Or English," Joseph whispered across her. "An Estonian girl, a recent arrival. She grew up a communist, just across the water from Finland. A Nordic princess. I'm sure she thinks you're a cop. She thinks everyone is a cop. We're dropping her off at her apartment, on the other side of the river, and then I have a business meeting."

Monsieur Claude remained beside Joseph. He would have alerted others through some electronic means, because there were now three men on the sidewalk. Only one was properly dressed.

"We can go, dear Monsieur Claude." Joseph waved at the others and they retreated back into the apartment. "All is well. All is well, isn't it, Christopher?"

"No, Joseph, I'm afraid all is not well."

Monsieur Claude entered the driver's side door and his seat squeaked with regret. He looked up in the rear-view mirror, dished eyes of fury at Kruse, and started the car.

Kruse reached around the Nordic princess and took Joseph by the hair. "It was a set-up. Why? Did the mayor order this?"

"Christopher." Joseph tilted his head in Kruse's direction so it wouldn't hurt quite so much. There was a faint grimace about his mouth but he spoke as though they were waiting for a chamber music concert to begin. "I know how good you are at what you do, I know. But if you—"

"You're going to threaten me? Make my life *worse*?"

Monsieur Claude shouted, "Let him go or I pull over and shoot you in the face!"

The Nordic princess scrambled between the seats, into the front. She wrenched on the door, to get out, but Monsieur Claude had locked her in.

"Why are you so angry with the only true friend you have in this country?" Joseph lay on the seat, like a napping child. "Why would you pull my hair like this, diminish me in front of Inga?"

Inga turned around. *"Vabandust?"*

"Oh my darling." Joseph reached into the front, touched her arm even as Kruse yanked his hair. "We'll get you some French lessons. Now, Christopher, what has happened? Is this about Monsieur Chatel?"

"You told me to go after Chatel but he knew I was coming. He was ready. Someone had warned him, someone who knew he was paranoid. If you want to get rid of me, why don't you—"

"Christopher. Take your hand out of my hair so we can talk like gentlemen. Someone fucks us, we fuck them back. It's a very simple calculation."

His calls to Joseph were routed through receptionists in Marseille, London, and Brussels, and each one required a password dropped into a simple request. He would not progress past the London receptionist, who worked at a genuine art gallery Joseph owned in Whitechapel, if he did not thank her for her "kind attention." Over his beer, five glasses in the brasserie on Rue du Bac, he came to understand that no breathy German woman could have phoned Joseph anonymously. It would have been easier to phone the president.

"You lied. This woman who called you—"

"The German."

"No one *calls* you."

"I will show you everything, tell you the truth as I understand it. But you'll have to let me go, before the affection I carry for you drains completely from my heart."

Kruse released him. Joseph sat back up in his seat, adjusted his hair and suit, and breathed. He could hear Tzvi: only a weak man loses his temper. Three blocks they passed in silence and hit the quay. At the Trocadéro, blooming in the morning sunlight, they turned right across a bridge that did not have to be pretty—the Pont d'Iéna—because it seemed to run under the Eiffel Tower. Joseph looked in the rear-view mirror, to adjust his tie.

"No one, no one in France, would pull my hair. Maybe our Nordic princess, in another context. But in anger! Only you, my friend. My friend with nothing to lose."

"Who has already lost everything, thanks to you."

"Not everything. Your little Anouk."

"She isn't mine."

"Let's just wipe out the editorialist, Étienne What's-his-name . . ."

"Bonnet."

"*Bonnet*, and you can be a beautiful little family. And let's not forget the Israeli."

Kruse told him about Agent Peach, what he had said about Tzvi.

"I'll send one of my Bilbao guys to look after him. Is that what's bothering you? You think I sent you off to wipe out an innocent terrorist? First of all, it wasn't me. Second—"

"Réné Chatel is dead."

"What are you talking about?"

"It's in all the newspapers, on television."

Monsieur Claude confirmed it and tossed a copy of *Le Figaro* into the back. It was on the front page. "He went crazy and pulled a knife on the police?"

"On me. Then the police. I asked him about Chez Sternbergh and he went bananas."

"So he *did* do it?"

"No."

"I don't understand."

"Someone told him I would come for him, ask him about it. Your German woman—"

"My breathy German."

"—who somehow just *called you up*, prepared him. He is—was—already wired for paranoia, which everyone in France seems to know. I don't think Monsieur Chatel was supposed to be shot by the police. He was supposed to try to stab me, protect himself from a scar-faced man who meant to harm him. Maybe the breathy German understood I would never allow him to stab me. Maybe she thought I would at least hurt him or that he would kill me. Either way, he was set up and so was I. Why?"

Joseph spoke to Monsieur Claude in Corsican and the driver leaned over. They were on the quay now. Monsieur Claude opened the glovebox and pulled out a pile of papers, handed them back. Joseph put on his reading glasses and went through them, found an envelope, handed it to Kruse.

It was an Easter card.

"I received it through the bistro in Marseille."

Inside was a short note. It was written in calligraphy.

Monsieur Mariani: I have information about the explosion on Rue des Rosiers. I can go to the police or I can go to you. Please call.

He read it a few times. The number was not local. "Where is this phone from?"

"Lorraine. Christopher, if I wanted to hurt you, wouldn't I just hurt you?"

"And you called?"

"I called. Let's call again, shall we?"

TEN

Place Stanislas, Nancy

THE FLAGS WERE AT HALF-MAST IN THE PLAZA, TO COMMEMORATE their lost mayor, Pierre Cassin. In the centre was the statue of Stanislas, the stout Polish king and duke of Lorraine. The duke leaned on a sword with one hand and with the other he pointed to the north, like an eighteenth-century Babe Ruth predicting a diplomatic home run. Plazas were comfortable and pleasant to normal people, but there was enough room on this expanse of cobblestones to land an airplane. Every rooftop was a perfect location for an observer, and Kruse had come to see himself as observed. The trees on the outskirts of Place Stanislas and on the low hills surrounding the old town were deep green, and the city itself smelled more like the countryside than his seventh arrondissement.

The bearded security man in the lobby of the ornate Hôtel de Ville was taking a photograph for a group of tourists wearing too much perfume, *un, deux, trois, et voilà,* so Kruse went for the stairwell as though he had been here hundreds of times. On the top floor the route to the

Office of the Mayor was lined with flowerpots and flags. A woman with black hair, her scalp evident as she bent over to work, sat at a grand desk in the entrance. There was no computer.

Without looking up she said, "*Oui*, Monsieur?"

"I am an investigator from Paris, serving at the pleasure of the mayor. I was hoping to speak with Monsieur Cassin's chief of staff."

She had looked up from her desk at the fourth word in his first sentence. As ever, his accent inspired all the French calculations of foreignness. She pointed at the new wounds on his cheek. "You? *You* work for the mayor of Paris?"

"Yes, Madame."

"But you are American."

He performed the Gallic gesture; he pushed out his lips just slightly and shrugged and said, just faintly, "*Ben.*"

"Your name?"

"Mathieu Gibenus."

The woman crossed her arms and appraised him like his mother on the day she caught him on the refrigerator eating from a bag of chocolate chips. *How did you get up there?* "You didn't think to call for an appointment?"

"No, Madame."

"And *that*, evidently, Monsieur, is why you people rule the world." She pushed herself away from the desk, on the wheeled chair, and asked him to wait while she spoke to Monsieur Lévy. He was alone for almost ten minutes, so he went through a big black book of condolence in the hallway. Citizens of Nancy, and visitors, wrote of their ruined hopes for Mayor Cassin and what he might have achieved were it not for *les Beurs*—the Arabs.

In the margin of one of these notes, someone else had written, "The mayor was half an Arab, you idiot."

A man walked tentatively into the reception area, through a heavy oak door. He was short and rotund, with a skein of sweat where his hairline once extended. He was ill or frightened. Definitely frightened. His handshake was soft but his eyes were not.

"What do you want?"

It was unusually abrupt for a Frenchman. Kruse tried on a smile. "Just a conversation, Monsieur Lévy."

"You work for the mayor?"

The way he said the word *mayor* was beyond Kruse's comprehension. "Yes."

Lévy took a step back, adjusted his tie, looked around. "I received no advance warning from your office."

"I don't work in the office. It's different, what I do."

"Of course. Of course it's different. I should have expected you would come. I knew someone would come, eventually." His skin was pale even for a cloudy northern spring.

"Can we walk and talk?"

"I would prefer to stay here, Monsieur . . ."

"Gibenus. It isn't raining. The air is quite warm and still."

This seemed to confuse Lévy. "I probably can't say no, can I? It's a dance we're doing. You didn't receive your scars at charm school, did you? As ever, we do what *you* want to do no matter what I say. Give me a moment." Lévy opened the heavy door, sighed, and it closed behind him. The building was silent but for the slip of Kruse's soles on the marble. In less than a minute, the chief of staff had returned, wearing a thin beige overcoat with something heavy in the right pocket. "I can give you ten minutes."

They went down an interior stairwell and entered Rue des Dominicains, a tidy commercial street of banks and boutiques. Monsieur Lévy hugged a beige folder to his chest with one arm and with the other, his right, he cracked his chubby knuckles.

"Gibenus. This is your real name?"

"No."

"But you genuinely work for the mayor."

"You know him, Monsieur Lévy?"

"Of course I know him."

"So as genuinely as one can work for him, I work for him."

"A very French thing to say. Bravo. What do you want?"

"The explosion."

He pushed out his lips and shrugged with so much style Kruse was jealous. "I was supposed to be there. My daughter is at Sciences Po in Strasbourg. Her Parisian asshole boyfriend broke up with her, and she was inconsolable. My wife was worried and wanted to go to her, but she was stricken with a gastrointestinal tragedy. Pierre, that is, Mayor Cassin, he insisted I go to Strasbourg to be with my daughter. And after all, the trip to Paris wasn't essential business. He was supposed to meet your man that evening, for dinner, to talk about Brussels."

"The mayor of Paris invited him?"

"Absolutely. Chez Sternbergh was an add-on, a little conference with a few party donors."

This was not part of the security briefing from the mayor's office. It wasn't how the mayor had described the meeting. "I thought you had requested a public announcement."

Lévy passed the folder to Kruse. The first page was a photocopy of a memo from the mayor's office, in Paris, confirming the details of a luncheon with party donors from the Jewish community. The second page was from Lévy's counterpart in Paris, requesting a meeting. It was not on City of Paris letterhead.

"Your daughter is okay?"

"Not her heart. Everything else is fine." He took a step back, painted in the air a few of the scars on Kruse's face. "How is it, Monsieur, that a trusted advisor to the mayor of Paris could be so ill-used? And look at those hands. The suit, however, is a lovely camouflage. It looks bespoke. The mayor must treat you well."

"Tell me about Pierre Cassin."

"Your employer knows everything there is to know."

"I don't. Please."

"He worked hard. He was always prepared for the questions. Jewish and Arab, all wrapped in French, you know the story. He was confident but not preening. He didn't care about money, not excessively anyway. I could go on. But of all the political jobs one could have, working with Pierre . . . well, we had the finest hopes for him."

"Brussels."

"According to the mayor, your mayor, yes." They passed a store devoted exclusively to cellular phones. Lévy looked in as they passed. "We did the deal for Brussels. But we had other ambitions. We would be in Belgium five years, then back here. Or maybe we wouldn't bother with Brussels at all. There was money. A lot of support."

"For what?"

He cocked his head at Kruse. "You must know." He whispered it: "The Élysée."

Kruse stopped walking. "This was common knowledge, that he had presidential ambitions?"

"Many assumed, of course. Party leaders, for sure. He was handsome, well spoken, young but not too young, the symbolic value of his ethnic background. We have this obsession, as you must know, an outsider yourself: *integration.* How do we make our immigrants French? My mayor, the mayor of Nancy, was a model for the old French and the new."

"And my mayor—"

"*Everyone* knows what your mayor wants. Pierre was more careful. Not careful enough, I guess."

"What do you mean?"

Lévy looked around, pretending to be lost. They were in front of a fragrant boulangerie-pâtisserie. "I've said enough. It was Arabs, they say. Islamists? I caught some of the news conference."

"That's what they say."

The dead man's chief of staff looked into the bakery. Then he whispered again. "There were death threats."

"When?"

"Over the past year or so."

"Letters?"

"Phone calls, unforgettable things."

"You took some of these calls?"

"We began recording them. They would torture and kill Pierre, rape his wife and children if . . ." He reached up to sort out hair that had fallen out long ago. Kruse had met men like this, policemen and soldiers who had seen too much. It seemed odd in a bureaucrat, the anxiety. He was about to offer to take him for a petit blanc when Lévy cussed. "Other calls were different. Pierre was supposed to retire from politics, take a job, if he wanted to . . . thrive. This wasn't ridiculous. He was probably the most employable man in France. He could have been very wealthy. These callers, two different men, two voices, were keen to encourage him."

A tall woman walked out of the bakery with a brown bag and Lévy reached for the door, went inside. Kruse followed. It was warm and smelled of yeast and sugar, of childhood. The line was long, a quiet horseshoe.

"It's made me crazy. I thought, I think . . . *They're everywhere.*"

"These men who made the death threats? Who were they?"

Lévy shrugged. Inside, they whispered. "Perhaps all I need is a week on the beaches of Egypt."

"Who do *you* imagine is listening, Monsieur Lévy?"

"Who do you imagine, Monsieur Mercenary?"

"You traced the calls?"

"Just one. The others were too short. These are sophisticated psychopaths. But they messed one up, missed the receiver or pressed the wrong button. There was a click but the line didn't go dead."

"Where did it come from?"

The chief of staff took the folder back from Kruse and turned the memo over. On the back, in neat handwriting, was an address and a phone number. "We gave it to the police as well."

"And what did they do?"

"I have no idea. Chez Sternbergh blew up two days later, didn't it?" Lévy addressed himself to the displays, to some vanilla cream and chocolate combinations. "You'll buy me a pastry now, I think. In fact, you'll buy pastries for my family. A box."

They did not speak for the next few minutes as they neared the cash register. There were two women behind the counter in white cotton dresses and aprons, somewhere between thirty and fifty. It did not appear as though either of them had smiled since the end of the 1980s. They wore matching deep red lipstick. Lévy looked around several times, for others in the shop. His right hand was in his pocket, awkwardly. At the register he asked for a box of eight pastries and stepped back so Kruse could pay. The box was white and tied with a red ribbon, the red of the women's lipstick, and sealed with a sticker.

Back on the street, he opened the box and offered one to Kruse. "There are only three of us in my family. And only because my daughter is visiting." They each chose one and ate as they walked together, back to city hall.

"Can you give me something else, Monsieur Lévy?"

"I don't know."

"A list of your staff. Actually, anyone who could answer a phone call to the Office of the Mayor of Nancy."

"Why?"

Kruse told him about Réné Chatel, the Lorraine phone number. Someone from his office had implicated Chatel in the explosion in Chez Sternbergh.

"In *my* office? I can't imagine who would do that. I fear this is a sabotage."

"We received instructions to phone."

"Who are *we*?"

"And when we phoned, it was your office."

"When was this, Monsieur Gibenus?"

"A few days ago. Do you have anyone with a German accent, a woman?"

"We've been having trouble with our phones. We thought perhaps it was the volume of calls of condolence, but really there weren't that many. For a day and a half we couldn't call out or receive calls. We were using portables, borrowing other departments' phones. Our security detail, ever the geniuses, took another two days to realize we had been hacked."

"When did this happen?"

"The day and a half?" Lévy pulled a small organizer from the inside pocket of his suit jacket and put on his reading glasses. Kruse readied his own notebook, where he had written the time and date of Joseph's call. They corresponded perfectly.

"Your security detail. Did they discover who had done it?"

"They're retired army men. Very retired."

They were a few steps from the side door. Lévy looked at him. "What are you really doing here, Monsieur Gibenus?"

"Someone killed your boss."

"Khalil al-Faruqi killed my boss. Now he's dead. There is no reason to think further upon it. But then, you're here."

"What do you think?"

"I've never benefited financially from my position, apart from my not-so-fantastic salary. I've been a faithful husband, Monsieur Gibenus. This job, it requires some travel and some late nights, but I am as good a father as I can be."

"How about Mayor Cassin?"

"What do you mean?"

"Was he faithful? A good father? Did he benefit financially in any unsavoury ways?"

"No politician is faithful. Pierre was not faithful, no. No politician is a good father, despite what he might tell himself. No politician who grew up the way he grew up can say no to money. It's entirely contrary. But he was as good a man as he could be."

"Any trouble there?"

"With money?" He shrugged. "No. It was all done slyly enough, impossible to trace. Affairs of the heart can be troublesome. Voters don't care in this country, unlike yours. But a mistress does. Love is love. I can't imagine what he might have told a couple of these women. But none of them were . . . Monsieur, when my assistant told me you're with the Mayor's Office I retrieved what I could. I don't have much. You have everything. Everything I know. So if there's anything else, anything you might think I know, please . . ." Lévy placed his half-eaten pastry on top of Kruse's half-eaten pastry. Their left hands touched. His eyes went moist as he spoke. There was a small blob of chocolate on his chin. "*Return to this moment*, Monsieur Gibenus. I know nothing. I suspect no one. With me, there are no loose threads. It has all been cut. I am only a servant of my city and my republic."

"You think I came to hurt you?"

"I am imagining the words Monsieur le Maire used, the euphemism. Research? Diplomacy?"

"To shut you up."

"Why else? To examine me? To see what I know? Your mayor, he is not a man to cross. I know this, I do, and I will not."

Lévy was close enough so Kruse reached down, touched metal. It was, as he had suspected, a small handgun in the overcoat. "You were going to shoot me in the street."

"Only if you cornered me."

"Monsieur Lévy, who killed Pierre Cassin, and the others in that restaurant?"

"You don't know, Monsieur? You really don't know?"

Kruse shook his head.

The chief of staff finished his pastry. He put his hand on the door, looked around to be sure no one was following them. Lévy would never be sure. "It's in your dossier, that address and phone number. These men who called to threaten Pierre—they were not Arabs."

• • •

At the end of the Grande-Rue there was an entry to a tunnel that looked, from a distance, like the medieval castle in a Bugs Bunny cartoon he had watched with Lily. There was a cross of Lorraine, the cross of the Crusades, to remind everyone, and below that a statue and the words "Porte de la Craffe, 1336." Evelyn would have been pleased with his first thought: the tunnel had been built two hundred years before Shakespeare was born. His second thought was less impressive: what was a *craffe*?

The varnish on the wooden door at number 94, Grande-Rue had been peeling for decades. It was between a real estate agency and an empty storefront that had once been a Turkish restaurant. A cracked intercom box affixed to the stone had three names for three suites. Kruse pressed number 2, the one on the address Lévy had given him, and waited. No one responded so he pressed 1 and 3, and an old-time buzz sounded.

The steps had begun to rot long ago. It smelled of wet wood and cigarettes in the stairwell, and a fluorescent light flicked on the upper wall. A door was open on the landing and a tiny woman with dyed orange hair and grey roots, wearing a polyester dress and fluffy slippers, stood with her mouth open in anticipation, her hands out. It took her a moment to see Kruse, and then she shrank even further. "Oh."

"Bonjour, Madame."

"I thought you were my grandson, young man. Why did you press my button?"

Suite 2 was across the landing from her door. "I am an investigator."

"You speak like you're from New York. Are you an investigator from New York?"

"Yes, Madame."

"I always thought I would see New York. 'When I'm a little older,' I said. 'When I'm a little older I'll have more time. More money!' Now I have plenty of time and no money and I'm too old for New York. I would just get in the way."

"You're not too old."

"Bah."

"Madame. I am investigating suite number two, your neighbours."

"Have they done something wrong?"

"I don't know. That is what I am investigating."

"One of them is from Austria, I believe. But neither is from New York."

"May I come in, Madame?"

"Of course. Of course, Monsieur. I will make coffee." The woman, four and a half feet tall, led Kruse into her apartment. He closed the door. It was a three-room suite, clean but cluttered with photos and Catholic knick-knacks and too much furniture. She filled her kettle with water and Kruse took over. She sat at the tiny table along the window, in her narrow kitchen, and pushed some of the envelopes and papers away. Music played from her bedroom. He knew, from Evelyn's teaching, that it was Vivaldi: cello, harpsichord, violin. "Just yesterday I bought some lovely raisin biscuits, if you want to pull them down from that shelf. No no, that one. I have heard, Monsieur, that Americans find us cold. Rude, even. It may be so in Paris, it may be. I doubt it. But one thing is certain. Here in Lorraine, our doors are open to foreigners who agree to work hard and contribute to France. I can see you aren't a *resquilleur*, a freeloader. You're wearing a good suit, and shoes, and you have nice clear blue eyes. That says a lot about a man."

The woman introduced herself as Françoise Flandrin, a lifelong Nancéiene who had lived here on Grande-Rue since the death of her husband in 1986. Soon, she understood, she would have to leave. Soon the stairs would be too much.

"Do they help you, the men across the hall?"

"You mean with groceries? If I press the buzzer and they are home, yes, of course, one of them will come down and help me up."

"Can you describe the men for me?" Kruse pulled out a small note-book. The water had not yet boiled. "You said one is Austrian. He *looks* Austrian?"

"Well, it's difficult to say how one can *look* Austrian. He does have a moustache, if that is what you mean, and his posture is very good."

"Light-coloured hair, or dark?"

"Oh, light. And thinning, the poor dear. Men worry too much about that, if you ask me."

"So neither of these men are, say, ethnically North African? Not Arab?"

Madame Flandrin looked at him as though he had declared her an Arab. "Of course not!" She chuckled. "Now, when I tell the boys you asked me *that*. It's funny because neither of them is fond of foreigners. Not foreigners like you but as you say, Africans, Lebanese and the like, Jews."

"They don't like Jews?"

"Oh I don't know. France for the French, that sort of thing. Though I suppose Karl is Austrian after all."

"So it's *Karl*?"

"Yes, he'll be the Austrian. And Victor is from Besançon originally. I've never been there. You?"

"No, Madame. I will have to visit."

She looked out her window, which had a view of a messy courtyard. A small tree was surrounded by bags of garbage and some children's toys had been abandoned to the weather.

"Might you have photographs of them?"

She snapped her fingers. "Open that drawer. The one below. Below that. Yes, there. You will find, right on top, a packet of them."

The packet was not right on top, but he dug through and found it—plastered with Kodak, just as it might have been in Toronto. He handed it to her and she put her glasses on and flipped through them. Madame Flandrin was quick when she wanted to be. She slapped three photos down on her messy table and handed them to Kruse. "*Voilà*, Victor and Karl."

The balding one, the Austrian, had grown a modest, pointed beard. The other had dark hair, cut short. Kruse could not say he recognized him as the man who threw the grenades but it was possible. He was the right age. They smiled in all three photos. "Do Karl and Victor have jobs?"

"Of course. They work at a Vigner."

Kruse had seen Vigner retail outlets in Paris and in Marseille: it was a chain of wine and beer stores that advertised on sandwich boards out front. It wasn't about quality or rarefied selection or atmosphere: they competed on price. "Nearby?"

"On the other side of the door."

"The door?"

"La Porte de la Craffe."

Two of the photos were taken in her apartment. The third was clearly not, as the wall was almost bare of decorations. It was Madame Flandrin with the men on either side of her, all three of them with glasses of white wine. Kruse was just about to hand it back when he noticed something in the top right corner.

"Is that a swastika? Your neighbours have a swastika on the wall?"

Madame Flandrin rolled her eyes. "Those boys are crazy about them. And I asked, during my first visit, if they admired Hitler or the Nazis, Marshal Pétain the vile collaborator. Because that is something I could not abide in a friend. But it's just a misunderstanding, you see. It's an old Indian symbol. Hindu, I think they said. Did you know that? Even the word *swastika* comes from Sanskrit."

"So they have an interest in Indian symbology."

"Perhaps that is what they said. But I did tell them, Monsieur, it's very easy to make the wrong assumptions about such a thing. The way it makes me feel, when I look at it! I lived here then. They were here, all around us, and if I close my eyes I'm there. I can't remember what I had for dinner last night but I can remember the war perfectly. Certainly I'm not alone, feeling sensitive about such things. Maybe they could find a symbol of old India that doesn't also mean 'Hitler had some terrific ideas,' which is what a Frenchwoman thinks first when she sees such a thing. I'm not sure if it's the same in New York."

"Do you know their family names?"

"Handke. Karl Handke and Victor Nodier. Victor says he descends from the author Nodier, also from Besançon, but I must say I don't know so much about literature. Literature and symbols from Old India. It's beyond me, I'm afraid." She closed her eyes for a moment as the music from her bedroom seemed to rise in volume, and she briefly conducted the small orchestra. She was so tiny, in the kitchen chair, her feet did not touch the floor.

"You rent this apartment?"

"But of course not. I am a landowner. I own this entire neighbourhood." She pointed at him, winked. "No, no, Monsieur. I rent it from the company that owns the wine stores, actually, the Vigner Group. They do own a lot of the property around here. In Paris too, I imagine. You could check into that, for your investigations."

"I could."

"The boys bring me wine from the store. I hope *that's* not why you're investigating them."

"No."

"If it helps, Monsieur, write this down: they are good boys. They help an old lady with her groceries, with wine, and with a leaky faucet."

"What time do they come home from work?"

"Oh, normally in time for dinner, before seven o'clock. But they have been on holidays for a week and a half."

"Do you know where they went?"

"They wouldn't tell me, as it happens. But I'm no fool. I'm not so old. I imagine Karl and Victor were off somewhere naughty, like one of those beaches in the Caribbean where everyone is naked."

• • •

He walked under a delicately carved triumphant stone arch south-west of Place Stanislas, stained by the weather and desperately in need of restoration. The city was newer on the other side of the arch, marked by an ugly rectangular 1960s glass office tower that looked as ridiculous in central Nancy as the Tour Montparnasse in Paris. Two men sat in front of it, huddled on a stained piece of cardboard with a magnum bottle of cheap wine between them.

It had not taken much: Madame Flandrin had simply produced her phone book. Above the drunks and through the windows, Kruse recognized the simple, elegant sign in the lobby: *Vigner*, in white letters. There was a directory at the security desk, offices and floors: Real Estate, Wine and Spirits, Human Resources. The top floor, the seventeenth, was not listed. He had put on his new suit, and the tie was freshly knotted.

The security guard, who wore military medals on his deep blue Vigner uniform, looked at *Le Figaro*. There he was on the editorial page: Étienne Bonnet's name on the right-hand column. Its headline was a play on words Kruse did not catch: something about Islam and houseguests. The plan was to speak with the security guard, to announce his arrival, the arrival of an important American business partner, but the man did not look up from the newspaper. The name Khalil al-Faruqi was in the first paragraph.

In the elevator, the button for the seventeenth floor would not work. He was about to press 16 when the woman next to him, who wore a business jacket and skirt, too much foundation, produced a key and inserted it in the panel. She pressed 17 for him, without making eye contact.

"I saw you trying to get the guard's attention."

"Thank you, Madame."

"You have a meeting with . . ."

"The Acquisitions Department." This was a trick Tzvi had taught him. No matter where she worked, legal or accounting, marketing, an *acquisition* would not reach her desk until the early negotiations were completed. "Just the beginning of a conversation."

"We're having more and more of those. Mergers, acquisitions."

"Isn't everyone, Madame?"

"This is why I fear, one of these days, we will learn Monsieur Alibert has had a massive coronary. If one can die of heartbreak."

"One can die of heartbreak, Madame. I'm sure of it."

Now she looked at him. They were about the same age and her eyes held just as much fatigue. Her engagement ring carried a large but not obscene diamond. "Have you met him?"

"Monsieur Alibert? No. But I do hope to on this visit."

"If he's interested in your company, you'll meet him. Fascinating guy."

"In what way?"

The elevator stopped on her floor, the tenth. "You'll see."

"You're a lawyer?"

"How did you know?" The doors opened and she stepped out into a modern lobby decorated with light wood, lit with honey-coloured bulbs. Three years earlier, only Denmark had looked this way. *Vigner*, the same sign, shone behind the reception desk. There was no need to respond to the woman, who turned back for a final, flirtatious look just as the doors were closing.

Alibert: he was pleased he had not asked about any Monsieur Vigner. If the company began as a wine retailer, the name was likely invented: a short form of *vigneron*. He rode alone to the seventeenth floor and the elevator doors opened into a much darker space. The reception area on the top floor had been designed like a British gentlemen's club: dark wood, dimly lit spaces, comfortable upholstery, and portraits of white-haired men in suits on the wall. The receptionist was a man in his forties, in a three-piece suit. *Butler* was his first thought, or perhaps the overly solicitous purser in the business class of a European airline. He stood up and walked around the desk to greet Kruse, to shake his hand.

"Welcome to Vigner Industries, Monsieur . . ."

"Meisels."

"Ah, Monsieur Meisels, of course. I was just scanning our appointment book for the afternoon and I somehow missed your name. May I ask whom you have come to meet?"

"Monsieur Alibert."

The butler looked genuinely confused. "Perhaps one of us is mistaken. I am confident Monsieur Alibert does not have another appointment today. May I ask what it is regarding?"

"I'm afraid not."

"Will you please take a seat while I speak to one of my superiors? Can I pour you a refreshment of any sort?"

"No, thank you."

"Just a moment, Monsieur Meisels. From . . ."

"Direction de la Protection et de la Sécurité de la Défense."

The butler stepped back as though he were a demon and Kruse had brandished a cross. "Well. An intelligence agent. How exciting for us." He held a key fob up to a box beside the door and exited without another word.

It was a relatively small reception area, yet four teardrops hung from the ceiling: cameras. He was tempted to wave, certain they were watching him, making phone calls, unwrapping his lie.

There were some magazines on a carved coffee table, none of them current but all of them featuring Henri Alibert—a bald man in his sixties who seemed, at least in the three glossy front-page photographs, to be a giant. Kruse picked up *Le Monde Magazine* and made it through the first five paragraphs before the butler returned. Henri Alibert was from a family of steel barons, had inherited his money, had trained at all the right schools, had played polo, and had used the phrase "protect my family's empire and save my country" when the journalist had asked him to sum up his mission in life.

The butler entered the reception area from a second door, nearer the wing chairs and the magazines. Kruse stood up and the gentleman handed him an envelope. "An invitation."

"To what?"

"Monsieur Alibert is hosting a dinner tomorrow, at his residence. He apologizes that he does not have the time to meet with you today, Monsieur Meisels. Were you planning to stay the night?"

"I was."

"And where are you staying? I have been instructed to send you a basket, a gesture of welcome."

"I do appreciate the gesture, but I am not yet sure where I will be staying."

"Well, then. Monsieur Alibert owns a hotel of very good standing. I would be delighted to reserve the finest room for you. Vigner Industries will take care of the cost, of course."

"Thank you, but we must preserve our independence."

"We, Monsieur?"

"La Direction."

The butler nearly smirked. "Monsieur Alibert went to school with the defence minister, in fact. I'm sure he would appreciate your integrity in this matter. Can I tell Monsieur Alibert you will come?"

"It's an honour, thank you."

"I can have a car pick you up, wherever you would like. If you provide me with an address, when you find a suitable hotel?"

"You're too kind, Monsieur." Kruse opened the envelope. The invitation was a gold-embossed card. "But I can find my way to the party."

Kruse excused himself with another handshake, and they exchanged more wishes and words of concern and absurd goodbyes, all of them laced with degrees of irony and distrust he could feel more than understand. He understood enough, and as the elevator descended he looked into the camera and wished Tzvi were with him.

There was a bank of payphones near the drunk men on cardboard. He slipped his card into the slot and phoned Zoé Moquin.

• • •

Kruse passed the courtyard in front of Nancy's public library, where a teacher and twenty students in black-and-white uniforms stood listening to a woman on a bench, reading aloud from a picture book. Since it was nearly five o'clock, he imagined it was an after-school program for well-behaved children. Lily would have been one of these, one of the rare ones who still possessed the ability to concentrate. There was a vast building on the next corner, the first private bank he had seen in France. A man and a woman in beautiful overcoats walked out, wealth in their posture and in the flat appraising looks in their eyes, and in the way the gentleman helped the lady down the stairs. Some of the richest people in the world lived in New York, and he had worked for them, but none of them looked like this.

It was bright inside the train station, all that was old and grand stripped away to lease retail space: a Vigner wine store, a mini-grocery, clothing chains, an electronics shop. He brushed his teeth, left the washroom, and returned to brush his tongue. The train arrived on time. A small crowd had formed: husbands and wives, children, parents, drivers. Kruse waited against a pillar, to watch her before she saw him.

The first-class car was at the front. At the back of a crowd of businessmen and businesswomen she walked slowly, with a small bag on wheels. From the waist up, her dress had three thick and repeating horizontal stripes: black, orange, beige. On the bottom half, the skirt portion, the stripes were the same colour but vertical. She wore a wide-brimmed black hat with a veil, and a lacy black cape over her shoulders, white Doc Martens boots.

Kruse had never said anything, out loud, about her clothes. But even in a country of women who took fashion seriously, Zoé was a flamingo. A security agency in America would never hire someone who looked and dressed like Zoé Moquin.

"Our appointment is in fifteen minutes." Zoé walked out in front of him, through the automatic doors and onto Rue Piroux. It smelled as though it might rain. She waved at the first taxi and opened the back door, settled into the back seat with her bag.

The driver stepped out of the car and looked at Kruse. It was as though a multicoloured thunderstorm had just sat in the gentleman's car. "Where are we going, Monsieur?"

"Place Carnot."

"But that is only a few minutes' walk."

Kruse opened the driver's side rear door. "Madame Moquin. The driver says—"

"I heard him. I know where it is. Perhaps he could just get in the car and drive."

The driver mumbled to himself as he started off, squealing his tires in frustration. It was as though Zoé and the driver had been married for twelve years and had just finished arguing about money. Kruse waited a moment.

"You had the press conference?"

"The minister of the interior had it."

"So how, officially, did Monsieur al-Faruqi meet his end?"

"A military operation."

"And the CIA, did they participate in the press conference?"

Zoé looked away from him, out the window as the first flash of rain hit the glass. "Of course not. Why do you ask?"

When he had phoned Zoé to tell her he had discovered a new line of inquiry, Victor and Karl, she had resisted him. When he had said the name Henri Alibert there was a long pause on the line. It was so long that Kruse had asked if she was still with him. Zoé had a contact at the university, one of the "best minds in European politics and economy." She could set up a meeting but—long sigh—Professor Saussure would not meet alone with a stranger. As busy as she was, Zoé would have to join him.

The conference room was on the top floor of the pretty mansion on Place Carnot, furnished not with office chairs but antiques from an old court. Zoé sat across from the ageless woman in enormous sunglasses, with grey hair bleached blond and wearing a blue dress that would best belong in a dark, smoke-filled cocktail lounge. There was a stack of books in front of her. She and Zoé had kissed, called each other by their first names.

Zoé accepted Marie Saussure's compliments on her dress, and reciprocated, but she did not want to talk about clothes.

"It was a huge loss."

"Yes."

"To *wear her*, in a sense, must be some consolation."

"Yes, Marie."

The professor removed her sunglasses. "I had wanted to be there, for the funeral, Zoé. I was ready to cancel everything. But the negotiations—"

"Funeral?" said Kruse.

Zoé wiped at the air in front of them, as though she wanted to clear away a puff of sewer gas. "A personal matter. I apologize, Monsieur Kruse. Shall we?"

Madame Saussure lit a cigarette. "Let me begin to answer your questions, as I understand them, with a bit of a history lesson. Yes?"

"Thank you, Madame Professor."

She started with the horrors of the Second World War, early conversations about economic partnership. It resulted in something called the European Coal and Steel Community in the 1950s. This led to the Treaty of Rome and broader economic ties between the countries of Europe. Did they follow? The road to economic integration was like the Autobahn. "There are, in any deal like this, winners and losers. Men who were already thinking about markets outside their borders, about cooperation and growth, they benefited radically. Some old families have become fabulously wealthy since the war. Others, who were focused on France, on the quirks of post-war France, did not. Why not? They were and in some cases *are* chauvinists. They would like to sell their wares internationally but they would prefer not to compete with foreign companies *inside* France, you see. There were legitimate concerns, then as now, that the Germans would do as the Germans have always done: use coop-eration to achieve a dominant position. Who won these arguments? I think we know. Slowly and cautiously, and now not so slowly and cautiously, we move toward *total economic union*—a shared market here in Western Europe. Europeanism as a step toward complete globalization."

Madame Saussure, who had spent twenty or thirty or forty years lecturing, enunciated carefully and spoke with a lovely singsong rhythm. Kruse had actually heard her before, on the radio. But he did not yet understand what this history lesson had to do with a couple of neo-Nazis and their boss.

"But Henri Alibert, in the articles about him, is the richest man in Lorraine."

"Perhaps in assets, Monsieur Kruse. But they're worth less and less every year. Every week, in fact. We have seen, since the seventies, a sharp decline in French families like the Aliberts. The old industrialist has not adapted. Some who cannot adapt go away quietly. Their sons and daughters spend the last of their fortunes on yachts and cocaine. Others, like Monsieur Alibert, they organize."

"What do you mean?"

"I mean a resistance movement, powerful people working against European integration and globalization. People who would prefer to protect the way things are. Better yet, the way things were forty years ago. We understood France then. We understood capitalism. Imagine what one hundred or five hundred Henri Aliberts could do if they pooled even one-tenth of their wealth. Each of these old European fortunes, even as they decline, are more than you and I or our children will ever see—by many multiples. Imagine if they put a fraction of their resources together to fight what is coming in just a few months."

"Maastricht," said Zoé.

"Precisely, Madame."

Kruse knew Maastricht was a Dutch city, but he didn't understand what they were talking about.

"And the mayor—"

"Yes, Zoé. Your beloved mayor of Paris supported Maastricht in the referendum. As did my late mayor."

Kruse put his hand up. "What referendum? What do you mean by Maastricht?"

"You said he was in . . ." Madame Saussure looked at her cigarette, switched to English for a phrase. *"American intelligence."*

"I don't think I used the word *intelligence.*" Zoé spoke slowly now, as though he had suffered brain damage. "Weren't you living here in September, Monsieur Kruse?"

In September he had lived in Vaison-la-Romaine. His life consisted of taking Lily to and from school, learning how to bake bread, training in the evenings. He did not watch the television or read the newspapers. When Evelyn spoke of politics, he would suggest an imaginary tea party with his daughter.

Madame Saussure cleared her throat. "No reason to feel any chagrin, Monsieur Kruse. A shocking number of my students, whose parents would have campaigned for or against Maastricht, don't understand its significance. In September, fifty-one per cent of French voters said yes to ratifying the Maastricht Treaty, which will create an economic union of European countries. Many people, like our Henri

Alibert, put a lot of money into the No campaign. They felt the mayor of Paris had betrayed his party and the Gaullists and, ultimately, France. They feel fifty-one per cent is not enough to hand over our sovereignty. They feel it's Mitterrand's legacy project and a socialist nightmare. They're sure Germany will soon dominate this union. They feel it will open, Americanize, and, as I said, globalize Europe. It will certainly hurt their business interests. And, most importantly, these people are not alone. They have fellow travellers in Denmark, whose referendum failed, and in the United Kingdom, in Belgium and the Netherlands, in Austria and Spain and Italy and Portugal and even Germany."

Zoé opened her notebook, raised her pen. "Is this an official coalition?"

"There are many official coalitions."

"I mean the one you're hinting at. One hundred or five hundred men like Henri Alibert."

"You will not find its address in the phone book, dear Zoé, but it does exist. You'll discover it has been active for some years. And it has failed, spectacularly. Maastricht represents its final defeat, yes? I will not be surprised to see acts of desperation."

"Does it have a name?"

"Surely not."

"Who is its leader?"

Madame Saussure removed her sunglasses and smiled. Despite the air of elegance about her, a spot of her lipstick had transferred to her perfectly white teeth. Dentures. "I have felt pressure from these men— and they are men, to be sure—for much of my career. It was only in the early days, the less careful days, that it seemed to originate somewhere."

"Where?" said Kruse.

"Nancy."

• • •

They had walked through a gilded gate into Place Stanislas and the 1950s. The bistro was of brass and heavy red velvet, carved mirrors. Three horse-faced musicians in tuxedos and unnecessary sunglasses, whom he imagined as brothers, played soft jazz in the corner: a mini drum set, an acoustic guitar, a clarinet.

Locals in suits and dresses filled the tables and banquettes. The tourist season had not yet begun; no one had cameras or dressed in what the French saw as the comically informal manner of Americans. Yet even for the French, who do not tend to stare in public, Zoé's striped dress and veil were irresistible.

Without asking, their waiter brought each of them a flute of champagne. A house rule, apparently.

"You must be accustomed to it."

She shrugged.

"Madame Saussure said something about you *wearing her*. What did she mean, if I may ask?"

For a long time, Zoé watched the musicians. When she answered she hardly answered. "My sister."

"You're wearing her clothes?"

"Yes."

On their walk from the university to the hotel, the air was still and charged and warm, though a heavy Atlantic mist had arrived. He knew the reputation of Lorraine—cold, cold, cold—and as a Canadian he sympathized and quietly cheered for the gentle weather of Nancy. The hotel was a vast house next to the cathedral. It had been a home for the prelates until they no longer merited such extravagance. When few believed in God, what was the purpose of the prelates' magnificent robes and rings and rooms?

"My sister was a designer, Monsieur Kruse. For a year, to honour her, I am wearing the dresses she created."

"She died recently?"

Zoé nodded, and for a moment it was quiet between them. She looked out the window. Kruse imagined lymphoma, leukemia, a miserable thing that can take a thirty-year-old. The waiter arrived with his notepad.

They ate white asparagus soup and salad with a lemony vinaigrette and capers. Zoé chose a bottle of Séguret, a village he knew well from his time in Vaison-la-Romaine. When there was a strike at the post office in Vaison, he and Lily would drive to the one in Séguret. He might have mentioned it, his special feelings for Séguret, but Zoé barely paused to eat. She stared intently at him as she spoke. If Kruse looked away, she would stop speaking and wait for him to return to her. They decided to give up Monsieur and Madame, to become Christophe and Zoé. He had met people like her at cocktail parties and receptions at the university, through Evelyn, people with a devouring sort of intelligence. Despite her beauty, Zoé would not have had many friends in school. She was too much.

It was dark, the light outside the windows of the bistro streaked. The weather had turned violent. Zoé spoke mostly of Henri Alibert and how Kruse ought to prepare himself for an evening with the wily industrialist who was probably a neo-Nazi. She did not want to talk about her sister and Kruse did not want to talk about Evelyn or Lily or Tzvi—any of their losses. In the morning he would go to the library and learn what he could about Alibert and far-right politics in Lorraine, antiglobalization movements. The dress code was formal. On the square, rain fell in an echoing roar that overwhelmed the horse-faced jazz brothers. When the wine was gone they decided they were plenty drunk enough.

Were it not for the wine he might not have mentioned it directly, but when Zoé returned from a visit to the washroom he asked about the threats to Annette and Anouk.

She leaned over the table, spoke just loud enough that he could hear.

In the washroom she had reapplied her eye makeup and lipstick. "I did inquire."

"With whom?"

"My superiors, Christophe. At the agency. I know it is nothing, nothing you could say overtly. But do you have a deal with the mayor of Paris?"

Kruse had assumed she knew this all along. "Of sorts, yes."

"You did something for him. And he has rewarded you."

"In my file you read about my daughter and my wife? How they died?"

"Of course."

"I don't know about the mayor, but the mayor's office was not blameless. I knew the story and Annette knew the story."

"When she worked for the newspaper."

"Yes."

"She spiked it?"

"For protection. For a better life."

"And by now you must know these sorts of deals are . . . what is the word?"

"Ephemeral."

"Yes, Christophe. Though Monsieur le Maire is a good bet. I imagine the gentleman is already picking out the furniture for his office in the Élysée. The heads of the agencies know he is the next president. The police. The armed forces. Monsieur le Maire can do exactly as he wishes. Everyone wants to be on his list of benefactors."

"So you're saying the threat, if it is a threat, originates with him?"

Zoé shrugged. "As we learned today, he has a great many enemies. And he is not sentimental. In times of war we think as warriors. Who are you, after all, to the mayor?"

Neither of them had taken an umbrella from the hotel so they had to walk under the awnings and cornices. The cathedral, at the end of the street, was lit with pale yellow floodlights. No one else was out walking, and there were few cars. When they arrived at the hotel, the strangeness between them undone by the grapes of Séguret and by the preposterousness of two adults soaking like children, they took the stairs and, on the third floor, she stopped at her door and leaned back into it.

"I'm sorry for what happened in Spain." The water had released her perfume. "Monumentally sorry for your business partner. And for you. You know I did not intend for that to happen."

Kruse didn't see what her intentions had to do with it.

"And thank you for tonight, Christophe. I've had a miserable year. It's rare for me."

"To eat?"

"No, no. I generally eat."

"My humour doesn't work in French."

"Perhaps it's your accent. We always assume you've made a syntactic error."

"To be funny, one must project authority."

"You project plenty of that. It just isn't through language, Christophe." With her heels on, she was only a couple of inches shorter than him.

Here again he was lost. The wine had not sharpened his senses but it had seemed, during dessert, as though she might at any moment take him by the collar and kiss him. Now it seemed even more likely, alone in the dim hallway. He had been with Evelyn so long he had forgotten about moments like these. Should he walk away? There was no uncertainty with Annette: they had been thrown together by violence, and Anouk had wiped away the possibility of flirtation. With Annette, a kiss was everything. Either move in together, share a towel, or don't bother.

Zoé took his hand in hers and whispered something he did not hear, but to ask her to repeat it would have ruined things. He thought of Annette again. It was ridiculous. He was ridiculous. He nearly laughed out loud.

"I feel like a teenager."

"If you were a Frenchman, Christophe, you would have already . . . well, I might already be pushing you away. I'm rather old-fashioned. I work for conservatives. I am a conservative."

"Most conservatives, in France, would be socialists in America."

"I'm not a libertine, that is all I mean."

Kruse did not want to talk about it. If Zoé was going to ask him into her room, he wanted her to do it. Now. The more they dissected and intellectualized it, the less likely it would be. Of course, Kruse could ask her. As she had already noted, if it seemed vulgar he could retreat and claim he had made a syntactic error.

When you are learning to fight, it is essential to throw the first punch. One day, you become good enough to believe the opposite. When your opponent throws the first punch, and you dodge or intercept it, he gives you all the information you need to defeat him.

There was a drop of rainwater on his nose. Zoé reached up and transferred it to her finger before it dripped.

"Let's think about this a moment."

"Zoé. Let's not think about it. If we have to think about it—"

"Quite right." She adjusted on her heels, stepped an inch forward so he could feel her breath on him. It smelled sweetly of wine. "You work for me."

"I thought I worked for the mayor."

"It would be unprofessional. And in the morning light, grey no doubt, in the fog of a champagne-red-wine headache, this time we are spending together now will be difficult to . . . to justify."

A portly man with a trim beard and a suit bag stepped out of the elevator and waddled past them, said good night. He was a lonely salesman. Industrial curtains, maybe. Kruse nearly made himself laugh again. He wanted to go into her room. He wanted to remove the veil from her and drape it over the back of a chair, slowly unzip her dress and kiss the back of her wet neck.

"No matter what happens here, Christophe, I have money for you. You've finished your job, at least officially. When you're back in Paris . . ."

"Back in Paris. And this is finished."

"Yes, Christophe. When this is finished."

He backed away, out of her orbit, and opened his mouth to say good night but some other sound came out of his throat. He needed a glass of water. A toothbrush. A symphony. At his own door at the other end of the hall, across from the curtain salesman, he watched her enter her room. She moved carefully, with grace, even after champagne and half a bottle of wine. Zoé took one final look back at him because she knew Kruse was watching and she closed her door, locked it with a snap.

ELEVEN

Rue des Brice, Nancy

FOR TWENTY MINUTES HE STOOD NEAR HIS DOOR, LISTENING FOR HER in the hall. He found himself believing, with the wine in him, that he could will her to come. In the morning, groggy and somewhat pained, as though a bottle had broken in his head, he stopped by her room on the way to breakfast and knocked. There was no answer, so he asked the woman at the front desk. Madame had checked out at six in the morning.

"What was she wearing?"

"Pardon, Monsieur?"

"Madame Moquin is my friend. She dresses elaborately. If you noticed . . ."

The woman tilted her head just slightly. "Have you been to Chenonceau, Monsieur, the castle on the Cher River?"

"No."

"There is a room where Queen Louise of Lorraine mourned after her husband died. It is black and decorated with white feathers and teardrops. I don't remember precisely what your friend was wearing but her dress reminded me of the queen's room."

Kruse thanked her and made his way outside. The morning smelled of last night's rain. It was cool but not cold. Steam rose from the wet stones. The library was on Rue Stanislas, busy with cars at this hour. He took a tartine and a coffee in a café where retired men in hats were already up for their morning wine and soccer highlights. He was tempted to join them, to chase his headache away.

In the library he tried to think of Henri Alibert and the mayor and Joseph, not Zoé Moquin in a black dress of white feathers and teardrops, walking to the train station in the dewy dawn. The back of her wet neck, how he might have kissed it. The Alibert family had owned coal mines and coke furnaces. They moved into iron and steel. Lorraine was not always a terrific place to do business, as it had passed back and forth from France to Germany and back to France. Henri's father, Georges Alibert, used this in his defence after the war, when he was asked why he had chosen to supply the Germans. He was a business-man. His other option, to flee and allow his factories to be nationalized by foreigners, was more distasteful. The Nazis and Vichy had been good to the Alibert family. Henri was sixteen when the war ended, and suddenly he was not so popular.

The Fourth Republic nationalized the coal industry immediately after the war, in 1946. The iron and steel business never returned to its prewar glory and in 1978 the government nationalized it too, without compensation. Vigner Industries was into wine retailing and real estate but it was selling off and, in some cases, shuttering factories. Kruse guessed the Alibert family had slipped, in one generation, from a place in the top ten in France to somewhere in the unfortunate end of the top one thousand. In 1978, when a centre-right president, Valéry Giscard d'Estaing, decided to seize his family's assets and his mother died "of a broken heart," Henri Alibert became a supporter of the Front National—financially and spiritually.

In the popular press, Alibert was rich and racist, right-wing, given to sweaty outbursts during political campaigns. There were two reports, in *L'Est Républicain* and in *Le Monde*'s Saturday magazine, linking him to the Parti Nationaliste Français et Européen, a neo-Nazi group that liked to smash up Jewish cemeteries and, in 1989, burned down a hostel in Nice filled with workers from Tunisia. Three of its leaders were in prison. Alibert denied it and sued both newspapers and lost. There were no mentions, in any media, of his wine-store employees—the men who had threatened to kill the mayor of Nancy.

If the mayors of Nancy and Paris were pro-Maastricht and Henri Alibert and his club were anti-Maastricht, perhaps there had been others—other Chez Sternberghs. Kruse changed his search terms. On his seventh newspaper, a copy of *La Repubblica*, he discovered that a pro-Maastricht leader from Italy, a politician who had made a fortune importing children's clothing from China, had died of heart failure a few days before his fifty-third birthday, while singing karaoke. He was physically fit.

The story speculated that the next president of the European Parliament would almost certainly come from one of the left-wing coalitions. A parliamentarian from Greece, Giorgos Kafatos, who had quite a following in his own country and in Cyprus, was in the best position to be the next coalition leader. Three weeks before the Italian died, Kafatos's car was run off the road in Santorini. Kruse looked him up: authorities had no idea who might have done it. He was well loved, apart from *people who oppose Greece's membership in the European Union*.

In January a handsome British parliamentarian who wanted to drop the pound sterling for the new European currency was robbed and beaten nearly to death on his way home from the pub. During the referendum fight in Belgium about ratifying Maastricht, two of the pro-Europe leaders died of carbon monoxide poisoning in a village hotel.

Joseph Mariani and the mayor of Paris were scoundrels but they were no more guilty in any of this than Khalil al-Faruqi. Kruse was sure he had found the man—the men—who had blown up Chez Sternbergh.

Just before the library closed for lunch, when there was nothing more to read about Henri Alibert, Kruse searched Zoé's sister—Catherine Moquin. There were short, nearly identical obituaries in *Le Parisien* and *Le Monde*, both celebrating her work at Chanel, her rare imagination, and her potential. There were quotes, in both stories, from Karl Lagerfeld and by the CEO of Chanel.

Neither of the stories mentioned how Catherine died. This nearly always meant suicide.

• • •

Henri Alibert lived on a street of art nouveau mansions. Kruse skipped the cocktail portion of the evening and walked in his new tuxedo up Rue des Brice as dusk turned to darkness. At this hour, the whimsical ironwork and stained glass dragonflies of the houses and fences and gardens were lit by floodlights. He passed two grey-haired British couples with cameras and guidebooks. "Brilliant," they said, "brilliant," pointing at details that reminded him of childhood nightmares: twisting figures, flowers drunkenly blooming, vampire awnings.

There were two men on the driveway at Chez Alibert, keeping guard: *les voyous*, bald thugs in suits and ties. They stiffened when they saw him, glanced at each other. Kruse and Tzvi had worked parties like this in Toronto and New York and Boston, for politicians, for visiting dignitaries who had offended dangerous people, and his favourite: the paranoid billionaires. He wondered where Alibert fit into this client profile.

The heavier and shorter of the two men, with a freshly shaved head, stepped forward. "This is a private residence."

"Of course. Monsieur Alibert asked me to come."

Kruse reached inside his jacket for the invitation, and the tall one reached for him and grunted into his lapel, *"Homme armé, homme armé."*

"He's finally here?" It was another man's voice in the guard's earpiece, loud enough that Kruse heard it as a whisper.

"Wait." Kruse put his hands up. "I'm a guest."

"*Homme*—" the guard started to say again as he took a handful of Kruse's tuxedo jacket. He reached back with his free hand, grunted, made a fist.

Kruse locked the guard's hand and his elbow in place, pulled, and slammed him into the sloped pavement. The guard's right hand, still preparing for the punch, was not available to soften the landing. He hit the concrete with his face, and Kruse, in one motion, dislocated his shoulder and went after the second guard, who had taken out a gun.

"I was invited."

The second guard pointed the gun and tried to disable the safety mechanism with a "*Merde, merde!*" just as Kruse kicked it out of his hand. He elbowed the second guard, to stun him, and took him down backwards. This one was not so tall, and a better athlete, and the fall itself did not immobilize him. Kruse put his knee on the man's neck and cranked his arm.

"I wasn't on the list?"

"*Nique ta mère.*"

"What did they say about me?"

The guard said something equally vulgar about Kruse's mother, so he cranked his arm harder, felt where the tendons would give way. Knocking a man out, without killing him or leaving him permanently maimed, was tricky. Kruse drove the guard's arm as far as it would go and kicked it the rest of the way. As the man screamed, Kruse jumped toward the house and hid behind the two cedars next to the front door. It opened and two thinner bald men in suits came out.

One of the two forward guards was unconscious, face-first on the paving stones. The other was on his side, immobile and delivering something in between a grunt and a scream. The two men from the house ran to him.

"He's here."

Just as they started to turn, Kruse was upon them. These two had less training but they did have guns. He disarmed them first and avoided using his fists. The tuxedo was five hours old. He didn't want blood on anything. Before he went into the house, Kruse gathered the three weapons and their communications equipment, tossed it all in the shrubbery.

The door was open. No one was in the foyer to welcome him. It was fragrant with poultry. Off to the left, in the grand salon, a woman played Erik Satie on a polished grand piano by soft lamplight—apparently for no one but herself. Another woman appeared in a red cocktail dress with a tray of four champagne flutes. She nearly dropped the tray when she saw him.

"Where did all the men go?"

"Outside, Madame."

"Are you one of the guests?"

Kruse took out his invitation and showed it to her.

"I'm so sorry, Monsieur. I had been told everyone had already arrived. Please, let me announce you."

Kruse followed her.

"What . . ." She looked back, a hint of annoyance in her voice. "What are the men doing outside?"

"Exercising."

The woman slowed and turned for a moment, examined his face. "What happened to you?"

"I'm prone to accidents, Madame."

There was historical art on the wall, royal scenes, but most of the frames held black-and-white photographs of battles he did not recognize and puffy men in suits shaking hands. He had seen these men before. The sounds of conversation grew as he entered the core of the house.

"Who are these people?"

"I never ask, Monsieur."

The music followed him and then, as he drew closer to the centre, transformed. In an anteroom another woman played not a piano but a harpsichord. A thin gentleman, the first he had seen who was not a bouncer, played a cello, and two more women, young twins, held violins. None of them made eye contact as they played a song that sounded, to him, like it had been plucked from the Middle Ages. At a sliding red wooden door the woman asked him to wait among the musicians. On the other side was a dining room, the sounds of laughter and conversation, men in tuxedos and women in cocktail dresses. She closed the door behind her and he was left with the musicians. It was the sound of long-abandoned courts of queens and kings, filled with dignity and sadness, long and careful notes. Evelyn would have adored this music of doom and the funhouse quality of the art nouveau house. From its core he could feel the bass and drum of boots: more bald men with weapons.

The conversations quieted on the other side of the door and it slid open. Henri Alibert, some years older than his photograph, was six and a half feet tall. He kept his chin aloft, not the sort to bend down to meet a shorter man's eyes. His white hair was cropped short on the sides, where it continued to grow. There were flakes of dandruff on what Kruse could see of his shoulders.

"Our American friend."

"Henri Alibert?"

"I am delighted to welcome you to my modest home."

"My name is Mathieu Meisels."

Alibert closed his eyes for a moment, as though the name was a spasm he had learned to endure, and opened them slowly. "You spoke to the men outside?"

"I showed them my invitation."

"And they were welcoming?"

"A typically warm, typically French introduction to your modest home, Monsieur, yes."

Behind Alibert, a crowd of seven women and five men in business attire stood behind their chairs. They were in their fifties and sixties. The scents of cooking blended with perfumes and colognes.

"I had neglected to tell my greeters you were coming. A terrible oversight, so I'm delighted they were so good to you. Please, join us."

"Why did you invite me, Monsieur?"

Alibert was not accustomed to this. His breathing changed and he reached back for the space between the pretty harpsichord and the wall. His forehead bloomed pink. "Perhaps you could tell me why you're harassing elderly ladies and bothering Cassin's poor old chief of staff." Alibert's lips trembled, as though he were on the verge of weeping. He was not a young man and, despite his posture, it was as though something within seemed ready to cut him down. "If you want to know about me, Monsieur *Meisels*, why not ask?"

"I tried. If you remember, I visited your office yesterday. You invited me to this party. And then when I arrived it seemed your men had been ordered to—"

The door slid open all the way now, and a fat man in a white tuxedo stepped into the anteroom. His eyebrows were enchanted forests.

"Come, Henri. Sit down. And you are?"

"Mathieu Meisels. *Enchanté*, Monsieur."

The man shifted his glass of champagne, clearly not his first, into his left hand. "A foreigner, yet. Henri Alibert, fraternizing with a foreigner on his birthday. And a handsome devil. A young something-or-other. Remember, Henri, when we were young and handsome and clever?"

"Monsieur Alibert, you did not tell me it was your birthday. What a magnificent honour to be invited."

The fat man with the eyebrows escorted Kruse into the dining room. "Everyone, this is Henri's friend . . . what did you say your name was again?"

Alibert walked in behind them. "His name is Meisels, an American business acquaintance of mine."

There was half a place setting in the middle of the table. A woman in black hustled in to complete it. If he were to sit here, his back would be to the door: a security man's least favourite position. The group quieted as Alibert took his place at the head of the table, calmed himself, stared at Kruse for a moment, and prepared to speak. He was like a priest before the congregation, the sermon already buzzing at the back of his throat. *"Alors, mesdames et messieurs—"*

Kruse waved at the man directly across from him. "Excuse me, sorry. I'm hard of hearing in my left ear. Would it trouble you terribly to trade places with me?"

"Not at all."

The interrupted host crossed his arms and watched them walk around the opposite side of the table and take their new places. Servants followed with their glasses. From here, Kruse would be easily trapped but at least he could watch the two doors. Alibert waited an extra ten seconds, after Kruse was in his place, to recommence.

"I grew up, as most of you know, in Gascony."

A small team of servers, men and women in white and black, came through the swinging door behind Alibert with bottles of white wine. As Alibert explained the history and provenance of the wine, and its significance in his life, Kruse watched the man who filled his glass. Servers had come from both directions. His was the first splash from a fresh bottle, and the other glasses were full by the time his waiter was finished with him. The man departed with a full bottle, less a glass.

The first toast was to Gascony. Kruse raised his glass with the others but did not drink. Alibert watched him with half a smile on his shivering lips. Over the table, elegantly hidden in the base of the dragonflies-and-swirls chandelier, was a video camera. The dining room door slid open again and another gentleman in a suit stepped in. There were many sorts of bodyguards but most were like this: men with giant chests and arms and necks, steroid men who ate carefully and spent three hours in the gym every day until they stopped and turned fat, slow, clumsy, angry. This bodyguard against the wall was in the middle of his transition, from a powerlifter to what a powerlifter becomes. Kruse was no statistician but he had noticed a high suicide rate in his business, as young fighters moved into middle age.

Alibert's guests were wealthy and well educated, powerful in their worlds, with the shine of happiness and confidence about them. But if he were to spend an hour with anyone in the room, he would choose this bodyguard with smart but melancholy eyes.

The first course arrived. Alibert watched Kruse watch the bodyguard. He waited for Kruse's attention before he introduced the plates of fresh oysters from the Arcachon Basin, where he had hunted for his own as a boy. These came out on platters, for diners to share, so Kruse ate one—the explosion of salt and slippery muscle and sweetness that would never taste the way it tasted to Alibert, like home.

When the swinging kitchen door opened he could see more men, some dressed in black bomber jackets instead of suits and tuxedos. They watched him. Two of them he recognized from their photographs. They were not hiding: Karl Handke and Victor Nodier.

One of the diners, a woman with the flesh of her face yanked surgically toward her ears, lifted her glass. "There may be a better time for this, my friends, or a better person to say it. But here is to the splendid Henri Alibert on the occasion of his birthday."

They raised their glasses once more, and once more Kruse did not drink. The next course was salad, also filled with memories and meaning from the southwestern corner of the country. Alibert used flash cards to remember his points as he presented the food and wine. The deep red Bordeaux arrived with the foie gras, the bread, the capon—a castrated rooster, the source of the odour in the house when Kruse had arrived.

There was a theme to the southwestern dinner. All of it, in some way, was in danger of being lost. Protesters disliked foie gras, oysters were being poisoned and harvested by foreign companies, and the Brits and Americans and Aussies were buying up the wineries. Alibert had read in *Le Monde*—why was he reading *Le Monde*? Good question!—that a socialist senator wanted to make it illegal to emasculate a rooster in your own damn country.

Kruse had not taken any wine yet he could feel the temperature in the room change. The guests' eyes went rheumy and they leaned more deliberately into each other, they laughed, they touched one another's arms.

"Tell us about yourself, Monsieur Meisels." Henri Alibert, whose eyes were no less rheumy than those of his guests, continued to watch him, but the anxiety had passed away. A team of men in bomber jackets waited in the kitchen to eliminate the foreigner. The main bodyguard had whispered good news into his ear. Kruse was sure they would not do anything with Alibert's best friends assembled in the same room but they would pounce the moment he left. There was a faint but jolly slur in Alibert's voice. "This mysterious stranger who has joined my birthday celebration. What brings him to France from his homeland?"

"Americans don't have a homeland."

"No?"

"It's an ugly idea."

"Tell us how a homeland is an ugly idea."

"Sacred space for special people. This is ugly to me."

Alibert repeated it, with Kruse's accent. "*For special people.* Now, please tell us why."

"I was lucky enough to grow up without any real ethnic feeling, of rituals and traditions. I can feel at home anywhere, if I am welcomed."

"Your real name, Kruse. Is it not German?"

"My real name?"

"*Allez.*"

"My ethnicity is irrelevant."

Alibert sat back in his chair. "You call this lucky, to feel rootless."

"I enjoy the freedom to focus on the future."

"So the past means nothing to you."

"I can choose to find meaning in it, if I like."

Again, the temperature in the room changed. The guests drank nervously. The flamboyant man with the wild eyebrows raised his glass, to make a toast to their new American friend, whatever his name is, but when Alibert did not follow along he faked a coughing fit and shrank back into himself, whispered an apology to his wife. Waiters and waitresses asked the guests for their serviettes, gathered them up.

"I am not a subtle thinker." Alibert pushed back his chair. "You're saying an American has an advantage over a Frenchman because—"

"Monsieur, I can only speak for myself."

"*You* have an advantage."

"I will not be undone by nostalgia."

"There is nothing in your history, in your culture, you would fight to protect?"

"I don't have a culture."

"Is it not painful, an abomination, when what you love, those whom you love, are taken from you?"

Kruse often felt he was falling behind, in not-so-hidden assertions and emphasis. "I am not a subtle thinker either, as it happens. Are we still talking about France for the French? If you're threatening *those whom I love* in some way, I have a rule about that."

"A rule." The industrialist watched Kruse for so long, without a word, that the quartet outside the dining room had time to finish one old song and begin another. "I know where you live and whom you love. I know exactly who you are. Who you really are."

"Tell me. I've been having some trouble with that myself."

A few of the guests started to laugh and stopped. Others gulped wine.

"You work for the mayor of Paris." He spoke to the room. "The former prime minister of France hires *secret agents* to stop citizens, active citizens, leaders, from campaigning against him and his plans to destroy the republic. My friends, you won't find this man, Christophe Kruse, on any list of employees. He doesn't exist. He is an assassin, sent to Nancy to destroy me and my cause."

"What *cause* is that, Monsieur Alibert? What cause justifies blowing up a restaurant in Paris?"

The man with the eyebrows, no longer chastened by the failure of his previous toast, asked if this were *un spectacle*—a performance of some sort. He had heard of "murder mystery dinners" in which a diner is "killed" and for the rest of the evening the guests must work together to find the criminal among them. It seemed only correct to bring in a stranger, a foreigner, to kill off. At Henri's birthday party anyway.

Alibert ignored his friend and continued to stare at Kruse. "What are you talking about?"

"Chez Sternbergh, on the Rue des Rosiers."

"Yes."

"One of your men blew it up."

"What man?"

A woman who had been drinking her wine too quickly, in a red sequin dress, applauded. "If you are an actor, professional or not, I say bravo. Your grammar is quite impeccable for a foreigner. Bravo two times."

"Monsieur Alibert, I will leave you to your celebration if you will speak to me alone for ten minutes."

"This is not the time." He gestured behind him, at the kitchen. "And besides, I don't think you're in any position to dictate terms. Your accusation is, frankly, insane. Your very presence here, the audacity of it . . ."

Guests were beginning to whisper nervously to one another. A woman took out a fan.

"The mayor of Nancy, Pierre Cassin. Why were your men harassing him?"

"Because he was trying to destroy France. Cassin and your idiot patron. But neither me nor my men tried to *kill them*. Who told you this?"

Kruse felt the way he had felt in Spain. "Monsieur Cassin's torment- ers are among your men, in the kitchen. Perhaps we could ask them."

New smells entered the dining room. A man came through with fresh serviettes for everyone. The host took in a deep breath and with his exhalation addressed himself not to Kruse but to the rest of his guests. "For hundreds of years, in the region of my birth, families have grown grapes and bottled wine. They have found oysters. They have raised cocks and chickens and geese. They have perfected foie gras. And, most singularly, they have captured a tiny songbird called the ortolan bunting for occasions like these."

With the words *ortolan bunting* a few of the guests gasped. Someone applauded and the others joined in. The man with the eyebrows declared the birds were endangered, as though it were the most splen- did news. Three of the servers, all of them men, brought long white platters into the dining room. On each of them there was a line of small birds, plucked and browned, sizzling and steaming. The obese chef, who slipped into the dining room in his white smock to address the diners, had not removed the birds' heads.

Alibert watched Kruse as the chef explained how he had cooked the birds, each the size of an oblong potato. They had arrived in a box, still alive, where they had been overfed with millet; the dark confuses the ortolans, encourages them to eat and eat and eat. Then, less than two hours earlier, the chef had drowned them in Armagnac. He then spiced them and roasted them. He instructed the guests to hold each bird by the neck and to bite into it, eating everything but the head. Alibert lifted and unfolded his serviette. He reached for a bird and winked at Kruse, mouthed "*Au revoir*" and placed the serviette over his head. The rest of the guests followed along. The chef watched Kruse, and when all the others had covered their heads he pointed to the ceiling.

"We wear the serviette, Monsieur, so God will not witness the act."

"Because it is shameful?"

The chef shrugged. "Perhaps it is to trap and concentrate the aromas, but the first man to do it was a priest. Me, I simply follow the rules."

"The roof, the insulation, the ceiling, this is all transparent. But the serviettes, God somehow can't see through those."

The chef put his hands over his belly, like a pregnant woman near her term. "As you like, Monsieur." He retreated back through the swinging door.

Even over the music Kruse could hear the slurping and scrunching of the other guests, sighs of pleasure under the serviettes. He thought of photographs of Klansmen and of watching *It's the Great Pumpkin, Charlie Brown* with Lily, the day she died. It was on television, dubbed into French. Charlie Brown and his friends throw sheets over their heads and cut out two—or twenty—eyeholes. Kruse tucked the serviette on his lap and put the bird in his mouth and bit into it, the fat and brittle bones. It exploded with heat, the salt and oil and flesh. The powerlifter in charge shook his head; Kruse was supposed to be under the serviette. He was not supposed to be here at all, ruining the boss's birthday. The bodyguard pushed himself off the wall, knocked once on the swinging door, and walked around the table. The two men from the photographs, the wine-store men, Karl and Victor, entered the dining room and followed him.

Both had handguns.

Kruse was not finished chewing when he pushed back his chair, stood up, and placed his serviette on the table. It was like foie gras, only sweeter and juicier and crunchier. When the thought arrived that he was eating the heart of a little bird he shoved it away.

"Let's allow these people to eat." The powerlifter stopped at the corner and invited Kruse, as a maître d' invites new diners, to follow him out of the room.

He lifted his hands, swallowed a little. "Monsieur Alibert has not yet answered any of my questions."

Behind the powerlifter, the Austrian—whose accent was stronger than Kruse's—spoke just above a whisper. "You will be the one answering."

Kruse did not move.

"Let's go. Last chance."

It felt wrong to do what he had so often cautioned his daughter against: talking with his mouth full. "Back away and take Monsieur Alibert with you." He lifted his finger, paused them. "We can the four of us retire to a salon and talk about this, fifteen minutes, with more wine or even an Armagnac. But I'm not leaving until we do."

A powerlifter cannot fake or feint, especially when he's gone chubby. By the man's stance Kruse could tell he was going to lead with a right cross. If it hit him it would kill him, but it would not hit him, and neither of the other men would use their weapons—not in here. The powerlifter swung and his eyes squeezed shut with the effort. Kruse lifted his elbow and aimed it at the big man's fist, accepted the blow with it. The powerlifter's knuckle, at least one, crunched and he yelped with pain and cussed and stepped back into the smaller men. The guests emerged from under their serviettes and cried out, squeaked. Someone applauded. "It's starting!" Kruse grabbed a brass candlestick from the table and slammed it into the big man's nose. With a burst mouse of blood on his face he fell back entirely into the wine-store thugs and a credenza; there was nowhere else to go. With the candle-stick, Kruse stunned the Austrian and the Frenchman as they crawled out from under the wailing powerlifter. He disarmed them.

The handguns were heavy and so new they had not yet been scratched. Kruse emptied the magazines. It had all happened quickly and without excessive shouting, so not all of the guests had witnessed the fight. The man with the eyebrows had not finished chewing but he had emerged from under the serviette. "Is this supposed to be happening? Shall I phone the police?"

"Absolutely not." Alibert turned to the chef, who had opened the door from the kitchen. "Is that all of them?"

"More are coming, Monsieur."

Alibert tossed his serviette on the table, stood, and picked up another of the ortolans. "God damn it. Follow me, Kruse."

Alibert bit off the bird's head and spit it on the floor, opened the sliding door into the hallway past the quartet. He put the body in his mouth all at once, like a marshmallow. All of the musicians looked away. In the foyer, the bodyguards Kruse had moved through on his way into the house reposed on chairs. One lay on the floor, conscious but barely. Others sat holding their ruined arms. Kruse had great sympathy for them; a security man who fails at securing a home can only stew in misery.

Still, only one of the men stood to greet him.

"Aha," said Alibert.

The man lifted his hands like a boxer and walked in a semicircle. Alibert gave him instructions. Kruse was smaller and thinner; why not just grab the fucker and choke him to death?

"He won't let me grab him," said the guard. "But I can hit him." He walked in and swung. Kruse ducked it and danced away, and the others cheered on the guard. One tried to trip Kruse, so he turned and kicked the guard in the face. His head slammed against the wall behind him and slowly he slumped forward.

Alibert laughed, though not because it was funny.

Kruse moved in closer to the big, bald guard with long eyelashes and faked a kick. Then he jabbed him, just once, in the nose. The guard fell on his ass and tried to stand, the first pill of blood dropping from his nostril.

"Don't stand up." Kruse put his hands down. "If you didn't see that one coming, you're not going to see any of them."

The guard looked at Alibert, who shook his head.

"It's a lovely house, Monsieur Alibert. Congratulations on all your success."

"Fuck you," Alibert said, in English, his full mouth juicy with bird. He opened a heavy door and they entered an office decorated like a law library, with gold-embossed leather books from floor to ceiling. A stand in the corner held a selection of spirits in decanters. The host slammed the door and poured something that looked like whisky into a highball glass and sat behind a heavy old desk. He was still chewing. "I'd offer you something to drink but, at the risk of repeating myself, fuck you."

"What was your relationship with Pierre Cassin?"

"No *relationship* of any sort."

"That seems odd. I just read, in your office yesterday, you're the richest man in Lorraine. Was he not your mayor? In my country—"

"A mongrel." Alibert swallowed, his eyes closed, and took a moment to open them again. "Two ortolans is one too many. You end up feeling gluttonous. And I'm not the richest man in Lorraine. My father was, before the war."

"A mongrel?"

"Cassin was a socialist microcosm of the future Frenchman."

"I thought he was conservative."

"Not a *real* conservative."

Evelyn, who had spent her adult life studying conservatism, adored lines like these. It was not so different from fighting, the way she drew her debating opponents into saying something stupid like "not a real conservative."

In a fight, he drew his opponent into making an error. And then he attacked. A *real conservative.*

"You're an outsider, Monsieur Kruse. You can't see the way we see."

"We?"

"The French. The genuine French. To you, Cassin must have looked French. He must have sounded French. It's a French-sounding name, isn't it?"

"The final *n* is silent."

"Yes, yes. *Very* French. But when you peel back just a little bit, you see the impostor."

"Your interests are not exclusively French. What about the Italian who had a heart attack? The Greek parliamentarian, mysteriously run off the road. The Brit, the Belgians."

"There is a phrase for you, in English. *A conspiracy theorist.*"

"Very good."

"I was no friend of Pierre Cassin's and your boss can go to hell but I'm just a modest businessman."

Kruse looked at his watch. The others would arrive soon. A thump of fatigue hit him. He had not slept and the light was dim in the office. His head ached. "And an extremist."

"I disagree with that word. Anyway, my political views are not a crime."

"Unless you bomb a hostel full of refugees."

"They weren't refugees, you socialist asshole. They were regular immigrants like you, here to ruin the country. The Greek and the Brit wanted to ruin Europe, like your patron. How are you feeling?"

Outside it was not raining but the floodlights in the front yard illuminated a gentle mist. He knew they were coming but the room smelled sweetly of pipe tobacco and the liquor Alibert had poured. It was unusual, to feel so calm. His head thumped, exploded with pain, and then it subsided to nothing. A bed was what he wanted, more than anything, a warm, dark room. This was the sort of office Evelyn had hoped to inhabit, where she might speak with a man like this about Edmund Burke and Chateaubriand and her dead hero Benjamin Disraeli and Charles de Gaulle, about real conservatism. He yawned.

"Was it the mayor himself who sent you, Monsieur Kruse? Or one of his minions? You've been set up, you see. You're a stooge."

He looked around the room. It was difficult to focus. He could not say why he was here instead of Paris or Toronto, where he belonged. To discover something. To end something. The top of his head tingled, as though it were raining rice on him.

"You came here to, what, kill me? To punish me? Then why am I here, in my office, drinking an Armagnac? You could have killed me

twenty times by now. And I know you're capable. My worthless employees in the foyer: I am not a warrior, but I imagine it would have been
much simpler to kill them than to destroy their spirits."

"I am here . . ." he slurred. "I'm here to ask why you had instructed
your men, Karl and Victor, to harass Pierre Cassin."

"Who cares? He's dead."

"You killed him. And the others. The Maastricht Treaty. You're trying
to stop it. Your man threw two grenades into Chez Sternbergh, one for
each mayor."

Alibert laughed. "I like you, Monsieur Kruse. Even though you're
just like him, another one."

"Another what?"

"A dishrag. A Trojan horse for . . . a Jew and a Mohammedan dressed
up like a Frenchman? You know Cassin was off to represent us in the
European Parliament. Think of it, the word *represent*. France represented by an impostor. A Trojan horse for globalization, Monsieur
Kruse."

"You're going to stop globalization? You alone?"

"This is what I know. My factories can't compete with those in
Spain and Greece, in Turkey, in China and Mexico, in Poland. My
children will inherit union enterprises that can only wither and die.
We don't make anything anymore. We say this, men like us, as though
it were something miserable that simply happened to France. But you
know what? This was a decision. Someone, somewhere in my country,
made that decision. And they're about to make it again. This European
Union . . ."

"So who *made that decision*, Monsieur Alibert?"

"Men like you and Cassin."

"So you wanted him eliminated. And me."

"Monsieur Kruse, I don't want you eliminated. Not necessarily. I
quite enjoy speaking to you. You're *sage* for an American, your accent is
charming, and I admit you are unusually good with your hands. Maybe

you could stay here in Nancy, replace my head of security. He's the man whose nose you just exploded in the dining room."

The fire was cozy. He wanted to ask Alibert something but forgot the question. It flew across the room like a paper airplane. Evelyn was calling him from the next room. Why didn't she come into this room and ask him a question instead of shouting from afar? You come *here*! The room spun and went fuzzy. For an instant he forgot where he was, whether it was day or night. Kruse bit the inside of his cheek to remain alert.

Alibert sat back in his chair, a new sparkle in his eyes. "Who had the most to gain from the violent erasure of a young, handsome, well-spoken, well-funded, pretend-conservative? You've not considered your mayor? Our glorious president-in-waiting? That he might use you to camouflage his dirty business? Oh poor boy. Can I make up a bed for you?"

"It was in the ortolan."

"You wouldn't drink the wine."

He braced himself on the side of the desk, sleep leaking into every pore. "You drugged us all?"

"Just your side of the table. And don't worry: it's only sleeping pills. You'll wake up in entirely different circumstances, of course. I imagine my men will be slaves to their vengeful feelings."

There was a screech of tires outside, on the horseshoe driveway. Alibert looked at his watch again. "*Et voilà*. Thank you for coming this evening, Monsieur Kruse, for ruining my birthday dinner and unmanning my staff. Now I will have the pleasure of unmanning you. I will have the honour of sending the note to your employer personally. With profound sadness and regret, Monsieur le Maire . . ."

Kruse reached inside his jacket pocket, for the package he and Tzvi had made up in Paris, before driving out to the suburbs. It was deep in his new pocket. Too deep. He stood up out of his chair and stumbled into the window. More men in bomber jackets jumped out of a white van. "Skinheads."

"Oh, that's an ugly word."

"You're Nazis."

"Even uglier. No one in this country was ever a Nazi, not ever. But looking back, we traded a German Disneyland for an American one. Are we better off? Are French people happier today than they would have been if the Germans had won the war?"

The sleeping pills had poked something in him. He remembered where he had seen the photographs of the men in the hall: Vichy men, collaborators.

"I am not against eliminating my enemies. But I would never do it with grenades, not as long as there are genuine French citizens in the same room. You've failed and you're finished. It's a pity no one mourns an invisible man but I do vow to propose a toast to you, a little later tonight. While it's not a funeral, it's something, Monsieur. It's something."

The window was a work of art, bordered at the top and bottom by colourful, almost hallucinatory panels of stained glass flowers and insects. There was a small but heavy statue on the corner of the desk, of an eagle. Kruse scratched himself, to stay conscious, and picked it up. Alibert shouted, and with what remained of his strength Kruse tossed the statue through the window and with his arm he cleared the shards away. The rest of what Alibert said were underwater sounds. The old man's hands were on him now, one gripping him for support and the other slapping and punching him. Kruse did something he had taught hundreds of women: he dug into Alibert's cuticles with his fingernails and dragged deeply toward his knuckles. As Alibert backed away, into the desk, with a roar, Kruse flopped out the window and landed in some shrubbery. He crawled as far as he could and reached again into the inside pocket of his suit jacket. Against every sleepy instinct, he pulled the pack out with the tips of his fingers and opened the Velcro. The needle was already loaded with the liquid. He shot the flumazenil into his arm and crawled as far as he could crawl, into the darkness.

When the flumazenil jolted him awake he could not tell if he had been asleep two minutes or a year. The men in bomber jackets were about him now, their flashlights scanning the side of the house and the garden. He was in the messy branches of a tree that had just begun to lose its spring blossoms, the fragrance a leap to his own childhood. Alibert was shouting at someone. Kruse had collected the little flowers for his mother, and she had put them in a glass of water and had smelled them and had said *I am so lucky to have a sweet little boy like you.* His head throbbed from the punches and slaps Alibert had dealt him, and his lip was bleeding. He was groggy but no longer dizzy. Tzvi had insisted they carry the flumazenil on every mission, as an antidote to sedatives, and though he never saw himself falling for any tricks, Kruse adopted it along with nearly everything else his teacher had taught him.

The man nearest Kruse wore giant black boots. He carried one of the new silver handguns. An elderly woman with a small white puffball of a dog walked past the property. Kruse picked up a handful of cedar chips and tossed them toward the woman and the dog, who barked. The skinhead turned toward the sound and Kruse stunned him from behind, in the neck. He went down with a moan just loud enough to alert the others.

He ran past the elderly woman, past the dog. Two shots fired behind him: one hit the van and the second broke a window across the street. The woman bent down and covered her head, screamed "Police!"

Heavy black boots clomped along behind him, on Rue des Brice.

Clarity returned with a jolt, and nausea. He leaned against an Audi and threw up and felt better. He slowed down so Alibert's skinheads could follow, south and east, until he encountered a stone wall. There were trees on the other side. With two men half a block behind him, Kruse reached a black iron gate and hopped it and landed in a cemetery. He waited until the men, smokers, huffing and wheezing in the mist, reached the fence and found just enough strength to get over the gate. One pulled a knife and Kruse kicked it away.

"Any more weapons?"

The bald men looked at one another, their heads shiny and slick in the pale light. One was more frightened than the other. Kruse jabbed the brave one in the eyes, and when the man reached with his hands Kruse went after his undefended genitals. The man fell to his knees and, watching the frightened one, Kruse kicked the man of courage in the head and that was that.

"Tell me."

The coward backed away, toward a headstone.

Kruse leapt at him, took him to the ground. "Tell me."

"Tell you what?"

"Henri Alibert, your boss. Does he order you to hurt people?"

"I can't talk about that." The man smelled of beer. He tried to squirm away, each effort another opening: his neck, his straight arms. It may not have been fair but Tzvi had taught Kruse to think of skinheads as bullies and rapists. He went to work on the man's left arm and put a knee on his face, ground him into the wet gravel.

"Yes you can."

• • •

He was not yet finished with the skinheads when he heard an explosion, softer than the one on Rue des Rosiers. Kruse hopped the gate and walked three blocks back toward the art nouveau home of Henri Alibert. The mist was now a fog and the red glow in the distance was a terrible sunrise. A young man walked stiffly past him without making eye contact, muttering to himself. Kruse was not yet around the corner when he saw flames roaring about the pretty house. Three men and a woman staggered out. The woman rubbed furiously at her smoking hair. Two of the bald guards walked out and kept walking. Neighbours were beginning to gather in their nightclothes. Kruse frantically scanned the crowd: six people escaped the dinner party.

None of them was Henri Alibert.

TWELVE

Calle Altamira, Santillana del Mary

IT WAS LATE AFTERNOON, AND THROUGH THE GIANT WINDOW OF
Tzvi's recovery room the sky was seamlessly, dreamily blue. The glass
was too thick to hear the waves crashing against the rocks below. A
friendly mist rose up.

"Have you heard of phantom pains?"

"Only the phrase."

"Close your eyes, Christopher. Do it! Now reach out with your left
hand and make a fist. That is not a fist. Are you a newborn? Strong.
Tight. Make it hurt. You can open your eyes. Now, you can see a hand.
Congratulations, you smooth arm-having bastard. This happens to me
every hour, my left hand *doing preposterous things*, only it is not actually
there. My brain betrays me."

Tzvi sat on the side of his bed, in a pair of cotton pants stamped with
the centre's logo and a hospital T-shirt. The bandaged stub of his left
arm moved like the clipped tail of a big dog. He moved it up and
down, made a circle with it. "I blame you."

"And you should."

"If you had just stepped in and hit her."

"And al-Faruqi. It's all I think about. If only I'd walked in like a robot and slit his throat. You could have snapped the photo. We might have hopped right out of the hacienda, undetected."

"Like vipers."

Kruse looked out over the Atlantic. Pink was sneaking into the afternoon light. "We have to go."

"Why?"

Kruse told him about Agent Peach.

"His security clearance is not high enough, Christopher. He does not know what he does not know, this is all. The man would never get permission to come after us. The DPSD hired us to take out al-Faruqi."

"He isn't DPSD. Besides, they hired us to find and eliminate the Chez Sternbergh killer. Not to murder Khalil al-Faruqi. We have no proof he did it, Tzvi. Your contact from Mossad, I didn't even speak to him. I don't think Khalil al-Faruqi did anything in Paris. In fact, I've done more work for the client."

Tzvi stood up off the bed. "Write this down before I forget: I want a fake arm with a knife at the end instead of a hand."

"Your contact in Mossad, someone fed him information about al-Faruqi. The information was wrong. Purposely wrong. And we—"

"One of your Corsican friends visited me. Biff or Andreus or something. He wanted to know if anyone was harassing me. We played whist for an hour."

"I don't know what whist is."

"You brought me a suit?"

"It's in the closet."

"It had better goddamn well be Italian. Or what's the point of anything?" Tzvi reached for the ceiling with both arms, to stretch. "Everything I do looks hilarious, doesn't it?"

Kruse told the truth about the suit—Canali—and then he lied about how Tzvi looked when he stretched.

"You think we have become stooges?" Tzvi unfastened his hospital sweats, stepped into the suit pants.

"I know it. But whose stooges?"

"The government lady, Zoé, did she pay you yet?"

Kruse told him about Réné Chatel, the unfortunate communist, and he told him about the mayor of Nancy's little chief of staff, the neo-Nazis, the club of establishment men who seemed to be killing off promoters of the Maastricht Treaty and the European Union. He told him about the night on Rue des Brice in Nancy, Henri Alibert and the explosion.

Tzvi looked in the mirror. "Who the hell blew up the house?"

"I don't know. I passed a man, but when I ran back after him he was gone."

"You think there were cameras? Pictures of you?"

"Possibly. Probably."

"Did anyone know you were meeting with Chatel?"

"Étienne Bonnet, the editorialist. The man who is with Annette."

"Jesus Christ."

Kruse helped him into the Canali.

For some time Tzvi looked at himself in the mirror. "The arm looks more ridiculous in the suit, hidden, than when it is just out there—the quivering stub. The children of the world will have nightmares about me." Tzvi moved what was left of his arm and his dangling sleeve swung about. "What does it say in the newspapers?"

"About al-Faruqi? Sweet revenge. So far, Étienne hasn't written anything about Réné Chatel. But I flew here. I didn't see the French papers' treatment of the Alibert business."

"You know what it looks like?"

"Your arm?"

"No, for Christ's sake. It is obvious what my arm looks like: a deranged puppet."

"I know what this looks like."

"If the newspapers put together that a scarred-up thug from Toronto has shown up on surveillance footage near Chez Sternbergh, then in Luxembourg Gardens, then in Nancy, you are a dead man."

Kruse didn't say anything for a minute. Behind him, Tzvi sat back on the bed and made the sound he made when he was thinking: he sucked at his teeth. "Your mafia man—Joseph."

It was Joseph who had organized the meeting with Zoé. It was Joseph who had threatened Annette and Anouk, Joseph who had steered him toward Réné Chatel. Kruse wished he had held on to his hair, in the back of the Mercedes, a bit longer.

"I thought he was my friend."

"Someone like that, he would not understand your definition of friend. He thinks only of his client. His protector. He is like us."

"No. Not like us."

"Pierre Cassin was not a genuine friend of Monsieur le Maire. Was he? It was make-believe. A bit of that political party nonsense, where we pretend to be someone we are not for the sake of theatre."

"The socialists are more or less finished. The conservative leader will be president."

"Your mayor, then. But then this Cassin shows up, young and handsome, full head of hair. Did he have support?"

"Plenty. And the mayor has rivals—a lot of them."

"Think like the mayor. If we start eliminating rivals, why stop at one? This Alibert, it sounds like he wanted to destroy Monsieur le Maire. He was organized. Fearless, with an army of skinheads, connections all over Western Europe. If he was planning something and your Joseph knew it, perhaps it was time to clean every room in the house . . ."

"Réné Chatel was no rival."

"You do not know what you do not know. Perhaps he had information on Monsieur le Maire. Or perhaps the poor raving communist was just designed to remove *you*."

Kruse waited as Tzvi fussed with his new suit in the mirror. Then he said it. "I bought you a plane ticket."

"For Paris?"

"Toronto."

"Fuck you, Toronto."

"Finish recuperating, safely, put on your spooky knife prosthetic, and come back if you like. But with Agent Peach and now with Joseph, we have two well-funded enemies who fear no one."

"They will fear us."

"Take a few weeks in Toronto. Even better, Montreal. You can stay at the Ritz-Carlton, as Hans Miller."

"What a stupid fucking name. Nice one."

"I insist. And so would you, in my position."

Tzvi tried to tie his tie with one hand, and failed, and failed again. He tossed it on the floor and cussed in Hebrew. "I'm not going back to Toronto."

Both of the doctors on call thought it foolish to check out of the hospital just as Tzvi's rehabilitation was beginning. They appeared to invent, on the spot, a number of administrative levies instead of refunding the money Kruse had paid up front. Tzvi slept much of the way to Guadalajara. It was just after eight when they arrived at the train station. Tzvi remained sleeping in the car, a Peugeot 405 Turbo, while Kruse retrieved the file, al-Faruqi's *proof*, from the locker. There was a queer feeling in the station at this hour: there were only a few people waiting, and three of them—two men and a woman, all in business suits—watched him. On his way out of the station, at the door, they stood up. He ran to the Peugeot.

"Who are they?" Tzvi had awakened and started the car. All Kruse had to do was put it in gear and go. "What is that?"

"Proof."

"Proof of what?"

"I don't know yet. I took it from al-Faruqi's place. It has something to do with the CIA."

One of the men and the woman had blond hair, and Kruse thought—but he couldn't be sure—he had heard one of the men say "Let's go," in English. He said so while Tzvi worked the map. The flight to Toronto departed from Madrid at ten the following morning, but Kruse didn't want to lead them to Madrid. So they left the city in a northwesterly direction, following the signs to Segovia.

Soon they were alone on a more or less empty secondary highway, apart from the Range Rover following them.

"This Agent Peach, are you sure he is a CIA man?"

"No."

"How did he introduce himself? What actual words did he use?"

Kruse told Tzvi what he could recall. The Peugeot was a luxury liner of a sedan, so despite the big engine there was no way they could outrun the Range Rover.

"That is not at all a CIA vehicle, Christopher. The CIA I know."

"Should we pull a McGeachy?"

"Perhaps it is our only option."

"You stay in the car, Tzvi."

"And you go ahead and fuck yourself."

One afternoon, they were following a man named William McGeachy on Highway 87 from New York City to Albany. He was head of a lobbying group for real estate developers, and according to their client a man who intimidated his enemies and near enemies with violence. Their client, a state representative with gubernatorial ambitions, had wept as he recounted stories of McGeachy threatening to turn his knees into baby food. And if the representative complained about it, he'd do the same to his wife and son. They had been hoping to meet with McGeachy in a public place, a café or hotel lobby. But as they were following him,

McGeachy opened his window and reached out, pointed at the shoulder, and pulled over. He got out of his car, an Audi, pulled up his pants, took off his suit jacket, and began shouting. Tzvi got out to speak to him and McGeachy made rather a crucial mistake: he took a swing at Tzvi. He was on his back, on the hardtop, seven seconds later. From then on, confronting someone on the highway was *pulling a McGeachy*.

Kruse made a U-turn and parked, facing the Range Rover. The landscape was entirely flat, with cultivated soil on one side of the highway and a hayfield on the other. In the distance there was a farmhouse and some outbuildings. The sun was about to set. No one exited the Range Rover. Kruse and Tzvi stood together just in front of the Peugeot. They would be difficult to see, between the headlights.

"Is there a word in English for after dusk but not-quite-night?"

"Gloaming, maybe."

"How do you use that word? It is gloaming?"

"I don't know, Tzvi. I'm sorry. I've never said it out loud. The gloaming."

"It is currently *the gloaming*? That sounds unnecessarily poetic. Useless word."

"Ask someone else, then."

The driver's side door opened, slowly. The blond man stepped out. He was speaking on a cellular phone. "Affirmative," he said. "Affirmative."

Tzvi spoke with a mock American accent, gave the vowels something special: "*Affirmative. Affirmative.* You just know he's an asshole."

The moon was three-quarters full. His conversation finished, the blond man folded the phone closed and slipped it into a holster on his belt. The other two doors opened. Sound carried well on the plains. "Okay, team. Let's be circumspect here."

"What does that mean?" Tzvi whispered.

"Cautious, I think," Kruse whispered back.

With his right hand, Tzvi waved. "Howdy, neighbours." He continued to speak in what he seemed to think was an American accent. It veered, at times, into his Indian accent and his British accent. "Seems like one hell of a night to drink brewskis, watch a game. Why are you all following a couple of yokels like us?"

The blond man stopped before he entered hand-shaking range and so did the other two. They blocked the light with their forearms. "We work with Agent Raymond Peach. I believe you had a conversation with him, Mr. Kruse."

"I did."

"We were involved in an information-extraction situation with Mr. al-Faruqi. That situation came to an abrupt halt. I don't want to outright accuse anyone of malfeasance. Perhaps you two can tell us what happened to him."

Tzvi whispered, loud enough for Agent Peach's friends to hear: "What language is this man speaking?"

"In addition, there are certain resources, our resources, we have reason to believe you have confiscated from Mr. al-Faruqi. We thank you for that, for keeping a watchful eye on assets of the American government. And while we would like nothing more than to take . . . *brewskis* with friends from Canada, we are on the clock here. It's against regulations. You can keep the money. I was hoping, gentlemen, we could take the file and be on our way."

"It seems you know us." Kruse had slipped one throwing knife into each pocket of his suit jacket. He bumped his wrists against them, for comfort. "But we have no idea who you are."

"Like I said. We work with Raymond Peach."

"Frankly, sir, I didn't see his badge or even a business card. You work with Raymond Peach of the . . ."

Tzvi patted his pocket square, a flash of pink silk. "We are taping this conversation, to be sure you three are not partaking in any malfeasance."

The blond woman did not move, but the man to her left, the dark-haired agent who had been shifting his weight from foot to foot, reached clumsily inside his suit jacket. His hand caught on the lining and he cussed. It was plenty of time for Kruse to pull out his knives. He threw one as the young man pulled out his gun, and it stuck into his right shoulder. The young man dropped his gun and called out in pain. The two blonds, the man and woman, ran back to the Range Rover to take cover behind the open doors. Hunched over, the black-haired agent did the same. Kruse ran for the gun the man had dropped and dove into the ditch. The straw was tall enough, if he crouched, to hide him. Tzvi tried to run around the car but he careened to his right and slammed into the hood of the Peugeot and fell on the pavement like a drunk.

With the doors open and the engine still running, the Range Rover's interior lights were on. The woman aimed for the straw while her blond partner stepped away from the four-by-four, his gun on Tzvi, who had fallen in the middle of the two-lane highway. The blond agent was shouting orders at Tzvi to keep his hands, his hand, visible. Kruse calmed himself and aimed. The gun was one he had used quite often, with Tzvi's Mossad friends north of Brampton: a Beretta 92. He had intended to hit the agent in the arm. Instead, the bullet hit him in the hand. There was an explosion about the gun, of blood in the head-lights. The agent fell to his knees and moaned.

The woman began firing into the straw. Two of the bullets missed him by less than a foot. Like quick breaths he heard them pass. At the Range Rover it was now chaos: the woman shouted at the wounded man, who took cover in the back seat.

"I can't see anything."

"Close your door. That's why he can see us, you moron."

Kruse liked the way this conversation was going. He shot the rear-view mirror, next to the woman, who screamed and ducked. She jumped into the Range Rover and slammed the door shut. The other door was open so he could still see her. He shot again, to break the window.

Kruse couldn't see much. Tzvi had hidden behind the Peugeot. He had abandoned his American accent. "You want to tell us who you are? Who you really are?"

The blond man stood up and limped into the flat pool of light at the driver's side door of the Range Rover, one destroyed hand cradled in the other. Once he was inside, it was as though all three of them had forgotten Kruse and Tzvi. The blond man and woman changed places, so she was in the driver's seat.

"What should we do?" Kruse stood up in the straw, walked over to Tzvi. "Just let them go?"

Tzvi took the gun from him and aimed: two pops and a double whoosh. The Range Rover slouched.

"As you like to say, my son: we aren't murderers."

The light inside the Range Rover had gone dark. Kruse could hear them talking inside, shouting at one another. The woman, at least, could still shoot, so Kruse took back the Beretta and kept it pointed at them. Tzvi stepped into the Peugeot and started it, reached over to open the driver's door.

Kruse jumped in, put the car in reverse, ducked and steered. He turned around. The back window of the Peugeot cracked into a spider web but did not burst, and a bullet hit the stereo between them. It went black. For a few kilometres, neither of them spoke.

Then Tzvi cleared his throat.

"When I was a boy I often visited my uncle's farm in the Hula Valley. Once, in the autumn, it was time to slaughter some turkeys. We cut their heads off with an axe, over a stump, and we released their bodies and they ran about for a while—headless. Running just then, when you needed me: I was a headless chicken."

"I'm so sorry, Tzvi, for all of this."

"It made no sense, so I thought it was God, giving the turkeys thirty crazy seconds of life after death. Here I am with no sense of balance, no—"

"Doing a hell of a lot better than headless."

"Let me say this was a proud moment—that asshole's hand blowing up. I saw a bit of bone in the gloaming. He would have killed me and you did not hesitate."

"Did you hurt yourself, falling?"

"I have felt better, Christopher."

"Should you see a doctor?"

"It would be foolish to pay someone five hundred dollars to tell me what I already know. Blood loss and trauma are bad for a body, deep revelation. This is also what I know: I am no longer a young man. Neither are you, my boy. My genuine boy! Armless in that bright room, I began to feel I am on the final leg of a journey to decrepitude. Thirty crazy seconds from God."

"No."

"Look." He wiggled the stub of his left arm in his jacket. "You're not looking."

"Those three. What should we have done, Tzvi?"

"Precisely what we did, only smoother. Without any falling down. We did not take a bullet and we did not kill them like a couple of panicked amateurs. Now they know we are serious. And I know I am not leaving."

"You are, at least for now. When you're ready to fight again, come back. Or just give me advice when I call and I don't know what to do."

"I had thought we were the hunters when I arrived in Paris. We are the prey."

"I thought I understood."

"It's coordinated, Christopher. The explosion at the restaurant. Al-Faruqi and his minions, the communist, the anti-Semite in Nancy. This woman from the DPSD. I am sure it is not personal, but the mayor and your splendid Corsican friend are using you as a grenade."

"What about Agent Peach?"

"If what we have in this file is so damned important, and the agency knows about it, we would not have been accosted by three fuckups in a Range Rover. If they are genuine I will eat my other arm. We will figure it out together, my boy."

"You're leaving."

"I am not."

"And I am coming with you."

"What?" Tzvi turned to him, said nothing more for a while. "What about your secret girlfriend who does not know she is your girlfriend? What about her daughter who does not need you? And the Frogs in general, with their love for blowing up Jews? You would leave all of this truth and beauty to go home to Toronto where you belong?"

In Madrid they spent al-Faruqi's pesetas at the Palace Hotel. They rented the Royal Suite, with its sitting room and dining room and library, a grand balcony overlooking leafy treetops and the church spires. Tzvi slept.

A basket on the dining room table was filled with meats and cheeses, a cakey local bread, small jars of jam, and a cool bottle of cava with two champagne flutes. There was a radio on the credenza. Kruse messed around on the dial until he found a station that pleased him, a romantic pop song from the 1980s called "More Than This." It had once seemed boring, music for old people. Now it pleased him, especially with the cava warming him and taking away the throb of his new wounds. He thought of Annette and then he thought of Annette and Étienne. He thought of Zoé Moquin in one of her sister's baroque dresses, nearly kissing her in the hallway of the prelates' house. He really should have kissed her.

French doors opened onto a vast stone balcony. The evening was warm enough to open the doors and sit half in and half out of the suite, with the music and the cava and Khalil al-Faruqi's file on his lap—the *proof of something* that had been valuable enough that two men and a woman had staked it out and had fired shots in the night to retrieve it. When the song was finished and a less romantic one began, Kruse took a long sip and opened the file.

• • •

They were a security company, not a training school. Perhaps it was time to give up the studio and take an office downtown. With the money from Zoé Moquin they could even buy something near the university and rent out half of it. At least half. Cash flow, my son. More and more of the calls came from the Americans these days. At some point they would have to decide between Toronto and New York. Would they expand or remain small?

"I am not sure I could say it to a client, or anyone but you, this word people use for small businesses: *boutique*. A *boutique* security firm. I feel like a teenage girl. Let's not put it on our business cards."

Tzvi watched him as he spoke, without pauses, all the way to the airport. He did not invite Kruse's thoughts or opinions on their future together. It was as though Tzvi had not spoken in months and had to make up for the awful lack. At the international departures terminal Kruse pulled in behind a taxi.

"So you will drop me off here, the old invalid, and you will return the rental and meet me inside. Let's upgrade to first class, yes? Why the hell not?"

"Last night, while you were sleeping—"

"Just wait." Tzvi stared at him in the Peugeot. His eyes were red and he was pale in the morning sunlight. "What was in the file, my boy?"

"Like you suspected. I don't think these are genuine CIA agents."

"We can sort it out in Washington."

"No."

"That is your counter-argument? No?"

"You don't want a counter-argument. You knew I wasn't coming. I'll collect the money from Madame Moquin, open an account in Zürich, and then maybe . . ."

"Then maybe what? I'm not your mother, Christopher, or your lover. You don't have to spare my feelings." Tzvi sighed. "I taught you so much, and I am so proud of you. Even in this frustrating moment, as much as I want to break your nose again, I am proud of you. But I knew in our first week together, back when you were a boy, I would never strip one thing from your fragile brain. Your heart, I suppose. It is the thing that will kill you. And you know it. You know one day it will kill you."

They got out of the car together and embraced. This is what they did now: they embraced. Tzvi kissed him three times and there were tears in his eyes even though he claimed he did not share any of Kruse's weakness. He blamed it on the mysteries of blood loss. Kruse made promises to him and from the car he watched Hans Miller of Switzerland walk to the Air Canada desk. He was lopsided and looked small. For the first time in his life Kruse felt the need to protect him.

At the rental kiosk, Kruse exchanged the Peugeot for another one. He claimed to have parked just outside downtown Madrid. In the morning, he had returned to a broken window and—believe it or not—a *bullet in the radio*.

"Kids maybe, or Basques." The man at the kiosk carried few teeth in his mouth. His lisp was stronger than most. "We like to congratulate ourselves. Democracy wins. Capitalism wins. But I see it coming. This country, the entire continent is eating itself."

THIRTEEN

Avenue Montaigne

THE APARTMENT SMELLED OF SPOILED DAIRY AND SWEET MUSK.
Couches and chairs and mattresses and pillows had been ripped open
with knives. Feathers and polyester fluff lay on the floor. Paintings were
broken. Every cupboard in the kitchen was empty and, quite unnecessarily, so was the refrigerator. There was a safe in his bedroom. It had
been blasted open. Kruse had never used it; he didn't even know the
combination. The room he cared about most was a special mess. The
bookshelves in Anouk's room, which was also secretly Lily's room, were
broken on the floor and the bed was upside down. The sketches from
Winnie-the-Pooh and *Alice in Wonderland* were ripped, the glass of their
frames shattered. There wasn't much to throw about in the bathrooms
but the toiletries he had left behind had been yanked from the shelves;
he didn't wear cologne but the bottle Annette had bought for him, at
Christmastime, was broken and stinking. He opened the windows and
cleaned what he could, took out the broken eggs and spilled yogurt and
closed the bathroom door. It had been like this for some time. Even if

the mattresses had not been disembowelled he could not imagine sleeping in his apartment. The smell was a clamp around his temples. It turned his throat sour.

He put the file in his briefcase and turned left on Rue Valadon. It was just after seven. Annette would have begun Anouk's bedtime ritual. The lights were on up there. Kruse pressed her button on the intercom and considered what he might say. He did not want to alarm her.

"*Oui allô?*" It was the aristocratic voice of Étienne.

Kruse backed away, off the sidewalk and onto the thin and shadowed street. He was exhausted from driving for thirteen hours and dizzy from the cologne. He scanned the windows, the doorways. He was sure someone was watching him. He was sure of nothing. His address book was still in the inside pocket of his suit jacket, from the trip south. There were payphones at Rue de Grenelle, across from the Café Rousillon. He walked backwards up Valadon, watching the windows on the top floor.

The last time he had spoken to the capitaine was in an apartment in Marseille. Kruse recalled another powerful smell, of bleach. That day it had felt like the insides of his nostrils were being cooked. Hours earlier, a young man named Frédéric had been skinned alive in the apartment and the capitaine had not wanted to believe him. The capitaine was a massive crow with a beard and a cigarette, he remembered that, and a stoop. Kruse had two numbers for the Marseillais. The first one, at the station, rang out. On the fourth ring of the second number the capitaine answered in the middle of a coughing fit.

"Who is this? Who?" The capitaine did not recall him until Kruse described the rainy day they had met on Rue de la Cathédrale: the smell of bleach.

There was a long pause. A rugby match was on and the home team had evidently scored. Applause and shouts of joy exploded from Café Rousillon. Even over this, Kruse could hear the giant policeman's raspy breaths.

"I didn't see you at Huard's funeral."

Kruse could not tell him where he had been at the time: in Paris, trying to destroy the men who had killed Lieutenant Huard. "He's been avenged."

The policeman laughed. "It's that simple, is it? He has been avenged. The world is in order. In my career I have not come across anything so clean and so pleasing, Monsieur Kruse. Thank you for this. You did the avenging, I imagine?"

"I have to ask you a favour."

"Do you know what Huard said you were? An assassin. Let me see. It is late in the evening. I am at home with a glass of wine. And an assassin calls to ask me a favour."

"I'm working for the mayor of Paris."

"Another assassin! Two assassins in one phone call." The Marseillais began and tentatively halted another coughing fit. "I am blessed this evening."

Kruse explained he had been hired to find the people who had blown up Chez Sternbergh. One of the agents who had hired him had left two phone numbers: an office number, which would be useless just now, and a home number.

"Why don't you phone this agent?"

"I have. I called her before I called you, of course. But she was not home."

"It is not in my power to make a woman go to her home."

"I need her address."

"This is against the law."

"How much will it take? I have money."

"Assassins always seem to have money." Over the phone came the sounds of the Marseillais lighting a new cigarette. "Monsieur Kruse, I'm not a young man anymore. The people who ruin my beautiful city and my beautiful country, our gangsters, our businessmen, our politicians, they are—I have discovered—unstoppable. All I can do is intercept their little stooges from time to time, rough them up, toss them in jail for a year or two. I have become a terrible cynic, I will admit it. But even so, I don't see why I should help a thug go around dispensing justice in my country."

"This woman: I won't hurt her. I want to help her. Help you. Help France."

"Help yourself." The Marseillais was quiet for a moment. Then he began to sing a song Kruse had heard somewhere before. *"Nous sommes des dégourdis, nous sommes des lascars. Des types pas ordinaires."*

We are sneaky. We are rogues. We are not ordinary men. "What song is this?"

"Mais, c'est 'Le Boudin.'"

"Blood pudding?"

"The fight song of the French Foreign Legion, Monsieur Kruse. This is where I started my career—as a commander. Men like you, lost men, would arrive. My job was to make something of you. But I have a feeling, listening to your voice, you are more lost than lost."

"You're probably correct."

The Marseillais agreed to search the address attached to Zoé Moquin's personal phone line and to call him back with it, at Café Rousillon. Kruse crossed the street and ordered a glass of Gigondas and waited for the call.

• • •

He had bought two of his suits on Avenue Montaigne, where many of the haute couture houses had addresses. It did not take long to get into the building, an extraordinarily well-kept nineteenth-century block with cut stone and, on the top floor, pretty domes and turrets. It was not a bureaucrat's building. The boutiques were closed at this hour but people were filing out of the door in fine suits and tight dresses, their perfumes a reminder of his apartment, on their way to opera and theatre.

Her suite was on the fourth floor but there were no addresses on the fifth. First he knocked and waited, and knocked again. One of her neighbours, a man in a tuxedo carrying a bouquet of flowers, said hello as he passed. When they released Kruse from the Lyon jail, after Evelyn was murdered, he was allowed to take her wallet. It was easy to throw some of it away but not her driver's licence. They had gone into the registration office together, to get their cards, and when it was her turn to have her photograph taken he had lowered his shirt to show his nipple. It was unlike him to be silly, and her smile—her laugh—in the photograph was so true that her eyes were tiny. It was flimsy and flexible, still valid for another eight months. For slipping locks open it was better than any credit card.

It was more like a warehouse loft in New York City than a Paris apartment. He did not turn on any lights but enough flooded in from the street. There were few walls on the vast floor, and instead of furniture there were tables of fabric and elaborate dresses on unusual mannequins. It smelled of hot glue. Kruse called out for Zoé, for anyone. The art on the wall was enormous and enormously moody, night upon night. He pulled out his flashlight and inspected it: crows and cliffs and houses and abstractions and white faces, dark eyes.

A spiral staircase led up to the second floor, the living quarters. Despite all the space, the apartment had only two bedrooms. Both had closets filled with elaborate dresses. The kitchen was black and silver with fixtures that looked like they had been pulled from an advanced alien civilization; like the dresses, he had never seen anything like it. He wondered at the sort of mind that could imagine and demand and produce all of this.

In the dining room there was a large black-and-white photograph from the era when we did not smile for the camera. It was a man with a moustache. His arms were at his sides. He had wrapped himself in thick fabric and there were poles behind him like the thin bones in wings.

He examined the photograph with his flashlight. Thunder cracked and rolled; a steady rain began. Kruse opened the window in the apartment's only typically French room, a spacious salon with antique couches and chairs, a grand piano, busy wallpaper, and portraits. From buildings on both sides of Avenue Montaigne, men and women dashed from doorways into luxury sedans waiting out front. He thought again of Evelyn, who had dreamed of this room and its warmth, the view of the generous street below, the promise of an evening of elegance and sophistication hand in hand. Of course, he doubted that she ever dreamed of it with him. Another philosopher, perhaps, or a banker. As part of Kruse's transformation into an escort she could take to a dinner party, Evelyn had signed him up for piano classes before Lily was born. It turned out he was good at it, that his training as a fighter had something in common with musical apprenticeship. The rhythm of it, maybe, or just focus. He was never a star at reading notes, and his teacher, Ms. Zipp, had recognized that about him, so she focused on teaching him how to play by ear.

To stay awake as he waited for Zoé he sat at the black shiny piano and slowly lifted the fallboard. The idea was he would play for Lily and with her, so when it came time for her to take her own lessons it would not seem a chore. Music was simply a thing we humans make, as natural as fighting.

He had memorized a bit of the famous Beethoven and Bach and some movie soundtrack songs. At Zoé's piano Kruse played the only Chopin nocturne he had learned, one of the easiest ones, opus 9, number 2, which starts quiet and mostly stays quiet. He had learned it because Lily had asked for a "song about rain" and this is what Ms. Zipp had recommended. He had not played it in more than a year, but it returned to him in the silence of the apartment. Near the middle he heard footsteps behind him and he made an error. His timing was off. He found his rhythm again and calmed himself and finished quietly and prettily. She knew to wait a few seconds after the final note. Then she clapped.

"To arrive home to music like this. A woman could get used to such a thing, Christophe. But you didn't have to do it in the dark."

"I didn't want to frighten you."

"Sincerely, there is not another person in my life I would have suspected."

"And this prospect is not at all worrying?"

She pulled the cord on a brass floor lamp with a shade that belonged in a Dr. Seuss book. Her dress was red, ruffled and short, with a thin strap that crossed over her shoulders. It looked like she had been out on a date but she was home too early for that. "I was just out for an aperitif in your neighbourhood. The mayor hosted an evening for Plácido Domingo and Charles Aznavour."

"Did they sing?"

"They sing tomorrow. They're doing a benefit concert for the families of sick children who have to stay in Paris for treatment. Hotels in this town aren't cheap, as you know. There were actual sick children at the party, bald ones with cancer. One, a twelve-year-old, spoke about her family's suffering. She didn't mention her own troubles. I was so miserable about it I drank three glasses of champagne and ate nothing, so I couldn't stay long." Her cheeks were flushed. "I would have embarrassed myself eventually."

"You get along well with the mayor?"

Zoé was going to answer immediately but then she stepped back from it, out of the lamplight. "Would you like a drink, Christophe? Or did you already help yourself?"

"I'll have what you're having."

He followed her into the black and silver kitchen, where she turned on a set of four hanging lights. She pulled a bottle of red wine from a humming wine cooler. "A colleague gave this to me last week. I don't know enough about wine. Perhaps it is good and perhaps it is not. A 1990 Bordeaux. He's quite fancy, so I imagine it's good. 'For your cellar,' he said. So I don't think he intended this." She slid the bottle and the corkscrew over the concrete counter, and Kruse opened it. She poured two glasses and they touched the rims softly and looked at each other. "Did you sneak into my apartment to ravage me, Christophe? Should I phone the police?"

"It's up to you, really."

"Is it?"

"Phoning the police."

"To ravage or not to ravage: that part is out of my control?"

Kruse turned away from her, to look at the rooms in the light. He walked into the dining room.

"Catherine, my sister, worked for Chanel, for Monsieur Lagerfeld. He may have said this to other young designers, I cannot know, but he had told her that she would be his successor. She travelled. Men loved her, of course."

"This was her apartment?"

"It was."

Kruse took his glass of wine and returned to the black-and-white photograph of the raven man.

Zoé stood beside him, her arm touching his. "Franz Reichelt. It was taken in 1911. He was a tailor obsessed with flight. He clothed dummies in this outfit and tossed them from roofs. They had flown gently to the ground. When he was pleased with his experiments he petitioned the Paris police to allow him to try something at the Eiffel Tower."

"He jumped?"

"On a cold February morning. There was a crowd. He went to the first platform and stood on a stool and made a declaration and hurled himself off. It isn't pretty, what happens to a body when it drops from a great height. There were plenty of photographers, even a filmmaker. All the newspapers had photographs the next day. They called him the Flying Tailor."

"It's macabre."

"Catherine was attracted to his ambition, of course, the audacity of it. You can see it in her clothes: elegance and absurdity at once. And the macabre. Her plan was not to be creative director of Chanel, no matter what Karl Lagerfeld said about her. She wanted to make clothes for regular people. She registered the name Flying Tailor, as her clothing line. She wanted to be in boutiques and department stores."

There was genuine pain in her voice. He imagined intelligence agents weren't supposed to feel pain. Perhaps it was the wine. He said nothing more and turned away from the flying tailor, even though he wanted to continue looking at him. There was more thunder, a quiet flash.

"The mayor did this, Zoé. All of it."

"All of what?"

"He's eliminating his enemies. And I've helped him. You and your agency are paying for it. When there are no enemies left, I become the enemy."

"How is that?"

"*I know about it.* And Monsieur le Maire will need a crazed loner, his Lee Harvey Oswald."

"A Canadian assassin who dislikes Jewish restaurants and Palestinian terrorists and communists and ultra-right-wing industrialists?"

"Close."

Zoé led him across the room. Her heels clicked on and off the parquet floor, interrupted by red Persian rugs.

"If I'm right, the mayor's team will have footage of me at Chez Sternbergh, in Sigüenza, in Luxembourg Gardens, on Rue des Brice in Nancy. When he is finished with me, he will send it to the Gendarmerie Nationale, a few newspapers and television stations. My friend Étienne Bonnet will get the scoop. I'll see myself on the news. There will be witnesses. Then, before I can make any official statements, they'll come for me. And they'll come for Tzvi in Toronto. There won't be a trial or even an arrest. They threatened Annette and Anouk, to make me do this. Maybe they'll assume I told Annette. Maybe they have to get rid of her, too."

She sat on the gold and red couch that was so magnificent he worried about going anywhere near it with his glass of wine. For more than a minute she said nothing. She looked out the window. "If you're correct, Christophe, he has manipulated us both. What will he do to me?"

"You're a professional. Perhaps nothing. Perhaps we both die in an accident."

"Then we shouldn't be in the same room together. It's too easy for him. All it takes is a gas leak and his problems are over. Did anyone follow you here?"

"No."

"Are you sure?"

"No."

There was only a hint of light on her face, from the adjacent lamp. He could not see her expression but she seemed perfectly relaxed, not at all perturbed by his revelations. Her question—*What will he do to me?*—was not a real question. Did she know? There was a flair about her voice, quiet as it was. She whispered, as though her parents were asleep in the bedroom.

Kruse had come here because he had thought Zoé could help. She could alert her superiors at the agency, launch an investigation, put him in some sort of protective custody. But she sounded amused by what he had told her, not frightened or even concerned. He had encountered this sort of cynicism in New York, when CEOs were threatened by lawsuits and criminal charges or even physical threats by the leaders of organized crime families.

"What's in the briefcase, Christophe?"

"Proof."

Zoé sat up. "Proof of what you say the mayor has done?"

"No."

"Proof of what, then?"

He had planned to tell her everything, to give her the briefcase. "Another matter, quite unrelated."

"Do you like the wine?"

It was delicious but he did not want to talk about wine. Why was she talking about wine? If she wore perfume he could not smell it. Now and then the wet air from the street would move through the room and it would take him, momentarily, somewhere else. The sleep in Madrid had helped but he remained exhausted. Exhausted and, now, confused. "It's fine. Thank you."

She slid closer to him, on the couch.

"You're a spy, Zoé. Is that right?"

"I don't pretend to be anyone I am not, if that's what you mean. No fake names, nothing undercover. But I do work in a clandestine service. The work you did for us—for France, Christophe, not for the mayor, at least not in any official way—did not actually happen. I'm not worried that you'll suddenly be charged with a crime for eliminating Khalil al-Faruqi. You did not eliminate him. You don't exist, you see."

"But the others . . ."

"This will take some research on my part, some activity, but it's late in the evening. The computers are turned off. The bureaucrats have gone home. It seems to me, Christophe, that you have entirely succeeded. You have done what we, the republic, asked of you. It's time to celebrate, not worry."

The way she sat on the couch, her short dress was even shorter. The fabric crinkled against the couch as she slid closer to him. She wore patterned stockings. Zoé watched him so intently he did not know where to look so he looked at her legs.

She whispered. "Would you like to be elsewhere?"

Kruse answered without actually saying it: no.

"I don't want to embarrass myself, Christophe."

He turned to her and she reached for his cheek and pulled him in for a kiss. He had forgotten how, how to really kiss a woman. But it returned to him and he did not think about the mayor and Joseph or his ruined apartment or Tzvi or Evelyn or Lily. Somewhere across the city, he imagined briefly that Annette was kissing Étienne, which only made him want to kiss Zoé better. She pulled off his jacket and pawed at him through his white shirt, still damp from the rain, and she lay back while they kissed and then, with a growl of frustration, she shoved him off. She stood up, one shoe on and one shoe off, breathing deeply, her hair wild.

"Wait. What are you doing here?"

"My apartment's destroyed."

"Why? Who destroyed it?"

"Some Americans."

Zoé looked at his briefcase. "Your proof."

"Yes."

"You could have gone to a hotel." She pulled down her dress, reached up to fix her hair. "Did you come here for the money? It's not here. Where is the Israeli, Monsieur Meisels? In Toronto, really? Or is he here somewhere, waiting with a knife?"

"No."

"I didn't plan this. This wasn't in my plan." She walked into the kitchen, drew a glass of water, drank it all at once, and returned to him. "Is this . . . What are you thinking, Christophe?"

If he were honest with her, he wasn't thinking at all. He had gone to Annette's apartment but she was with the editorialist. There were a thousand hotels between Avenue Bosquet and Avenue Montaigne. He had hoped Zoé would say he had nothing to worry about. Joseph's men would not come after him or Tzvi. The mayor would not punish Annette and Anouk. Until he saw Zoé, in her dress, Kruse had planned to share al-Faruqi's file with her. He could hide here, in this carnival apartment, and she would take care of everything.

He stood up. "I came because I wanted to see you."

Zoé put her hand on her heart. "That means you have to go."

"Why?"

"If you are in earnest, Christophe, and I do hope you are, we cannot . . .

I cannot make love to you until all this is settled. Tomorrow I will see about what you have told me. I will get your money."

"Should I . . . ?"

Zoé looked at her watch. It wasn't late. "You should go."

• • •

Three taxis were lined up at the end of her building, in front of a white-walled boutique. Scarves and handbags were posed under loving spotlights. Kruse stood in the rain for a few minutes to cool off, to clear himself of desire, before he rapped on any windshields. In the rain and in the wind that came with it, his feelings for Zoé twisted into fury. They had made a murderer of him: he was not free to fall in love. He looked up at the windows, to see if anyone was watching him. If anyone was watching him, they were in darkness.

The driver took him west in the rain, to Joseph's impossibly quiet neighbourhood. Kruse asked the driver to wait for him a moment and he ran out to press the buzzer in the dark and the wet. One of the giants who acted as gatekeeper opened the door. He wore a shirt and tie but his blazer was on his chair. His partner sat at a small card table, waiting. It smelled of pizza in the foyer. A checkerboard was open and the second giant sat studying it.

"Good evening, Monsieur Kruse."

Kruse apologized for coming without any notice and asked if Monsieur Mariani was home. He felt like a nine-year-old asking if Joey could come out for a bike ride.

"No, no. He's out."

Without looking away from the checkerboard, the second giant called out: "At his fundraiser!"

"What fundraiser?" said the man at the door. "I thought he was at church."

"He is in a church but it isn't *church*. It's a church with music inside. That old stuff he likes."

"You can't make a church not a church. It's still a church even if it isn't church. If he's in a church he's at church."

"Jesus Christ. My point is—"

"What church is it?" Kruse interrupted.

This inspired another back-and-forth that reminded him of married couples he and Evelyn had known back in Toronto. They would be over for dinner and the husband and wife would argue without emotion about items in the news they had remembered differently, or the way they had met, the caterers at their wedding, summer holidays, what they had been wearing that cold night in February. There were so many Notre-Dames and so many saints in the Roman martyrology, Kruse thought it could go on all night. *Notre-Dame de Passy, non non, de l'Assomption de Passy, non Notre-Dame-d'Auteuil. Non. Non? Saint-Honoré de Something, Saint-François, Sainte-Thérèse.* They agreed it was somewhere in the sixteenth arrondissement. The one at the little card table closed his eyes in concentration, clapped his hands.

"I remember him saying something about choosing the church because it was on a street named for a player."

"A football player?"

"No, you idiot. A music player. It's a music night, for Christ's sake."

Kruse doubted a street in old Paris would be named after a non-French musician, so he named all the composers he could remember. Chopin? Berlioz? That was close but no. Satie or Debussy? Saint-Saëns didn't sound like a street but Saint-Saëns? He had read somewhere that Stravinsky had become a Parisian. No? Kruse was about to open it up to other European nationalities when he remembered Georges Bizet.

"That's it!"

Kruse ran back to the taxi. His driver, a handsome young man from Côte d'Ivoire, did not know of the church but he knew of Rue Georges Bizet. Just that morning he had taken a woman to a business meeting at the Egyptian embassy on Bizet. They entered from its northern tip, at a quiet plaza full of cars. It was a residential street with few shops. They passed a clinic with some trees out front and then the street grew thinner and older, the details on the front of the mansions more magnificent. There was one restaurant on the corner, probably Italian, and a dry cleaner. Kruse tried to calm himself, tried to wipe the memory of his ruined and reeking apartment away. If Tzvi were with him he would suggest subtlety and stealth: sit at the back of whatever room it is, or stand. Wait for the right moment. Let as few people as possible see you.

It was not a church but a Greek Orthodox cathedral, and it surprised both Kruse and the driver. From eye level, on the street, it did not appear to be much. Kruse paid the driver, who said he did not look at all Greek. "But I haven't learned to tell the difference between you," he said, sincerely.

Kruse reached for his briefcase and realized there was no briefcase. He had forgotten it, in his dreaminess, back at Zoé's apartment. The cab had already pulled away. He waved but the cab did not stop.

It didn't matter. Not now.

There were more elegant strategies. Perhaps Tzvi was right: doing all of this from Toronto, somehow, might have been better. Joseph would be well guarded. He would deny everything. But Kruse wanted him to know he had ruined the wrong man.

Joseph had started all of this on the evening of the explosion, an explosion he himself had planned. This is why the mayor was standing close to the door: so Kruse could save him. If he had faltered, the mayor might simply have run out. Joseph or one of his retired armed forces staff would have told him how many seconds to count after the grenades had toppled to the floor. One, two, three. Only a diabolically paranoid journalist or investigator would consider the mayor a suspect. Politics were always competitive. The mayor had won many races in the past without resorting to violence. And why would a man go anywhere near a restaurant that was going to blow up?

To be certain.

From the beginning, the plan would have included false suspects. The traditional route might have been to plant evidence, but there was always a chance—a good chance—that all other suspects had wonderful alibis. Police and military, bound by laws and processes, would have delivered men like Khalil al-Faruqi, Réné Chatel, and Henri Alibert into the nimble hands of lawyers. A couple of foreign mercenaries, however, would be quiet about it and allow the government to build a story of clandestine triumph. We cannot tell you, for security reasons, how we found and killed al-Faruqi. But he was an enemy of France, the murderer of noble Pierre Cassin and other innocents.

The cathedral was named after a saint named Stéphane. He could hear the music even before he opened the door. Nearly every pew in the cathedral was full. A soprano sang under a massive chandelier and a mural of Jesus. There were nine or ten chairs at the front of the cathedral, in the raised altar. Zoé's shampoo, the scent of it, remained about him. One of the people seated on the altar was Joseph, his legs crossed, in a grey double-breasted suit. One of his girlfriends was next to him, in a simple but elegant black dress. Joseph saw him, made a subtle gesture of surprise with his hands, and smiled. In his perfectly symmetrical smile he carried health and a boyish joy that probably made it easy for him to meet women even if they had not yet seen his car and his apartment.

In the rain, on the evening of the explosion, Joseph had found Kruse in the café and he had taken him to the apartment on Rue d'Andigné. This is the smile he had worn that night. Now that they had killed the mayor's only authentic rival, they would have to find—and eliminate—some other possibilities: the terrorist, the communist radical, the right-wing extremist.

The vast room and its echoes magnified the single violin and harpsichord. The music was somehow light and dark at once, happy and tragic. "*Selig ist der Mann,*" the soprano sang. Blessed is the man. And then she sang of death, how happy she will be to depart this earth. *"Hier hast du die Seele, was schenkest du mir?"*

You have my soul. What do I get?

If there was an answer in the aria, Kruse did not hear it. He thought of Tzvi, grotesque lines of muscle and vein and skin hanging where his elbow ought to have been, the terrible woman and al-Faruqi, the smell of the unclean hacienda. The smell, now, of his own apartment. What he had mistaken as his own. Perhaps the mayor was here too. They had killed his daughter and they had killed his wife and now they had removed the arm of his true father and here they were smiling with God.

Zoé's lipstick was on his lips. *Calm, calm.* He breathed and remembered the word for the neck of the cathedral: sanctuary. The woman sang of death in the sanctuary.

He walked up the centre aisle like a priest with a tall candle, like a husband.

"What do you get, Joseph?"

Everyone turned. He was sensitive to it, with the exploded bottle in his apartment, but the sudden movement in the pews had released a new cloud of perfume. He had said it in English. The harpsichordist stopped but the violinist continued. The soprano looked about her.

Joseph stood up. The smile was gone.

Kruse had hoped to embarrass the truth out of him but Joseph did not seem to care what anyone else in the cathedral was thinking. There was something else in his eyes. He looked up past Kruse for an instant, at the bodyguards. *Wait.*

"You did it. You did it for the mayor."

Joseph stepped down and into the aisle before him, his hands up in surrender. His skin was more tanned than the last time Kruse had seen him. His pocket square was expertly poufed.

Men were behind him now. He could hear and feel their weight, the eagerness in their heels on the old floor. Kruse turned and prepared himself. The music had ended now but its ghost haunted the room.

This is what he most loved: three large men stepping in to take him. They were hired goons in the uniforms of hired goons, not Joseph's staff. "Monsieur." The one in front reached for him, spoke in a bored voice as if this were the tenth time he had retrieved Kruse from a church. "Let's step out into the street." There wasn't much room between the pews. The big men were lined up single file.

Joseph called out to them. "No no, don't try—"

Like too many men who frequent the gym, this one didn't bother with his legs. They were cartoonishly thin compared with the size of his upper body. Kruse knocked his reaching hand away to throw the man off balance and went after his right knee, where he was carrying all his weight. His kick made a dull, unpleasant sound. The security guard's howl of pain was worse. Joseph's guests called out in horror. Some on the opposite sides of the aisle stood up to leave. The big man tumbled onto a white-haired couple and went down calling for an ambulance.

"My goodness, Christopher." Joseph stepped between Kruse and the two remaining guards, over the fallen man, switched to French. He pointed to the guards, who were in that miserable place between wanting to run away and wanting to shoot someone. They panted, mouths open. "Back away. This man means us no harm." Now he spoke to everyone: "Please relax. This was a simple emotional disturbance. It's over now! And really, as we listen to this music, let's pause for a moment to remember Monsieur Bach wrote it to turn us away from violence and destruction and toward the best of our natures."

For a moment, it worked. Some of those who had stood up to leave returned tentatively to their places in the pews. Joseph turned to the front of the room, to the musicians and the soprano.

"We're terribly sorry for the interruption, Madame."

The soprano raised her hands, to block the apology. There were banners at the back of the room, advertising for Les Petits Frères des Pauvres. Kruse had seen them at work in his neighbourhood, helping isolated and hungry senior citizens with money and companionship. Three women and a man, at long tables below the banners, were standing to watch him. Everyone watched him. On the floor, the security guard moaned. It was otherwise silent for long enough that the guard called out to the room again. "An ambulance, lord please. He broke my knee."

Someone called out, a man with a shaky voice. "Leave us, you *con*."

Others joined in, ordered Kruse to leave. There were enough voices now that Joseph could speak without being heard. "What's happened to you?"

"The mayor happened. You happened."

"This is a fundraiser for—"

Kruse did not want to hear it. He knew. There was no room to walk past the remaining beefy guards, and he did not want to step over the man on the floor, so he walked to the altar. The soprano shouted "No!" and closed her hands in prayer. She seemed to be looking for someone to embrace or shield her. No one sitting on the altar stood up to comfort the soprano.

He could do it at once, in three seconds. Maybe five. Joseph would have just enough time to feel it and know it.

The philanthropists watched him as though he was the opposite of a priest, and he was the opposite of a priest. He had told himself otherwise, as an answer to his parents' accusations, but he was no one's saviour. He comforted and shielded no one. The guards helped the big man with the spoiled knee to his one good leg and they walked him sideways down the aisle. He moaned and asked why. The men and women at the Petits Frères des Pauvres table had settled back into their folding chairs. They looked miserable. He had made them all miserable.

Joseph stood alone in the aisle, watching him. The philanthropists had gone quiet. Kruse was a jack-in-the-box and this was the final turn of the crank.

The Mariani cousin who would take his place as chief murderer, if Kruse broke his neck in the aisle, would not spend any of his free time with the little siblings of the poor. There was nothing Kruse could say to these people. He was not made to be at the front of the room, on the altar or under the chandelier of the sanctuary. When they were still teaching self-defence, young men who had seen Bruce Lee movies or popular bits of preposterousness like *Gymkata* would come into MagaSecure because they hoped it would transform them. Learning to fight, and actually fighting, would make them powerful and sexy because that's what it did in the movies. In real life, it's abominable. Tzvi would shout at him when Kruse tried to dissuade teenage boys with wealthy parents. Fighting is not what you think it is. It will impress no one. If you do not quit within a month, like most do, it will make a horror of you.

It was finished. Joseph had succeeded, as he had always succeeded and always would. Pierre Cassin was dead and Khalil al-Faruqi, the main suspect, could not answer for himself. Réné Chatel and Henri Alibert could not defend themselves. There was no side door, so Kruse walked around the left side of the cathedral. The words were returning to him, now that his heart had slowed: the epistle side of the nave. No one said anything. His footsteps echoed and they watched him. The lunatic, the monster. On Rue Bizet it was raining again and he did not have an umbrella and it didn't matter.

Three doors of a silver car opened at once and three men in suits pointed pistols at him. Agent Peach was in the lead. He wore a bullet-proof vest and his cheeks were red. He shouted orders. Kruse did not run and he did not fight. They wanted him on his knees so he fell to his knees and put his hands behind his back and his forehead on the wet stone. It felt like he ought to pray but he did not know how to begin.

FOURTEEN

Parc de Belleville, Paris

THE BLACK HOOD WAS STITCHED TIGHTLY WITH WOOL. IT MADE GOOD sense. His balaclava in elementary school, when winter blew in off Lake Superior, was loosely knitted, permanently wet cotton. It didn't matter if the eyeholes were in place; he could still see in a snowball fight, or sliding down that hill on the east side of Riverdale Park. The agents, or whatever they were, didn't want him peeking through the stitches. The handcuffs were real even if Agent Peach and his crew were something else. If he was under arrest, no one had read him his rights. One of them had kicked him in the face after the hood was over his head. It had hit him on the right cheek, which was better than his nose or his mouth, but he could feel the heat of an ugly bruise forming. He suspected they would kill him before it amounted to much.

His family was gone. Tzvi was back in Toronto. Annette and Anouk did not need him. His only real friend in France had betrayed him. The apartment was a smelly ruin. It would have been nice to make love to Zoé with the windows open to the thunderstorm.

When he was a kid he had made lists of girls in the neighbourhood. When things were really bad between the Americans and the Soviets and he was sure a nuclear holocaust would be going down any day, he was moved to find the girls, in their backyards or walking home from school, and pitch them. Do you want to die a virgin? I don't. Maybe we can work something out. Luckily, he had lacked that sort of boldness.

The van was the tall, thin, top-heavy sort that was unlike anything in America, the baby giraffe of vehicles. While he did not see the van before they had shoved him inside, he imagined it was white. It smelled of new plastic. On the corners, as he toppled about, the tires squealed. In the back of the van with him, near the doors, was a box. Inside it, there were desperate scratches and squeals.

They went up a hill. Kruse could not hear much, through the strip of metal that separated him from the cabin, but two men spoke English. They shouted directions to one another, argued over them.

It was not a terribly long drive—between twelve and fifteen minutes. Five doors opened and closed, echoed. The air changed. They were in a garage of some sort, or a warehouse. He felt the way he had felt in the early days of MagaSecure, when Tzvi had signed him up for underground fighting competitions in Toronto. The only rule was to stay away from the groin. On the way to these fights, on Saturday afternoons in boxing gyms that had closed for *maintenance and renovations*, Kruse was always nauseated. He never lost a maintenance and renovation fight, not even close, because Tzvi was his teacher and no one else's, but he never stopped feeling sick before the match began.

The door opened. He was both nauseated and ready. Though he had been convincing himself that dying would be all right, he had still counted the distance. He had learned the captors by their voices. There were five of them. At least three had semi-automatic pistols.

"Out."

Kruse knew it was Agent Peach but he wanted him to say it, to confirm. "Agent Peach."

"Pull him out."

There was nothing he could do, not now, so he concentrated on remaining conscious. He tried not to fall as they pulled him out. Someone whispered, "Can he see through that thing?"

The floor was concrete. There was a slippery layer of grit on it. He could hear birds up high, in the rafters. Someone else dragged the wooden box. Even through the hood he could smell dust in the air, and shit and mould.

His captors, four men and one woman, spoke English quietly. He could tell by the way the echoes changed that they eventually reached a wall. The hands released him and gently pushed him against a brick wall. "Okay," a man said. It was not Agent Peach. "One, two, three."

In one pull the hood came off his head. It was a delicious relief to escape the heat of it, the moisture of his breath. The woman from the rural road in Spain was the first he spotted, on the far left. In the middle, Agent Peach. Both pointed guns at him. Both were frightened, which pleased him. It was dim, from the fading daylight and whatever leaked in from the street. Then, with a pop, a spotlight flashed on him and he saw nothing but bright yellow.

"Where is it?" Now that he heard Agent Peach's voice, without seeing him, it was obvious. Something had felt wrong.

"You're not an agent."

"Where's the file, Chris?"

These were his people. No strangers in Europe, not even jerks with handguns, would call him Chris. "What file?"

A shot echoed through the warehouse and the instant of it stretched. He was dead. He was not. Not even hurt. The shot had missed. Another shot, this one a few inches from his feet and a puff of dust rose up. They laughed on the other side of the light and there were more shots. Two of the men ordered him to dance.

He did not dance, and when there were no more gunshots and the echoes stopped, the laughter faded from the warehouse too. No one spoke. There was something embarrassing about their demands to *dance, dance,* even for Agent Peach. Too many cowboy movies.

Agent Peach cleared his throat before he spoke again. "We'll find it whether you tell us or not."

"You're wrong about that."

Agent Peach entered the beam of light. "Now I know you're thinking: this asshole hasn't met me yet. I'm *me,* Chris Fucking Kruse. But here's the thing. You all think you're the toughest and the baddest before you remember that in your heart you're a kid who wants to make it all go away. I know about you. You've had a hard run, and—"

"I'm quite aware of my biographical information."

With a sigh, Agent Peach backed out of the light and spoke softly with his compatriots. There was at least one door to the warehouse, where they had come in. If he ran, it would take time for his eyes to adjust. They would shoot, but they too would have to contend with darkness. He had to assume at least a couple of them were trained. Given the light, the open space, and uncertain exits, the odds were not good for him. But the odds were worse in the spotlight.

"You noticed you weren't alone in the van, Chris."

If he went left, there would be less room to run. He was sure the van had entered the warehouse from the right: he counted the paces.

"That hood we put over your head—we're going to use it again. What I want to do, Chris, is ensure you understand us. Our personality. Where we're coming from."

"New England?"

"Honestly, in different circumstances you and I could be fabulous friends. New England, he says."

Two of the other men, the ones who had been asking him to dance, laughed a bit too enthusiastically at this. They were not here for their intelligence.

"Near Les Halles there's a little shop that specializes in traps, poisons, consulting services. Some of their do-gooder clients, bless them, don't like the idea of *killing* rats. So the exterminators will instead come out and *catch* your rats. These are honourable people. It would be easy for them to drown the rats, or poison them in the shop, but instead, once a week, they drive southwest of the city and dump the rats in a field. Unless, *unless*, someone from a university comes by with a good reason to buy the rats. Now that's what we did. The CIA Research Consortium."

"You can stop pretending."

"How did we know about the file *we gave* to al-Faruqi?"

"You're blackmailing someone."

"Where is it?" Agent Peach shouted the question. It was powered by frustration. "Where? Where? Where?"

The others joined in, shouting and threatening him in all the usual ways: fucking his ass, fucking his mother, fuck fuck fuck.

Agent Peach told them to shut up and sighed, allowed a pause, and continued. "We bought ten mean-looking rats for two hundred and fifty francs. Some street-fighting rats. Real pricks. That was three days ago. They've been in this box ever since, without any food or water. They are going nuts, Chris."

On the other side of the light, he could hear them now: the squeaking and the scratching. One of the men cussed and another said, "Oh I'll do it for Christ's sake, you tit."

"What the idiots are doing, Chris, is putting three of the maddest, hungriest rats in your hood. Then we're going to shake it up nicely, really rattle them, and tie it back on your head. How does that sound?"

Agent Peach went on but Kruse didn't fully listen. After the rats ate his face for a while, he would have another chance to tell them where to find the file. Then, if he still refuses and Agent Peach gives up, well, that is when things get tasty. They tie him down and open up his stomach with a paring knife and put the rats in him and leave him there. Goodbye, goodbye.

Since he was a child in church he could not imagine death as darkness, as the end. He could not even imagine dying. Even when he gave up on what Allan and Nettie Kruse believed, he held on to the idea that his thoughts and, when Lily was born, his love were so powerful, so *everywhere and everything*, that the world could not go on without him. Of course it would. The world went on without Leonardo da Vinci. But it would not. Somehow he would live forever.

His magical feelings died with Lily. A bullet could kill him, or lymphoma. Or starving rats. He was a failed protector with no one to protect.

Agent Peach had asked him a question, but it didn't matter. None of it mattered. One of the dullards entered the light with the hood full of twisting rats. He shook the bag and stopped briefly and said, "Quit fuckin' scratchin', for fuck sakes." Kruse decided not to wait. He took two quick steps forward, into the light, and kicked the distracted man in the face. Three shots boomed and echoed.

"He's coming your way!"

All he could see were shifting blots of yellow as he ran.

The yellow faded into white—the white van. He had thought he was running toward the warehouse door but he was still far from it. With his hands cuffed behind his back he struggled with his balance. On the opposite side of the van he leaned on it and waited for his eyes to adjust to the dark. It was cool on his forehead, and wet. They had shot at him so many times he could not believe they had not hit him. Then he realized they had hit him. A chunk of his pants was gone and the skin on the right side of his hip throbbed and burned. Blood ran down his thigh. They ran from behind, with the spotlight turned in his direction. And from the door three more approached, their flashlights shaking about. If he had started in the correct direction from the beginning, he would have run into them.

Glass shattered beside him, in the passenger side window. Agent Peach screamed that it was a *goddamn rental* and for a moment all was quiet. There was no running board around the van so he couldn't jump up on anything, hide his feet. And soon they would come around.

There was nowhere else to hide, that he could see, and the route to the warehouse door was blocked. The big light shifted and yellow flooded under the van. His feet made shadows. It began again, with a single shot that ricocheted to the right of his feet and then many shots. It seemed to come from all directions, like July 1 fireworks. They shouted and he couldn't hear. All he could do was run, so he ran again: a chicken with its head cut off. They would shoot him before he hit the far wall. They would shoot him in the back and he would fall to the ground and Agent Peach would stand over him and ask him one last time for the file and he would insult Agent Peach and think about Lily, think about Lily, *think about Lily, think only of Lily* because he had been wrong about what happens to people when they die with love about them and there was a place he could go to be with her.

All at once the shooting stopped. Kruse was four metres from the wall. The only wound he could feel was on his hip, thumping and bleeding. There were footsteps behind him. He could hear heavy breaths. For a moment he thought perhaps he was dead and invisible to the world. When you die instantly it doesn't hurt. He was sure he had seen a ghost in the basement of the house on Foxbar Road one night when Evelyn asked him to find a bottle of white wine. It was a child, an adolescent or teenager, a girl. He hadn't told anyone.

The flashlights were on the concrete floor. Bodies had fallen nearby. The woman dragged herself along. "I'm so fucking thirsty," she said, "please," but no one was listening to her. There were sirens in the distance.

Kruse returned to the light.

"Christopher!" Five footsteps: leather-soled shoes on gritty concrete. Joseph put his hands on Kruse's shoulders. "They didn't get you. Oh— they got you a little."

Agent Peach was on his knees, just outside the spotlight. Two of Joseph's men stood over him. "Please, please, *arrêtez. Je suis américain. Je suis CIA.*"

• • •

He understood why people went to the top of the Eiffel Tower—to say they had done it—but the view was disappointing. Paris is not like New York City. It is most magnificent from below, *à pied*, from the parks and plazas. In Paris, social class is a subtler affair. There are no kings and queens on the penthouse floors, looking down on their subjects. They share the sidewalk. It's not that they don't judge. They simply don't see you.

This is why the view from Parc de Belleville, which he had seen only in the daytime, was not terribly *belle*. The apartment blocks on the edges of the park were made of concrete, a flashback to the least beautiful architecture in Canada. The city below was a rippling sea of rain-rusted roofs.

Kruse sat in the back of the car, next to Agent Peach. Joseph had removed the agent's handcuffs. They had taken a tarp fron the warehouse; Kruse bled on it to spare the Mercedes. Monsieur Claude explained that when he was a police officer, here in Paris, Belleville Park at night was one of the top five places to buy drugs and sex. He didn't know if it was like that anymore. Agent Peach, who was not fluent in French, sighed and lowered his face into his hands. He *did* work for the CIA but he wasn't an agent and his name wasn't Peach. He was an archivist and researcher. Nothing much happened in the Paris office, but it was an information hub. Agent Peach knew how to intercept communications destined for the actual agents, who were thirty-year-old drunks with well-connected parents. None of the real spies wanted to be in the Paris office. But every month, one or two briefs would come through that could topple a government.

In the past eighteen months Agent Peach and his team, all from his hometown of Louisville, had worked with Khalil al-Faruqi to, yes, blackmail the American government for $100 million. They supplied the information. Al-Faruqi would run the scam.

Of his seven comrades from Louisville, four were dead in the warehouse. The others were wounded. César, one of Joseph's largest and most powerful bodyguards, had pulled Agent Peach out of the warehouse by his hair, and he kept reaching up and touching the top of his head, to examine what he had lost.

When they were sure no one was watching, César exited from the front passenger side of the Mercedes and opened the door for Joseph, helped him out. Then he reached in, much less gently, for Agent Peach.

He had finished begging. Now he was threatening them. He would bring the full power and menace of the American government down upon them, crush them into a fine white sand.

As they walked into the darkness of the park Joseph informed Agent Peach in a calm voice about his own contacts in the agency. He was a source, in fact. He had his own core collector, who would be keenly interested in this file Agent Peach had collected. Agent Peach was quiet for a time. They found a poorly lit spot.

"I'll do anything you want," Agent Peach whispered.

Kruse leaned against a plane tree, touched his new bruise.

"Yes," said Joseph. "You will."

"Don't kill me."

"Tell me what you can do for me," said Joseph.

The car was not so far away. Kruse walked back to it, to the American folk song Monsieur Claude played with the driver's door opened. They did not speak, but Monsieur Claude reached out and put a hand on Kruse's shoulder. The rain had stopped but it remained humid and cool.

It was not long before Joseph returned, alone.

"Thank you."

"You're welcome, Christopher."

Monsieur Claude had watched Agent Peach and his friends from Louisville kidnap Kruse in front of the church. He had followed the van and rental car behind it to the warehouse and he had called César and the team. By then, the fundraiser Kruse had ruined was finished. Joseph joined the expedition.

"I don't even care, Joseph. I don't even care if you started this whole thing, sent me off to ruin. All I care about, now, is—"

"My friend, what are you talking about? This is why you accosted me in the cathedral? You think I betrayed you?"

"You're a businessman. You have your reasons."

Joseph took his hand. "Christopher. I am a crook. I descend from a long line of crooks. You know that about me. But I don't betray my friends unless . . . unless they decide they no longer want to be friends."

On the drive across the Right Bank, to Rue d'Andigné, Kruse told him what had happened in Spain and in Nancy. It was obvious what came next: he would be arrested for mass murder. And there was only one person it could possibly benefit.

Joseph picked up his car phone, dialed. "I need to see him tomorrow. No, it cannot wait. Monsieur, I have never made a demand like this before. Either we see him tomorrow or something rather untoward happens. Yes. Yes, that would be fine. I've always been fond of gravel quarries."

• • •

The mayor of Paris stood in a quarry on the outer limits of the Boulevard Périphérique, twelve kilometres west of the Seine. His bodyguard remained at the car. A young woman with a clipboard stood behind the mayor, not speaking to him. The sun was in its natural position for April, once again hidden by blankets of white-grey cloud, and a wind was up. What remained of the mayor's hair stayed in place, slicked back with a concretizing solution. In the car, César begged Joseph to ask the mayor what extraordinary cream he used.

"I'm not asking that."

"Come on. Mine never stays in place. It can't be Brylcreem."

"No, César."

"Please."

"No."

"Damn it."

It was a Sunday, so the actual workers were at home or at church. Surrounded by piles of rock and sand, by tractors and transport trucks, in his suit and with his public posture, the mayor made him think of a prisoner of the Roman circus waiting to be devoured by lions. From across the street they watched him, and scanned the hiding places about him. There was no way the mayor could allow him to continue, knowing what he knew. This would be the end of one of them. Kruse had been less than careful and he would not make a similar mistake. He designed their security arrangement: Joseph had sixteen of his men and women, dressed for pretend industrial work, monitoring the quarry.

Everyone called in to report there were no snipers or clandestine service agents in the area. There was no one at all, unless they were hiding under the gravel. It made no sense. Kruse and Joseph got out of the car and walked across the street. The mayor pointed to his watch. He shouted into the wind.

"I have nine other appointments today. And why did we have to meet in person? There are secure lines."

Joseph did not speak until their hands met. "We have *reason to believe*, Monsieur le Maire, that very little is secure."

"What reason to believe?"

"We . . ." Kruse was bashful about his grammar in front of him. "I began working on a project the day we last saw one another."

The mayor had avoided eye contact with Kruse until now. "What project?"

"Khalil al-Faruqi. Réné Chatel. Henri Alibert."

"What about them?"

Kruse had not expected a plea of ignorance. "You asked me to—"

"I asked nothing." The mayor turned to Joseph. "What is he talking about?"

"Monsieur le Maire, our friend has been led by the republic to find the people who blew up Chez Sternbergh."

"You mean Khalil al-Faruqi?"

"It wasn't him," said Kruse.

"Who was it, then?" The mayor looked at Kruse, then at Joseph. "And what does it have to do with me?"

Kruse didn't answer the question and neither did Joseph.

"How is your apartment, Kruse?"

"It's a mess, Monsieur le Maire. A group of men and women from the CIA destroyed it."

"The CIA. Are you saying the CIA blew up Chez Sternbergh? Why?"

"I'm not saying that."

The mayor touched the knot of his tie, examined it. He asked his assistant, without looking at her, to order an immediate and thorough cleaning and furniture redesign of the apartment.

"At luncheon on that day, Monsieur Kruse, when you rushed at me with that look in your eye, I thought for a moment you had gone mad. I thought: my life is over. You shoved me out the door and onto the street and I hit my head with such terrible force. The sound of it, the curious *kak*. I wondered if you would keep coming, perhaps with a knife. I know your reputation, after all."

The keeper of his reputation, at least with the mayor, was Joseph.

"Then you ran back inside, as though I were nothing. I couldn't think. I didn't have time to do much else, even to stand, before the restaurant went up. That sound. Your ears must still be ringing with it, in the quiet. I know mine do."

Kruse watched him.

"I have many enemies. I have a few paid defenders, though it seems you're the only one who's any good at it. But until that day, sincerely, I never once imagined I was in real danger. Or at least until some appalling malediction strikes me, cancer of the pancreas." He looked across the street, away from Kruse. "That is to say, thank you. You had only a moment and you might have focused on yourself. Like my chief of security, for instance, whose resignation I accepted that same day. Do you know what he was doing, when he should have been standing at the door? Reading his newspaper in the car."

The mayor had no idea. Kruse felt as though he had eaten another ortolan laced with sleeping pills. His legs were hot and unsteady. "You didn't direct the DPSD to hire me?"

"They called my office that day. They wanted to know if I knew any freelance men. Men like you. So I phoned Joseph." The mayor extended a hand of help. "Are you all right?"

"Yes, Monsieur le Maire."

He turned to Joseph. "What's happened here? What's happened to his face?"

"Monsieur le Maire. There is much to explain, but someone is working against you in this. Against us both."

"How?"

Joseph looked at Kruse for a moment, and back at the mayor. "The DPSD, on the day of the explosion, sought your help. You sought mine. But—"

The mayor placed his hand gently on Kruse's shoulder, as though their roles had shifted. The mayor was the benevolent protector of these lost boys. "I plead ignorance. I certainly carry no love for Khalil al-Faruqi but I'm only the mayor of Paris. I lack those powers."

Kruse knew what Tzvi would say at a moment like this: *What the fuck are you people talking about?* Kruse didn't think he could say it with authority in French. So for a time he simply stared at them, one and then the other, hoping they would be undone by absurdity.

"Monsieur Kruse." The mayor was nearly whispering now, in the quarry. "Why did you want to speak to me today?"

"I'm here to find out why I was hired to murder your rivals."

"What rivals?"

"Yesterday, Monsieur le Maire, I thought Joseph had done this to me, that he had blown up Chez Sternbergh on your behalf. To get rid of Monsieur Cassin. You hired me to eliminate al-Faruqi, to cleanse the nation's palate and to lend you a veneer of mysterious strength. Then Réné Chatel. Then Henri Alibert. I assumed you made a pigeon of me."

The mayor did not interrupt him. After Kruse spoke, a dust devil moved through the quarry. The men and the woman with the clipboard covered their faces as the dust rose up.

"Kruse, I have been in this business since 1962."

"Yes."

"First as our prime minister's chief of staff. I was still a young man then, filled with passion. Passion inspires the good, clean work of destroying our political enemies. Not with violence, not ever, not in France. But with tact and strategy. Of course, this will not mean much to you. You live in a beautiful apartment—and I vow it will be beautiful again—and you receive a generous stipend because you are the victim of the *one instance* where my staff, my office, broke this rule. I will be president of the republic very soon. And as president I will be a friend to you. Why would I risk destroying everything to be rid of a few rivals? Men whom I have already defeated?"

Joseph walked a few steps toward a pile of gravel, looked away from them.

The mayor continued. "When I spoke at Pierre Cassin's funeral, every word I said was sincere. Was he an ambitious man? Did we want many of the same things? Was he, in this, my political ally or my enemy? This is irrelevant. My instinct would be to defeat him and reward him at once. And frankly, when he is ready, to make him my successor. I am no longer a young man."

Kruse had spent the night in one of Joseph's guest suites. The wound on his hip and worries about today, confronting the mayor at the gravel quarry, had kept him awake. Dreams with claws and howls came with the sleep he did manage; he had seen far too many dead people since the fourth of April. He could not imagine what was next. "I am sorry to have wasted your time, Monsieur le Maire."

"So many people waste my time but so few of them apologize for it." The mayor smiled. "Thank you, Kruse."

"But if I have seen this, surely others will too."

The mayor stopped smiling. "What?"

"If a detective were to unravel it all—"

"That I have hired you to do away with my rivals, ever so quietly. Yes. Have you spoken to anyone about this?"

"Only the woman from DPSD. My handler. Zoé Moquin."

"I have not heard of her."

Kruse led him a few steps away from the others: from Joseph, from anyone with a clipboard. "Monsieur le Maire, I don't know how careful you have been with me, if our relationship can be traced. Whoever organized this organized it carefully."

The mayor looked into the wind.

From behind him, the woman with the clipboard waved. "The apartment will be back in shape by early this evening, Monsieur Kruse." She handed him her card. "If there is any trouble, please call."

On their way back to the Mercedes, Joseph put his hand on Kruse's back. "You see?"

Kruse was beginning to see.

FIFTEEN

Rue des Francs-Bourgeois

THE SMELL OF THE EXPLOSION LINGERED ABOUT CHEZ STERNBERGH, behind paint and freshly cut wood. Men and women in coveralls and masks were removing the final charred guts of the restaurant. Others were on the street and in the little plaza, preparing new window frames and refinishing the exterior. The bright blue awning was already up, protecting the new paint from the light rain. A short strip of police line was tangled in the wet hedges on the corner.

Kruse called the city museum of Paris, the Carnavalet, from a payphone across the street. Annette worked every second Sunday. He asked if she was in. The receptionist said yes and asked him to hold. He hung up.

When he arrived at the museum ten minutes later, soaking wet, Annette was standing in the courtyard with a black umbrella. "You should get one of these."

"I've had four since moving to Paris. I keep forgetting them in cafés."

"What happened to you? Your face . . ."

"I'd like to tell you."

Annette sighed and rolled her eyes. "But of course you can't. What do you want?"

"Help."

"A funny thing happened yesterday evening, Christophe. The buzzer rang at the apartment. Étienne had come with dinner. He answered but no one responded. I looked out the window. Who do you think I saw slouching up Rue Valadon?"

"Can we go for a walk?"

"I'm at work."

"You can say it's an emergency. It is an emergency. Or perhaps you're feeling ill. Please."

Annette took two steps closer to him. The skepticism she nearly always carried when they spoke melted into something else. Without a word she turned and folded her umbrella and walked back into the museum. Kruse waited in the rain. Five minutes later she returned and they walked out of the quiet courtyard together, turned left on Rue des Francs-Bourgeois. She shifted her umbrella so it would cover him as well. Kruse moved her hand back in place. "Don't imperil your left side. I'm already wet."

"Start talking."

It was only a few blocks, along charming boutiques, to Place des Vosges. But it was far enough to tell her things she should not know, beginning with the day of the explosion on Rue des Rosiers, the mayor and Joseph, Tzvi, Pierre Cassin and the terrorist, the communist, the ultra-right-wing industrialist, the CIA. By the time they reached the plaza, she had gone pale.

"Is that what you were, before we met? An assassin?"

"No."

"Then why did they think you *were*?"

"The mayor owns me. They own us. I will be anything he wants. They asked Joseph to say something, something that had seemed benign to him, that your life, your life with Anouk, your protection, your safety, depended on me. On what I might do for them."

"Them. I thought *they* were the mayor and Joseph."

"Me too."

Annette pulled him out of the rain, under the arcade. A man sat in a well-lit art gallery, in a baby blue suit, reading a newspaper. Kruse had been sleeping so poorly since this began, since before it began, he was beginning to feel paranoid. Everyone was an agent of potential doom.

"So who are *they*?"

"The DPSD."

"The Ministry of Defence threatened you again? Us?"

"Not exactly." He did not want to say it because it didn't make sense. "An agency of the ministry."

"Why would they not have one of their own agents do all of this ugly work, if it served some national security purpose? Why you?"

Kruse was midway through explaining why and stopped. The agency had wanted some distance. If he died, they had never heard of him. But of the three assassinations, it only made sense for Khalil al-Faruqi. If he had been caught by the police in Luxembourg Gardens or after the explosion in Nancy he would have told the truth as he saw it. He had been hired by the mayor of Paris. "I don't know."

At the end of the arcade, in front of one of the finest restaurants in the city, two men leaned on a pillar smoking. Annette told them she needed a ride to the National Library. The shorter of the two, who carried a large belly, leaned back and said he was on his break. It was one of those moments Kruse would have liked to share with Evelyn or with Tzvi, maybe even with Joseph: this conversation would never happen in Canada. A taxi driver does not take breaks. The look on the man's face was of triumph.

Today, it was something more than a sociological observation. Kruse slapped the cigarette out of his hand. "Get in the car and take us to the library."

The taxi driver's friend laughed nervously and backed away. For a moment it seemed the driver would lift his hands to fight, but only for a moment. He shrunk into obedience and opened the back door. "Of course, Monsieur. Madame."

Annette stared at Kruse in the back seat as the driver turned north on Rue de Turenne. The rain had stopped. For a moment the clouds broke and the day turned bright. Most of the shops were open, couples and families were out. In the Marais, Saturdays and Mondays were more likely days off than Sundays. They passed an old stone church that shone wet in the light. He made a promise to himself that if he survived this he would try to notice more of the beauty.

Every time the driver turned, they leaned in to one another. He tried to close himself to the scent and the heat of her, the slight damp of her clothes and her skin. What had she expected him to do when he rang her buzzer and Étienne answered?

"I have two theories." He held on to his door handle with both hands to avoid sliding into her.

"What's the first?"

"There is a group of wealthy men and women who don't want Maastricht."

"The treaty?"

"Henri Alibert was one of its leaders. I have a feeling they killed him rather than have it exposed."

"They're against European integration? So you mean the currency, open borders . . ."

"Globalization in general. Men like Alibert have benefited monumentally from trade restrictions."

"We can start there, Christophe. But what does it have to do with the Ministry of Defence?"

"Maybe Alibert's group has leaders inside the ministry."

"What group?"

Kruse told Annette what he had learned from the professor in Nancy.

She was quiet for the rest of the trip. The driver kept an eye on them through the rear-view mirror. Kruse paid him and they entered the courtyard of the library, his library. At the statue of Sartre Annette reached out for his arm. She was about to speak but said nothing. She walked to the door.

"Annette. What?"

"Let me show you."

• • •

His librarian wore an off-white dress with a flower in her hair. She was unusually polite and did not allow him any of his usual perks. Today she was far too busy to help, she said, though she appeared only to stand behind the circulation desk watching Annette with her arms crossed and her head tilted to the left. From time to time she twirled her wedding ring.

In Nancy, Kruse had already researched Henri Alibert. Mysterious and menacing things had happened to other supporters of Maastricht. Alibert may have been part of a secret group with members across Western Europe, but secret groups don't send out press releases. What was not so secret about Alibert: he supported, financially and other-wise, the Front National and a number of smaller parties and groups that made the Front National look moderate and philosophical. Once they had amassed everything, it did not take long for Annette to place a hand on his arm: "I don't buy it, Christophe."

There had been so few sunny days, but new freckles had already appeared on her nose and under her brown eyes. Her black hair was longer than it had been when they had first met. She carried herself with quiet confidence. Kruse could no longer imagine her as the cowed and miserable copy editor he had met at *Le Monde*, ashamed of her own ambitions.

He had wanted her to buy it. "Tell me why."

"Alibert was a racist. He encouraged other racists. He abused three wives. He ran his family empire into near bankruptcy. We know all this about him. Why? Like most of us, he lacked discipline. How could a man like this lead a secret conspiracy? He was rich, yes, but it was all inherited. Henri Alibert was a buffoon."

"Then why was he killed?"

"I don't know him like you do, but if we made a list of everyone he has hurt, over the years . . ."

"There wouldn't be enough paper."

"I'm sorry, Christophe."

Kruse stood up and walked to a wall of periodicals. One of the magazines had a photograph of the mayor of Paris on the glossy cover, his eyes sparkling. He had tremendous poise. Even after the explosion at Chez Sternbergh he had carried himself royally. He had only once seen a slump in the mayor's shoulders: when he was forced to admit that his chief of staff had orchestrated the ruin of Kruse's family.

"I haven't been paid."

"What?"

"For the ghastly work they forced me to do."

"Who are *they* again?"

"The agency. The DPSD."

"Who are your contacts there?"

"Zoé Moquin."

"One person? You've met others in the agency?"

Kruse sat back down.

"Tell me about her."

Twenty minutes later all of the material on Henri Alibert, Euroskeptics, far-right ultranationalist groups, and unfortunate politicians was in the cart. The librarian arrived with a huff and pushed it away. They had split a list of material on Zoé and Catherine Moquin in half.

Annette made notes. There were several photographs of Catherine with designers and models. Zoé was in only one of them, in an article from *Le Parisien*.

"Your Zoé is very beautiful."

Kruse pretended to read when Annette looked over at him.

"I didn't know intelligence agents could be so elegant. Don't they work in dusty, windowless basements surrounded by soda and potato chips?"

"The American ones, maybe."

She continued to watch him. "How old would she be? Zoé?"

"Our age. Perhaps thirty-five, forty."

"Where did you meet her?"

"At Joseph's place."

"You and Joseph and the agent." Annette leaned back in her chair. "Have you seen her since?"

"Yes."

"Many times? Always with Joseph?"

"Alone."

"You and Zoé, alone."

"In public, usually."

"Sometimes it was not in public? Where was it that time?"

Kruse turned to her finally. "Her apartment."

"An intelligence agent invited you into her apartment?"

"Not exactly."

"Are you . . . having a relationship with her?"

"No."

"That was unconvincing."

"Not really."

Now Annette crossed *her* arms. "I don't understand."

"Her organization hired Tzvi and me to . . ." He had trouble finding the words. "To find out who had blown up Chez Sternbergh and do something about it. We were led, by someone, to *do something* about Khalil al-Faruqi. Then, when it seemed he had not done it, the investigation continued."

"You said you agreed to this assignment because Joseph hinted Anouk and I would be in danger if you refused. But Joseph was working for this woman, responding to her demands. So what you meant to say is Zoé Moquin, your sort-of-girlfriend, hinted we would be in danger."

"Yes."

He felt a familiar anxiety. Like Annette, Evelyn was given to intellectual pursuit. When she had caught him in something she did not like, a secret that left a trace of betrayal, Evelyn would stalk and trap him at the dinner table or in bed, take him apart, leave him there.

"Have you made love to her? This woman who means us harm?"

"No."

Annette nodded. "You've kissed?"

"Yes."

Annette returned to the newspapers and magazines. So did Kruse. His hands were cold. He wanted to tell her what he knew about Étienne, that her boyfriend carried on a number of affairs.

"I regret . . . not being with you, when I had the chance."

Annette did not look away from her papers.

"I don't like it, that you're with Étienne. I want . . ." He decided not to say what he wanted. "I could tell you things."

Though she heard him, Annette did not register it with anything more than a delicate nod. She tucked her hair behind the ear closest to him, her left ear. Though she was now rich, in a relationship with a man who was beyond rich, Annette still wore a cheap brass earring. She licked her lips, prepared to speak, but it was not for some time that she said it. "We're in a fine fix, aren't we?"

There was nothing about Zoé in anything he had read. Catherine popped up every fashion season in the last five years, in stories and less often in photographs: at launches and parties and an industry showcase or two, in Paris and in Milan and beyond. In every photo she wore peculiar yet sophisticated, sexy dresses. She was in the French and American editions of *Vogue* several times. Apparently, it was customary for female fashion designers to dress with restraint, to leave the flamboyance for the models and the runway. Catherine was an exception, and the fashion journalists seemed to like that about her, especially the Americans. They nearly always mentioned she would soon be the creative head of a large house, if not her own. None of the stories mentioned the Flying Tailor, her line-to-be. After a while, Kruse began to skim the articles. They revealed nothing important and neither did the photographs.

His chair, like all the chairs in the Salle Ovale, drained the blood queerly from his legs. He stood up, walked in a circle, and at the limit of it the librarian was upon him. "Can I help you with anything, Monsieur?"

"No, Madame, but thank you kindly for the offer."

"Is this your girlfriend?"

"I'm afraid not. My friend."

Her eyes brightened. "A fellow investigator."

"She was a journalist for much of her career. She knows what to look for."

"And what are you looking for today?"

"I'm not sure."

"Do let me know, Monsieur." The librarian winked and returned to the circulation desk. She walked slowly, with careful posture. She knew he watched.

Kruse returned to Annette and stood over her. "I don't think there's anything here. At least there was nothing in my pile."

"Fascinating woman. The obituaries are vague. Cancer?"

"Zoé didn't say."

Without another word, Annette stood up and walked to the circulation desk. She spoke to the librarian, who sighed and led her to a computer. Kruse continued to skim his material. The second-last newspaper article was not about Catherine. He didn't see, immediately, any mention of Zoé. The headline was: *Ramadier accusé d'être au coeur de la corruption.*

The article, dated June 6, 1983, was about a candidate in the legislative elections named Christiane Ramadier. She had been accused of taking a bribe from a property developer. Réné Chatel, her Communist Party competitor, who held the seat, was quoted extensively in the article. "It is only an accusation, of course. We shall see what happens in court. But I would say it is an accurate reflection of Madame Ramadier's values, her social circle. If these are the people one travels with and fights for, how can we trust her to stand up for us—regular people—in the capital?"

Ramadier did not represent herself in the article. The only quotation was from her twenty-two-year-old executive assistant, *Zoé Moquin*. "We're flabbergasted," she told the reporter. "Madame Ramadier was obviously set up. The charge is ridiculous, based on a fabrication by her political enemies. She looks forward to defending herself."

The next article was a follow-up, after the election. Réné Chatel had defeated the incumbent Christiane Ramadier, who had fallen into scandal. There was no comment from her executive assistant.

Kruse put the articles aside and flipped through the rest of his material. Nothing. There were another four newspapers on Annette's desk. On top, an account of Catherine Moquin's triumphant show in New York. Next, a copy of *L'Est Républicain*—the regional paper from Nancy. It was a photograph, from a fundraiser at the Muséum-Aquarium, of Catherine Moquin arm in arm with Pierre Cassin. The mayor of Nancy's hand was up, as though to stop the photographer from pressing the button.

Annette leaned over him. "You look pale. Are you all right, Christophe?"

"Fine. Yes, I'm fine."

"You found something?"

"We have to look at bit deeper into Zoé's past."

"There are bulletin boards on the Internet—newsgroups. There's a newsgroup for everything. Some are absolutely ghastly. One of them is a gathering place for suicide obsessives. All I had to do was search her name."

"What did you learn?"

Annette didn't say it right away, as though she wanted to suck the juice out of it first. "Catherine Moquin jumped off the Eiffel Tower."

SIXTEEN

Avenue Bosquet

THE RAIN HAD STOPPED AND THE SUN HAD COME OUT. WITH IT:
genuine heat, a hint of hope, of summer. Kruse carried her jacket and
they walked along the Tuileries, through Place de la Concorde. It was not
pleasant, what he had learned, but he could slow the engine of paranoia.
No one would shoot at them, run them down with a Citroën, hide on
the bridge and toss them into the Seine. He allowed himself to pretend
they were walking for the sake of walking on a pretty afternoon.

"It would be nice if Anouk were with us."

Annette shook her head. "You do know, Christophe, that Frenchmen
aren't supposed to say things like that. Even if they believe it. Even if
their hearts are bursting. They do not want to appear weak. You can say
it to me, of course, but if you are courting a Frenchwoman you should
beware. Loving children the way you do—it has a maternal aspect."

"Not paternal?"

"At its foundation, *paternal* in this country is really just sperm and
money."

"That's unfair."

"Perhaps I've been blessed with a certain kind of man in my life: a father who ran off with a woman from Bangkok and a husband who took up with a teenage ballerina. Anouk's father, he doesn't even call."

"And now? What about the current man in your life?"

They entered the giant sidewalk of Pont de la Concorde. Dancing rollerbladers grooved to techno music from a silver stereo plugged into a diesel generator. A crowd watched them, clapped along. Annette pretended she didn't hear his final question. She ignored the performers. While Kruse did not worry about appearing weak before her, or maternal, he did not want to seem heartbroken and humiliated. In his pocket was a list of people he had helped destroy on the left column. On the right, Zoé's reason for having them destroyed.

His own name was the imaginary final entry at the bottom.

For years he had wondered why Evelyn, an elegant and beautiful and intelligent woman, would have anything to do with him. The answer he feared—youthful indiscretion—was probably correct. In the beginning, when she was still a graduate student, he would have seemed a peculiar mystery. She had liked his muscles and the simple way he saw the world, divided into only a few sorts of people. Everything at the university was complicated. Kruse was not. He was supportive, even—the word did not insult him—*maternal* when she was working long hours on her PhD and teaching and maintaining a relationship with her parents. If he was in Toronto Kruse would cook her dinner, clean the house, prepare take-away lunches for her, run errands. When Lily was born he became the primary parent. Of course, there was little left of mystery about him. *Peculiar* and *refreshingly simple* were no longer attractive. All that remained were muscles and take-away lunches. The world she entered, as a professor, was no place for him. Her efforts to turn him into a man of culture were, she occasionally admitted, clownish. He had read about Evelyn's affair with Jean-François de Musset in the newspaper—not in her eyes. Jean-François would not have been the first.

Zoé Moquin was not an adventurous graduate student seeking the opposite of the men she knew in school. She knew exactly who he was; she had hired him. Kruse had far more scars on his face and hands than in the mid-1980s, when Evelyn had met him. He still couldn't carry on a conversation about Stravinsky or David Mamet or Virginia Woolf. Zoé had kissed him despite all of that, and had hinted that she wanted more. This had been a glow inside Kruse since he had left her strange apartment: that he might see her and touch her again.

He felt a fool.

West of the National Assembly, along the Quai d'Orsay, the sun warmed a wet bush of blooming lilac and Annette stopped to smell them. She leaned for a moment against the fence, closed her eyes. "I'm a kid again."

"How old?"

"Nine, maybe. Just old enough to go exploring on my own."

Annette had wanted to take the story of Zoé Moquin to her former editors at Le Monde, pitch it as an exposé for the weekend magazine. With the connections to America, through the rogue CIA group, it would surely spread around the world. All she needed was the briefcase Kruse had forgotten in the apartment on Avenue Montaigne. The trouble was: the mayor and Joseph. There was no easy way to leave them out of it. Annette thought of herself as a journalist, but she also understood how her deal with the mayor had improved her daughter's life and prospects: an apartment in the seventh arrondissement, a space in the city's best private school, a group of peers that would—by 2020—run the country.

Hundreds of Parisians were out on the fields and grasses before Les Invalides, playing soccer and throwing Frisbees, laying out picnics, reading paperbacks, drinking wine out of plastic glasses. Annette talked herself through the story as Kruse imagined himself out here with a simple goal: have fun with his family. His daughter. Her daughter. Anouk was with her au pair, a student from Ho Chi Minh City. At the apartment on Rue Valadon, Kruse asked if he could come up and see her, and Annette looked at him with something like pity.

"I want to be careful."

"What do you mean?"

"She's a little girl. It's easy to confuse her. She has a father in Bordeaux. I'm with Étienne. She prefers you, of course, but *what are you to her?* Is it fair to Étienne, or even to Anouk?"

"You don't need an au pair, Annette. I'd do it for free. It won't confuse Anouk if I have a role that makes sense in her life. Babysitter is enough for me. I'll feed her whatever you like, continue her English lessons, take her on trips, teach her—"

"I don't think so, Christophe."

Annette kissed him on each cheek and gently pushed him away, down the street and toward the sun setting on Rue du Champ de Mars. When he reached the end of Valadon, Kruse turned to see if she was watching him. She was not.

Children shouted from open windows, from the balconies and court-yards, from the park in the distance, from the cafés and bistros on both sides of Avenue Bosquet. On the other side of the ocean, Tzvi was learning how to live with one arm. Men and women had died in Spain, in Luxembourg Gardens, in Nancy. But it was finished now. He hoped, as he had hoped in December, that the simple noisy pleasures of life in the seventh arrondissement could restart for him. Maybe, one of these days, Annette would see Étienne was as much a rascal as her father and her husband had been. He and Annette and Anouk could join these families at sidewalk cafés and worry, simply and gloriously, about money and stomach aches and holiday destinations and office politics and pets and public art.

Or he could do the right thing: walk into the travel shop and buy that ticket to Toronto, where he belonged.

Kruse opened the heavy door off the sidewalk, and the smell of cologne in the stairwell was a stiff jab to the forehead. But it came with paint. As he walked up the stairs, three men in white overalls walked down, carrying buckets and toolboxes. After them, a woman on a cellular phone. She said, into it, "Let me call you back, my little cabbage." And she shouted down, over the men, waving: "Monsieur Kruse. Christophe! What luck, that you've arrived just now. Please, come up."

It was a narrow stairwell but he was able to negotiate past the three men. The woman, who spoke with a Québécois accent, referred to him as *tu*—not *vous*; in Montreal fashion they were immediate friends. She took his hand and pulled him up the stairs. Two more men with paintbrushes and clear plastic tarps, their overalls splattered, waited silently for them. The woman, who introduced herself as Julie, asked him to be sure he thank his generous patron on her behalf. Imagine: a girl from Ville d'Anjou designing for the mayor of Paris. At his door she asked him to wait a moment, not to look yet. She walked into the apartment and closed the door behind her. Kruse could hear her high heels clicking on the parquet.

"Entrez!"

She had put in his Yo-Yo Ma disc, so *Carnival of the Animals* played as he entered—the one about the swan. The apartment smelled as the stairwell had smelled, of cologne and paint, but less powerfully. The walls were white. In his sunken salon the couch and chairs, the tables, the lamps were new.

"I was thinking for you, a bit of an enigma, a man who knows winter, some Nordic cool."

The kitchen was the same, but with new paint and a new toaster and an espresso machine. The dining room table, as well as he could remember, had not been ruined but she had moved in a new one— apparently, Nordic cool. She explained the goons had ripped the telephone cord from his wall but that France Télécom had reinstated it an hour ago. The art on the walls was entirely different. Nothing came from before the nineteenth century. His own bedroom was all white. Lily's bedroom, or Anouk's, the little girl bedroom, was far too pink and princessy for what he had imagined them liking, but there was a small table with an elaborate porcelain tea set and a much grander library of classic children's literature. Both bathrooms were immaculate. Julie had even replaced his broken bottle of cologne, which he would remove from the apartment at his earliest opportunity.

Afterwards she stood in the hall, her little hands clasped at the thin leather belt that cinched her dress around the waist. She wore diamond rings so large and fingernails so long he did not see how she could peel an orange.

"Thank you. It's beautiful."

"I know it smells, Christophe. Let's just open the windows."

"Oh that's okay. I can do it."

"Are you sure?"

"I'll tell Monsieur le Maire, next time I speak to him, that you did a lovely job."

"Would you? My God, Christophe. My God!"

He wanted to be alone so he looked away from her, pretended to evaluate the art in the hall. It was an abstract blob. Before he went to bed tonight, he would take it down. When she started to tell him about the artist he walked away, back toward the door. She followed him and, in the foyer, had no choice but to give him two more kisses.

"I'll be back to check on you, Christophe."

"I am blessed."

Julie winked and walked out, and he could hear her through the door ordering the last of the men to carry the ladder *doucement, doucement,* down the stairs. She called someone a monster. Kruse was pleased to have the smelly apartment to himself. There was a set of French doors, looking west. He opened them and every other window in the apartment, found his stack of business cards, and dialed the numbers of his two contacts at the Direction de la Protection et de la Sécurité de la Défense, Madame Lareau and Monsieur Meunier. The last time he had seen them was in Beaujolais. He had hidden from them in a vat of white wine.

Neither of them answered. It was France and it was after five on an unusually warm and sunny spring Sunday. He stood on his balcony, to breathe in unpolluted air. There were two hotels on Rue du Champ de Mars. He would leave these doors and all the windows open for three days, and pretend to be a tourist.

The knock on his door came with a voice: Julie again, surely. He did not hurry to unlock it. On his way he scanned the dining room, kitchen, and salon for what she may have forgotten: her address book, cellular phone, a few more giant rings. He opened it to Zoé Moquin, who performed her best rendition of a smile. Her matching shoes snaked up nearly all the way to her knee. On each side of her there was a briefcase.

"Christophe. I'm sorry to just *show up* like this. I had tried to leave a message on your telephone. I thought I would hear from you after—"

"I ran into some trouble after I left your apartment last night."

She reached up to his face. "More wounds."

"They're noticeable?"

"Does it have anything to do with our work together?" Her green dress was high in the front and low in the back, with sequins along the top—where her bra would be. There must have been a word for that part but he could not ask her. The straps were thin. It was, he imagined, her sister's interpretation of a spring dress.

"Can I take those?"

"Of course. They're yours. One you forgot in my apartment. The other is your fee. Would you like to count it?"

"I don't have to count it. Thank you."

"No, thank you, and Monsieur Meisels. I know money is no consolation for what he has lost, but . . . What, Christophe?"

"Would you like something to drink? I don't know if I have anything as nice as that wine you served me."

"Perhaps something cold?"

"Sorry for the smell. A cologne bottle broke. Then the cleaners . . ."

Kruse opened the refrigerator. It was clean, with the less complicated scent of a swimming pool, and empty but for a bottle of Krug Grand Cuvée. Julie was a thoughtful woman. He pulled it out.

"Well." Zoé put her hands together, rubbed them. "That's not so bad, is it?"

The plan he had worked out with Annette was simple enough: he would phone the DPSD, tell them what he and Annette had learned about Zoé, and send them off to discover the rest. He had briefly fallen in love with the idea of confronting her at her offices, of punishing her. While every one of his clients had *used him* to do what they could not imagine doing themselves, none had been so deceitful, so murderous. Certainly, none had kissed him. Why had she done that? Now that she was in his apartment, he was not at all sure what he ought to do.

He pulled two champagne glasses down, wiped them with a cloth, and opened the bottle with a pop. Wind blew into his apartment and ruffled her dress, layered like a green cake. She wore eye makeup and a ring on her left thumb.

"Your driver is downstairs?"

"I released him, for now. I am to call when I'm finished here."

"How did you know I was home?"

Zoé tilted her head. "You figured me out. My driver and I were parked across the street, watching. When we saw you arrive . . ."

"You waited until I was alone."

"Yes, Christophe."

"Why?"

"I'm here to deliver three million dollars. I wasn't terribly interested in speaking to your interior designer. Quite a flamboyant woman."

Kruse poured the glasses. On his balcony there were two chairs and a small but heavy table, designed to mimic Parisian café furniture. Zoé followed him outside and he handed her a glass. She straightened her posture. "To the families who lost so much on April fourth, in Chez Sternbergh."

"To the . . ." He took a breath of the fresh air, cool now as the sun hinted at setting on the other side of the tower. "To the families."

He could not tell the difference between Krug Grand Cuvée and the cheap Vouvray Pétillant they served at Café du Marché. They sat, first Zoé and then Kruse, and for nearly half a minute they looked out over the neighbourhood. The upper half of the Eiffel Tower was visible, the Paris version of a mountain or a sea view.

"Who threw the grenades, Zoé?"

"Pardon me?"

"The grenades, in Chez Sternbergh. Who threw them?"

"That was your job, to figure it out. It's what we paid you to do. Khalil al-Faruqi's men, officially. But perhaps the new-Nazis working for Henri Alibert. I'm not sure, in the end, if Réné Chatel was capable of it. I know you looked at the mayor himself, and there's still a chance—"

"Pierre Cassin said he would marry your sister, didn't he? He would divorce his wife and marry her."

She would not look at him. When she did respond, there wasn't much energy in it. "I don't know what you're talking about."

"Please."

Zoé took a deep breath and a longer than elegant drink of champagne. "I know there is nothing peculiar about a politician having a mistress. It would be bigger news—would it not?—if a French politician did not have a lover. Catherine was not his first girlfriend. She knew the rules. Pierre was devoted to his wife and family. I warned her. She did seem prepared."

"But . . ."

"She was pregnant."

"Couldn't you have destroyed him without . . . *destroying him*? And all those other people? Madame Sternbergh herself. If Cassin hadn't jumped on the grenades, so many more would have—"

"I can imagine the calculation in his disgusting mind: I'm going to die anyway so why not die a hero?"

"Zoé . . ."

"I did try. But you can't stop someone from falling in love." She continued to look out over the city, not at him, as she spoke. "This is what made Catherine Catherine. She committed fully to an enterprise—a dress, a job, a holiday, a love affair. When Pierre told her he was unhappy *but committed* in his marriage, she interpreted it as an opening. She would save him, change his life. When she discovered she was pregnant, Catherine phoned me. She was ecstatic."

Her glass was empty so Kruse went back into the kitchen for the bottle. Its dark neck was cold and sweating in the heat. Soft music continued to play. With every step it felt as though the stitches on his hip would open. The window in his kitchen, at this hour, was as reflective as a mirror. Since the night in Clichy-sous-Bois, when the young militant shot him in the face, he had tried to avoid looking at himself. He wondered how many of history's grand conspiracies and tragedies were really about an affair of the heart that had turned.

Kruse opened the heavier of the two briefcases. It was filled with brass bars wrapped in white facecloths. He carried the bottle of champagne to the terrace.

Zoé sat with stiff posture, her left leg crossed over her right. She did not appear nervous.

"I cannot call him a coward. No coward jumps on a grenade, even if it is for glory. But Cassin cussed and hung up the phone when my sister told him about the pregnancy and he refused to speak to her again. The secretary, who knew her, who had helped plan their liaisons, suddenly pretended she had never heard of Catherine. Her work suffered. She closed herself up. While I despised him and the situation, I agreed with him in one sense. The only thing to do was to seek an abortion and forget about him. But that was not Catherine. One morning she took the train to Nancy, to see Cassin."

"She went to his office."

"Imagine her in there alone, her steps echoing in that great hall.

While she had learned to take risks, she had rarely been humiliated. She had never been ignored. You will have seen photos of her, in your research."

"Yes."

"I wear her clothes but poorly. She was an abnormally beautiful woman. Her eyes were a translucent blue. When we were young it was not easy to be her sister. We would enter a room together and everyone would turn to her. It was fine training for my eventual career, to learn to be content with invisibility. On the day she travelled to Nancy, to meet Pierre Cassin without an appointment, Catherine wore her loveliest dress. It was the one that made her reputation in New York. Pierre walked past, with Monsieur Lévy, to the car waiting for them out front. For a moment his eyes rested on her and without a flinch he turned away. This lovely, talented, sensitive, smart, mysterious girl had become nothing to him. And that, I imagine, is how she felt. Like nothing. This is how Pierre Cassin murdered my sister."

"That was the day she jumped?"

"Catherine did not phone me or come see me. She didn't leave a note. We had become so close, after our parents died, that even now it seems unimaginable. If she poked her finger with a sewing needle or broke a heel she would phone me. That day she took a taxi to the airport north of Nancy, bought a fantastically expensive one-way trip to Orly on Air Corsica, and hired a limousine to the Eiffel Tower. It was dusk when she did it, on a wet and windy day. There weren't thousands of tourists to witness her . . . shame."

"I understand vengeance, Zoé. When my daughter was killed—"

"There is a point when you become nothing and your mission, your only mission, is justice."

"But each of those families who lost someone in Chez Sternbergh, don't they also deserve justice? Madame Sternbergh's children will want justice."

"I gave it to them. Or you did. Khalil al-Faruqi, a mass murderer, a career killer of Jews, died so they might all sleep tonight. Thank you, Christophe."

When Kruse and Annette widened their search of the name Moquin, and went back in time, they discovered Zoé and Catherine were not the only children in the family. The oldest sibling was their brother Lucas, who had died on December 8, 1988, in a Douglas DC-7. He was an economist completing a study of the Western Sahara for the U.S. Agency for International Development. The small airplane, deployed to spray insecticide for locusts, was shot down over the Moroccan border by a group called the Polisario Front. Leaders of the Polisario Front released a statement apologizing for the accident. They had thought it was full of Moroccan military. The American magazine *Atlantic Monthly* had published a long story about the crash. In 1988, the Polisario Front was a military client of Khalil al-Faruqi.

Leaders of the movement blamed the incident entirely on al-Faruqi.

In the western sky and in the air, there were hints that the interlude of summer would be brief. A gust of wind knocked Kruse's flute off the table; he caught the glass but lost the champagne. Behind him, there was noise in the apartment. New things fell from new furniture.

"Your brother . . ."

"Was a saint. He was better than all of us."

"But it was a mistake."

"It's never a mistake to shoot down an airplane."

Her top lip rose in a new way, above her teeth as she spoke, and seemed to quiver. Kruse had not noticed it before but she wore a great deal of foundation under her eyes. Her hands shook. His apartment no longer felt like his. It felt haunted by strange men and women, by designers and workmen and spies, by the dead. Now that Zoé was with him he didn't know what to do with her. He wanted to phone Annette, for advice. But then Étienne would answer, smugly. *Yes? Can I help you?*

"Are you all right, Zoé?"

"I did not expect to be interrogated when I entered your home." She turned to him, for the first time since they sat, and placed a hand on his chest. "Let's go back to when you didn't know what you know. It wasn't me. It was . . . invisible forces."

"If I can discover this, anyone can."

She whispered. "No one else is looking."

"Henri Alibert—"

"Every gendarme, every lawyer, every journalist in Nancy will be pleased, Christophe. Besides, you didn't find any connection between Monsieur Alibert and me."

"The others, yes."

"All *solved* crimes."

"But not Alibert. Unless it was just his odiousness in general."

"My parents were middle-class people. My father worked for the government, and my mother, when we children reached a certain age, ran a candy shop. But my father did have ambitions. He had saved a percentage of his salary, as a retirement fund, and in 1979 he bought a plot of land outside Paris. His plan was to find a partner and develop the land."

"He found a partner."

"Alibert's lawyers put together a byzantine contract for him to sign. Now, I will admit my father did not have to sign it. He might have taken it with him, for his own lawyer to inspect. But they had trapped him in a large conference room with a pen and this notion that a clock was ticking. But it wasn't a partnership agreement."

"He agreed to sell."

"At Alibert's price. This sale was executed automatically two years later, when they broke ground on the land. So instead of my parents owning one-third of a residential and business development south of Paris, they soon owned nothing but a bit of cash. My father was entirely humiliated, of course, and it was too late for his own lawyer to do much of anything. It would have cost him the entire amount to seek retribution, and Alibert had been clever. All my father could do, really, was claim ignorance and naivety. He was too proud for that. My sister had inherited her capacity for obsession from him. He mourned that day, that deal, the way other people—you, perhaps—mourn a lost child. He died two years later. Officially, it was a heart attack."

"So when you decided to go after Cassin, you thought . . . why not make a list?"

"It's a good list."

"Why me?"

"I don't understand."

"You decided to destroy some people. Why the Office of the Mayor?"

"There was a special file on you, Christophe, after what had happened last fall. You and your company, your business partner from Mossad. I knew the way to find you was through the mayor and his gangsters."

"Who called Tzvi?"

"Your Joseph. I told him he could negotiate up to four million."

"We left a million on the table." He looked away from her. "How did you convince Joseph to help?"

"Anything for his boss. His boss wanted to catch the killer. They think highly of you."

"Why pretend to like me?"

"I wasn't pretending, Christophe. Please, no matter what happens now, you must believe that."

"What happens now?"

"It's up to you, I think. You had planned something, I imagine, before I arrived today."

"Yes."

"And what was that?"

"I was going to your superiors at the agency."

She laughed. "My superiors have not likely heard of me. I'm an analyst, not a spook. And there's no need, Christophe. You have money you didn't have before. The world is rid of four odious men."

"And others who happened to be in the same room as them."

"I studied war craft in university. What I learned is we cannot allow ourselves to be undone by sentimental feelings. Was every citizen of Dresden, in February 1945, a Nazi? Every citizen of Hiroshima a kamikaze? No, but we must force ourselves to include those deaths in the larger project. It ended the war."

"It's not the same thing."

"I ended the war. I know the world is safer today than it was on the third of April."

"You're a murderer, Zoé. And thanks to you I am a murderer too."

"Many great men and women were murderers, by some calculation. I do hope, Christophe, you can accept my apology and keep our secret a secret. You haven't told anyone else. Have you?"

His long walk home from the library with Annette: of course she had watched. Zoé reached for his hand. "Our kiss . . . it's all I've been able to think about." Her hand was cool and moist, from the wine. He reached with his index finger for her wrist and felt her pulse. Her heart was beating quickly. When they had kissed in her apartment she had been calm. "We can forget all of this, address ourselves to the future. The war is over."

"Zoé. I opened the briefcase."

She sighed. "May I have some more champagne?"

Again over the soft horns and violins he heard something behind him, from within the apartment. One of his ghosts. The wind had calmed. He finished pouring her glass and stood up, to investigate. "Excuse me."

"Of course," she said, and adjusted her position to let him get around her. She reached into her purse and he thought, first, of lipstick or a small makeup kit. By the time he saw what she had pulled out it was too late. He moved quickly enough that she missed his stomach, where she had aimed. But she did plunge the knife deeply into the top of his left leg. She was quick and strong. He put his hand over the wound and she cut his wrist. Kruse backed into the stone rail. There, next to the gauzy curtain that covered the door to his balcony, stood the answer to his first question. He recognized her driver. Without his hat, Kruse saw it: this was the young man who had thrown two grenades into Chez Sternbergh. He pointed a handgun.

The driver helped Zoé around her chair and into the apartment. A splash of Kruse's blood was on her hand and arm, on the sleeve of her dress. She looked down at it and tsked. "Do you have any soda water?"

The blood ran down his leg and into his shoe. It dripped from his fingers. It would pool on the soft stone pad of his balcony. "Try the champagne."

"It's ruined."

There was plenty of blood but she had not hit a major artery. He leaned on the rail, to preserve his strength.

Zoé tossed her champagne flute back into the apartment. It crashed on the parquet floor. She fished around in her purse and pulled out a pair of gloves and an envelope of photographs. "Christophe in Chez Sternbergh." She pulled out a picture. It was too far away for him to see. "Christophe in Luxembourg Gardens, on Rue des Brice."

"You were there that night, in Nancy."

Zoé looked at her driver, back at Kruse. "I had the camera and Franck had the bomb. The things I've been able to find in the agency warehouse! I'm sorry. Let me introduce you two. Christophe Kruse, this is my younger brother, Franck."

"Bonjour, Monsieur." Franck spoke slowly, as though a wad of cheese were in his mouth, and waved his gun. He was a small and curiously misshapen man.

Kruse made his way around the table. Zoé's chair was bloody now so he sat in his. He filled his champagne glass. On television, one evening, a guest on a talk show damned champagne flutes. They were not wide enough to let oxygen in. Good wine needs oxygen to come alive. Flutes were an insult. But Kruse liked them anyway, the daintiness of them. He drank and looked up and wondered how much time had passed since they had last spoken. Had he said this bit about champagne flutes aloud, or had he just thought it?

And really: perhaps the man who had vilified champagne flutes on television was simply selling his own version, his clever update. The fat flute. What was wrong with Franck? His head was somehow too thin, and his black suit jacket hung crookedly off him. Kruse could not say what it was about Franck but he felt charitably toward him. The kids would have teased Franck, who lacked all of his sisters' beauty and grace.

They had to kill him now. It would be a simple matter for Franck, who had become rather good at it rather quickly. Kruse added up the grenades in Chez Sternbergh and whatever he had done to Henri Alibert's art nouveau funhouse. In only a few weeks Franck had killed fifteen people. Soon, sixteen.

Perhaps he *could* tell the difference between good and bad wine. As the blood left him, the champagne tasted better. Or perhaps the oxygen had done its work.

"What?" said Zoé.

He had almost forgotten she was there.

"What about oxygen, Christophe?"

The breeze was genuinely cold now. He turned back to the city. What was left of the setting sun had been overwhelmed by new Atlantic cloud. Soon the streetlamps would pop on below and the children would go to bed and only the whispering adults of Paris would remain. A group of Japanese tourists in matching fleece jackets, with heavy cameras over their necks, walked across Avenue Bosquet—from the Eiffel Tower to dinner. Their leader spoke into a miniature megaphone. Kruse wanted to go back in time, to *hold everything* and start over with Evelyn and Lily. It had been a year since they had arrived in France to change their lives, and while it had certainly worked—within minutes the last of the Kruse family would disappear from the continent—he could not have imagined any of it. He closed his eyes and tasted his champagne again, and made a wish. Why believe in wishes and not the God of his parents?

There was one thing. "Zoé?"

"Yes?"

"I've not yet told Annette or Tzvi anything I've discovered. Maybe you and Franck could just . . ."

She looked at her brother and back at Kruse. "I'm afraid not, Christophe."

The Québécoise had worked so hard on redesigning and refurnishing the apartment, he didn't want to bleed on the floor and furniture. He remained on the stone patio, with the bottle.

"Annette helped you find what you have found."

"No, she didn't."

She sighed and whispered something to Franck, who took a step forward and kicked Kruse's chair over. The bottle of Krug fell off the table and smashed next to him. Zoé slapped her brother, who backed away from her like an abused child. She stepped onto the patio and cleared her throat and shouted down: "I am so sorry, neighbours. Clumsy!"

The fizz of the champagne on the patio was the sound of sorrow. While they had worked hard, the cleaners and renovators had not swept out here, so bits that had fallen from his flowerpots, and dust, and a dead fly floated in the wine. He lay in it and then slowly raised himself on his hands and knees. The champagne was cold and fragrant. Zoé seemed to realize all at once that he could reach up and snatch her. She scrambled back into the apartment in her Roman heels.

When he first heard her voice, echoing behind Zoé and Franck, he thought he was imagining it. When he was tired, or jogging in the cold mists of the park, he could hear Lily. Perhaps this was a call from another place.

Then it happened again.

He looked up. Both Zoé and Franck had turned away from him. They were looking into the near darkness of the apartment.

"Bonjour, Madame." Zoé spoke calmly. "Where is your lovely little girl this evening?"

• • •

If he had acted on his first and most powerful instinct on the night his daughter was killed, he would not have been on his hands and knees in a puddle of blood and champagne on Avenue Bosquet. He would have taken her hand, pulled her off the side of the medieval road, and lifted her up on his shoulders. Jean-François de Musset, their drugged landlord, his wife's lover, would have crashed his Mercedes into a plane tree instead of Lily.

"Is . . ." Annette paused a moment. "Is Christophe here?"

"He is, Madame. But unfortunately, he's in no position to receive you."

"Perhaps I'll come back."

Kruse did not wait to hear Zoé's answer. He knew what it would be.

Before he had heard her voice, he had wanted to sleep. It was his only choice. They continued to speak in the apartment but all he could hear, now, was his heart beating in his ears. His face was hot. It hurt to move but he raised himself to his feet, reached for the door jamb.

"But you said she has a lovely little girl." Franck spoke as though he had just learned each word.

"Do it."

He lowered his gun. "No."

"I promise this is the last night. This woman, and Christophe, and you're finished."

"I can't."

"Then you're going back."

"No!"

Kruse sprinted into the room but the long muscle at the top of his leg failed him. He fell on the parquet.

"Shoot him."

Franck aimed but shook his head. "I'm not going back to the home."

Zoé took the gun from her brother. Franck fell to his knees. His face was in his hands now.

A few minutes earlier, Kruse was certain he was going to die. It had come with freedom, a syrupy end to pain, a feeling of dreaminess. He would enter, however briefly, a warm and blameless place.

Now he could not pause. Whatever there was left in him, of blood and honour, was for them. He leapt up. Zoé had time to shoot once but he did not feel anything. He tackled her into the end table and a vase toppled on them as they hit the floor. Kruse stripped the gun out of her hand and it slid across the polished floor. Someone ran above him: Franck, maybe. Beneath him, Zoé squirmed and scratched and slapped but he was too heavy and even weakened he could control her. Any minute now Franck would shoot. Zoé's eyes opened wide and then she closed them.

"Do I call the police?" It was Annette.

He rolled off Zoé, stood up and took the gun from her. He didn't know how to answer. The police? No, not the police. He told her the number to call, the passwords in London and Marseille. Her voice turned sour. She made it all the way through to Joseph, or to his man. "Yes. The apartment on Bosquet."

Her voice trailed off and Kruse slid closer to Franck. He rubbed his back and tried to console him but he couldn't summon the energy to speak.

SEVENTEEN

Place des Vosges

THERE WAS ONCE A PUPPET THEATRE IN PLACE DES VOSGES. IT WAS a miniature leaf-shrouded cottage with a wooden carousel on one side and a waffle trailer on the other. He had seen the theatre ten years earlier on a client trip, long before he imagined living here, and he had thought: Someday, when I'm a dad. Now he was a Parisian, not quite a dad, and the puppet theatre was gone.

"I'm sorry, Anouk." Kruse stood in the middle of the damp square holding her tiny hand, warmer than his. There was a scrape on her wrist, from a recent tumble on the cobblestones in front of his apartment. It had pleased her to have a small version of what he carried on his face, his arms and chest, the new one on his leg.

She shrugged. Too sad, he thought, to speak.

"I was certain."

A pigeon slowed and landed on the head of the silver statue, a king on horseback. They had come a long way, fourteen metro stops, and he had promised. For a week he had been preparing Anouk for this trip to

Place des Vosges. There were no tears, in the end. She did not ask for an explanation but she looked keenly into his eyes. The world of our imagination does not always match the world we live in, he said. The daughter he had lost, his own daughter, Lily, would have cried. She would have launched an assault of questions. If he was certain the theatre was here, why was it not here? How could he have been *certain*? Where had they taken the puppets?

Anouk simply stared, as though she knew all along this would happen and only came along to see how he would react to the truth. It broke his heart a little, how she had been wired for disappointment. He worried it was his fault.

Lunch was not for an hour but there was nothing else to do in Place des Vosges. Paris is designed for adult pleasures: it had rained that morning and the aged, austere playground equipment was wet. It would rain again soon enough; the smell of wet soil hung drearily in the Marais. April blossoms in the flower garden would not interest her. Neither would a historical note about the statue, the fountain, the age of the linden trees.

No one could say when the theatre had last been here, if it had ever been here, not the white-haired woman with the yellow scarf and the Yorkshire terrier, not the war veteran on the bench with the missing fingers.

"Perhaps you're thinking of the Champ-de-Mars, Monsieur?" The war veteran had caught Kruse's accent in the question. "It is much more touristic."

There were cafés on the arcade. They could sit and watch the rain when it rained, drink hot chocolates for twenty minutes. School was always out on Wednesday, a delicious French tradition, so Kruse—the only male au pair in the seventh arrondissement—took no jobs on Wednesdays.

He had done his research: Victor Hugo had lived in one of the pretty houses facing the park, and a marquise had written memorable letters from here. Kruse had read about the letters somewhere, in a book Evelyn had included in her list of great works that would make him into a man of culture, a giant novel in which almost nothing happened. He abandoned the novel. There was nothing he could say about Victor Hugo that interested her. It was too cold to splash one another with the water from the fountain.

There was nothing wrong with her raincoat, a red one with yellow polka dots, but her fancy white suede shoes were all wrong for this weather. He squeezed her hand and led her down Rue des Francs-Bourgeois. The rain began to fall just as they reached a children's boutique. A woman welcomed them and asked how she might help. Kruse pointed to Anouk's feet. Did she have pretty options for a pretty girl?

He sat and watched Anouk interact with the woman in the store, which smelled of peaches. Her confidence, speaking to the woman and choosing what she liked and did not like, made him proud. Forty minutes later, Anouk walked out of the store with a pair of yellow rubber boots with red polka dots.

It was not easy to get a reservation at L'Ambroisie. The mayor himself made a call for him, and had promised the maître d' that Anouk was an unusually quiet and well-behaved little girl who would not ruin anyone's luncheon. Annette waited for them in the dry arcade, leaning against a stone pole. The end of April was upon them. Soon it would change. The sun would win. But for now, under the heavy cloud, it felt like evening and all the soft lights of the art galleries and boutiques were on. Kruse had bought another dark suit when they released him from the hospital, to make up for the one Zoé had ruined in his apartment.

Zoé had not waited for Joseph and his men to arrive in the apartment, to do what they quietly do with betrayers. She had stood up, even as they shouted at her to stay down, and she had walked to the balcony and had climbed up on the chair and had adjusted her posture and had silently jumped—dived, like her sister. Another flying tailor.

She had not said goodbye or anything else to her brother, Franck, doomed to return to his group home for the mentally disabled in Neuilly-sur-Seine. Zoé had landed on the curb between the sidewalk and the boulevard, and when Annette had walked over to see what had happened everyone in the café on the other side of Avenue Bosquet was standing as though a national anthem was about to play. She broke her back and some ribs, and suffered a severe concussion, but the fall had not killed her.

The moment she spotted her mother on the arcade, Anouk ran to show off her new boots. They argued, quietly, about how appropriate they were for L'Ambroisie. Anouk lost and hugged Kruse to launch an appeal. She looked up at him and whispered, "Please?" in English, knowing how it would delight him.

Kruse put the boots in the bag and promised they would splash in some puddles in Place des Vosges right after lunch. The sun might be out by then. Did he promise promise *promise*? He did, and he taught Anouk how to pinky swear. He knew these moments of regular beauty were nothing to regular people but if he could capture them and put them in a bottle, to hold and sip forever, he would. He held Anouk's pinky and her eyes sparkled with the crazy novelty of their locked fingers and Annette sighed.

"It's time for us to go in, Monsieur Au Pair. Mademoiselle Polka Dots."

Kruse followed with the wet boots in a white plastic bag. Inside, Annette greeted the maître d', an aggressively handsome man in a tuxedo. She had been here before, with Étienne. Today, thanks to the mayor, they would have a finer table. They would have more fun.

At the door, Kruse turned. There was an orderly black fence around the plaza. The trees were clipped. A man on the corner walked a Weimaraner and wiped the rain from his eyes.

He hoped their fine table was against a wall, so he could watch. The door opened behind him. Annette did not sound impatient or exasperated.

"No one is there, Christophe."

"I want to be sure."

Annette reached for his arm, gave it a gentle pull, and released it. "Wanting will never make it so."

ACKNOWLEDGEMENTS

Thank you to Martha Magor Webb and Jennifer Lambert. Thank you to the Canada Council for the Arts and to the Alberta Foundation for the Arts, for their support and encouragement. Thank you—yes, you—for reading and (I hope) recommending this novel and this series. Invite me to your book club and if I can come I'll bring hummus and a decent bottle of Côtes du Rhône. I'm not joking, ask around.

And thank you to Gina and Avia and Esmé, for allowing me to do this.

Someday I will design and perform an opera for you, Martha. Or something.